A TIME TO RUN

A TIME TO RUN

Darleen Turner

To order additional copies of this book, contact:
Xlibris Corporation
1-888-795-4274
www.Xlibris.com
Orders@Xlibris.com
95478

Acknowledgments

*T*hank you to all my family, friends, and fans—it wouldn't be complete without you. Thank you to my publisher Xlibris for all their hard work.

Sincerely,
Darleen Turner

Prologue

FORTY-FOUR

Sitting off to the side of doctors' lounge, he pulls out his envelope from Emma and runs his finger back and forth along the edge.

"Oh, Emma. I have missed you so much, but I don't know if I can bring myself to read this and open the wound that isn't quite healed but has become livable. You know you were my love, and every day that goes by, I think of you. There will never be another you, and I am not able to move on this time without you.

"Your daughter and granddaughter are both going to have surgery tomorrow and are in need of me, and I have to be able to be in my right mind to help. If I were to read your letter, it would put me in such a state that I would be letting not just the girls down but you. So I know you are watching over us, and I know you understand what I'm saying. So if you don't mind, I will keep this until Kate and Angel are out of surgery and recuperating before I take time to wallow in self-pity."

"Dr. Adams, Angel was asking to see you."

Slipping his letter back into his pocket and getting up, he says, "Okay, I will be right there." He goes to see what is up with Angel. She should be sound asleep by now. He had requested that they both be given sedatives so they wouldn't worry all night. Pushing

Angel's door open slowly so he wouldn't disturb her if she had fallen asleep. Finding her sitting up in bed.

"Hey, kiddo, why aren't you sleeping?"

"I can't sleep, Dr. Adams."

"Well, how about telling me what's on your mind?" He climbs up and sits on the side of her bed.

"I don't know, really."

"Are you scared about tomorrow? It's normal to be scared. This is a big thing that you will be going through."

"Yea, I am, a little. But I know if I don't do this, I won't live to raise my babies."

"That is true. You have to remember your children and that they love you as much as you love them."

"I do love my children. Very much."

"Of course you do. All mothers love their children, and there isn't anything you wouldn't do for them because you are their mother." He waited a bit, and Angel didn't say anything. She just sat with her head hung. So he decided to go further.

"You know, Angel, your mother loves you as much as you love your children."

"But Mom doesn't like Chris."

"That may be true, but it doesn't mean she loves you any less. As a parent, we usually never like our children's choices in partners. It is only out of love, and it is because they have been responsible for you for so many years, it is hard to see someone else take our place. You will see. You will have the same problems, and if you don't, I want to be the first to hear about it."

"I wasn't very nice to Mom."

"No, you weren't. And I understand you haven't been for quite some time. Do you think deep down you really have a justifiable reason to be treating your mother this way?"

"I thought so."

"Honestly now, Angel. What has she done that has been so horrible that you would go this long before talking to her?"

"I can't think of why I was mad at her. Then Chris just kept telling me that my mother wasn't nothing more than a tramp. That she didn't love me because she didn't love him. He said she couldn't have one without the other. At first, I got mad at him for saying those things about Mom. But then I guess I believed it, and I didn't know how to stop it all." She starts to cry, and I take her into my arms and rock her as if she were a baby. In some ways, she was just a baby, and the man she is with has forced her to grow up to his standards.

"You know, Angel, it is not too late to tell your mother that you love her. She would love to meet your little girl and help you with your son."

"Maybe after my surgery."

"Angel, don't wait too long. It has already been long enough."

"I know, and I really wanted to tell her that today, but I keep hearing him in my head."

"How about after you are well? I'll take you and your children to see your mom."

"Chris won't let me go home. He says I don't need my family."

"Well, I'm here to tell you that you do, and I will tell him where he can go and how to get there the fastest way."

Angel chuckles. "Dr. Adams, you wouldn't do that."

"I sure the hell will. Your mother needs you and your children in her life. She loves Jake, but you have always been her Angel, and she has been sad ever since you left. She almost quit living, Angel. She had me very worried for a very long time."

"Is Mom okay now?"

"She is trying to accept the fact that you don't want anything to do with her. She has loved you from a distance long enough, it is time you came home."

She nods her head in agreement.

"Okay, young lady. I want you to get some sleep, and we will get this all straightened out after surgery."

"Do you think Mom will be here tomorrow?"

"I don't think a team of wild horses is going to keep her away." He kisses her forehead and says good night. Angel couldn't help but replay the last time her mom had come to see her and how terrible she had treated her. She couldn't get over the horrible feeling that she had caused her mother so much grief. She knew that her mother had seen a lot of grief in her lifetime, and she had just added more to it. How blind she had been, and how selfish and self-centered. Why had she let this man come between her and her mother? They were always close and had always been there for each other. God, with Grandma gone and me gone, Mom has been left alone. We were all she had besides Jake, and I still knew in my heart that I was her number one.

"OH, Mommy. I wish I could see you now. I need you, and I need to be able to tell you. I love you as big as the sky, Mommy." Angel rolled over on her side and curled up into a ball. She thought about how it was going to be when Dr. Adams takes her and her children to see their grandma. Angel knows her mother will be ecstatic to see her and the children. It's what she is going to have to put up with at home that scares her. She feels she has let it go on long enough, and she must try to fix what she and her mother used to have. The trust, the love, and the friendship that they had banked on all those years. It was what got them through the time when her dad died and baby Ben died and Grandma died. Mom has had it hard. With that thought in mind, she fell asleep.

Just to be woken up by the OR nurse. She was prepped and ready to go within a half hour. It was early, but Angel knew she was going right back to sleep. She was so tired that she didn't have time to get scared. When she woke up, she would have a new lease on life. Thanks to some poor soul who had lost their life. She had thought she should have asked the age of her donor. But she didn't want to know if it was a young person like herself or younger.

Kate had been prepped as well, and both ladies were in their own OR rooms. Their surgery was going to be hours, and both Jake and Dr. Adams waited in the halls of the hospital. They had asked

Dr. Adams if he wanted to stand in and watch, and he decided that Jake would need someone, and so he chose to be with him. After all, both the girls had several doctors working on them and didn't need another in the way. The two men walked the halls and went for coffee and walked the halls some more. They made a few trips to the nursery to see the baby; neither one had much to say. Of course, their minds were on the same thing and were scare to mention it to each other.

Jake was sick at heart and knew that he couldn't have stopped Kate if he had tried, and Angel didn't have a choice. In her case, it was do or die. Throwing them in the basket and picking one still wasn't giving her much of a choice.

"I'm taking Angel to see her Mother when she has recovered from this." Dr. Adams tells Jake just out of the blue.

"You are?"

"Yes, I am. Enough is enough."

"Angel know about this?"

"Yes, she does. We talked it over last night. She was feeling bad about how she treated Kate when we went in to see her."

"So she should have. She has been doing that for a long time."

"That's what I said. Told her it was over. She was worried about Chris. I told her I would deal with him. But I was taking her to see her mother and the children to see their grandma."

"Good for you. Thank you. Did you tell Kate?"

"No, I think it will make for a good surprise when she wakes up. It will give her the motivation she will need to recover."

"Oh, for sure. I don't know how you did it, but thank you." They shook hands and patted each other on the back.

Hours had gone by, and they knew it was going to be a long day. The day was coming to an end and still no one has come to tell them what was happening. Jake was starting to get antsy and didn't know what to do with himself. He thought he would try to reading one of Kate's books that she had in her bag. When he took the first one out it had the white envelope in it. Looked like Kate was using it for a book marker. So instead of messing with that book he took the other and it was also a James Patterson book. Kate had a lot of his books she was a great fan of his. She said she could never write like him but loved his stories. Taking her book and finding a place to sit and read wasn't easy. This was a very busy place and Jake liked it quiet when he read. He ended up out side under a tree. He found that Kate had very good taste in books and he got right into the story. He forgot to tell Dr. Adams where he was going but had mentioned it to a nurse. She had told him she would find him when the doctors came out.

The recovery rooms were busy with them checking their vital signs every ten minutes and working on get the women awake. It took some longer then others to come around. Some almost took a whole day to really wake up.

"Can I have a drink please?" She says in a whisper.

"You sure can, Angel. How are you feeling? Is there much pain?"

"No, it's not too bad."

"The drugs they gave you for surgery will be wearing off and you don't be afraid to ask for something. You also have to drink lots and lots. We want you to pee as soon as you can. That will tell us your kidneys are working on their own. For now you have a bag, and we are measuring the fluid you are discharging. We are keeping track of how much you drink as well. It is very important to drink, Angel. So ask for whatever you want, except milk."

"I will, thank you."

And she dozes off again just as Dr. Adams comes through the door. He didn't know where Chris was, and he didn't care. He was going to sit with her for a while before going to see Kate. He knew that they would call Jake in to sit with her. Kate was still sleeping deeply, and so he thought he might as well come in here. They had told him Angel was awake off and on. He pulls up a chair and takes her hand in his. Angel has always been the closest person to a grandchild that he had ever had. He didn't miss many of her school functions or special occasions. He had watched her grow up from the beautiful brown-eyed baby to the beautiful woman she is today. It saddens his heart to know that she hasn't seen her mother in all these years nor spoken to her. He knew Kate had tried to text her but never got a good response from Angel. He had even thought about hiring a private detective to find her and check this guy out that had her so brainwashed that she walked out of her mother's life.

"Mr. Sanders, you may come see your wife now." Jake scrambled to his feet, dropping the book and cursing. Turning all read in the face as the nurse stood by and watched him get his bearings.

"Are you going to be all right, Mr. Sanders?"

"Yes. Sorry I was startled by you and excited to hear I can see my wife. How is she doing? How are they doing?"

"Angel has been awake off and on, but your wife hasn't come around yet."

"Is that normal for Kate not to be awake yet?"

"It takes some people longer to come out of the anesthetic than others. Your wife is one of them." Jake said no more and just followed the nurse into the room where they had Kate. He goes over to her and takes her hand and starts to squeeze it. He is watching the nurse and she is taking Kate's vitals and they are calling her Name and telling her it's time to wake up. Kate wasn't having anything to do with them.

"Mr. Sanders, please just keep talking to her. This will bring her around faster than if we leave her to come around on her own."

"All right. I can do that."

"We will be back in fifteen minutes, unless you need me before that. Please just ring that bell."

"Okay, I can do that too." The nurse leaves, and Jake stands staring at his wife lying there so lifeless. It pulled at his heart.

"Okay, Kate, you heard them. It is time to wake up now. Angel is already awake, and you can't see her with your eyes closed."

Kate can faintly hear a voice. She can see Ben off in the distance, and she feels the pull toward him. Ben is calling her, and she finds she is drifting his way. Then she hears her name called again, but this time it's not Ben, but Jake that is calling her. Her eyes are so heavy. In her mind, she says "I hear you Jake."

"There's still nothing from your wife?" a nurse asked.

"No, nothing. I keep talking, but she just doesn't want to wake up yet."

"Dr. Anderson is coming back in to check her out. He should be in right away."

"All right. I will talk to her until then."

"Good man. That's what she needs." It was just a couple of minutes, and Dr. Anderson came in and he went over Kate. Done all kinds of things and in the end says.

"Jake, your wife has gone into a coma."

"What? Why? How long will this last?"

"Sorry. We have no way of knowing these things." Jake drops his head into his hands, and Dr. Anderson saw the tears hit the floor.

"Jake, we have to keep talking to her. And the more we talk to her, the better the chance of her coming back to us faster are." Jake just shook his head in agreement. This went on for days, and then Dr. Adams says to Jake.

"We should bring Angel in to talk to Kate. I think it would do the trick."

"You really think so?"

"It did before."

"Angel doesn't know Kate did this for her. Kate didn't want her to know."

"You're right on both accounts, but I think this is one time you can override what Kate wanted and do what is best for Kate."

"All right, let's do it."

"I will go talk to Angel and come back as soon as I can."

"OK." Entering Angel's room, he saw the man that she was living with, and his blood boils right away. He continues to go over to Angel, not making eye contact with the guy at all. For one thing, he couldn't remember his name, and also, he didn't give a damn. He was here to help Kate.

"Angel, I need to talk to you in private."

"Whatever you have to say to Angel, I can hear."

"I'm sorry. I'm her doctor, and no, you cannot. Now please leave."

"I will not."

"Then I will call security. You decide. Angel can talk to you later if she wishes, but for now, it is her and I."

"Go ahead, they won't remove me."

"All right then, have it your way." Dr. Adams picks up the phone, and before Chris knew it, he was being escorted out of the room before the next words were coming out of his mouth. Next step.

"Angel, I have to tell you something, and I want you to stay calm. You can't be getting all upset, but I need your help."

"OK. But how can I help you?"

"Your kidney donor has gone into a coma, and we hoped you would come and talk to her."

"Wait a minute—my donor wasn't someone who had died?"

"No, Angel, you had a live donor."

"Who the hell would do that?"

"Your mother?" Angel went pale, and I thought she was going to be sick. So, grabbing the bedpan, I stuck it under her chin.

"Mom gave me one of her kidneys? Why would she do that?"

"Your mother knew it was a death threat to you if you didn't get one, and she was a perfect match. She loves you, Angel. Can't you see that? There isn't anything. Anything at all she wouldn't do for you and your children. I think she has proven that to you. Don't you think? She has put her life on the line to save yours." Angel's tears are rolling down her cheeks as she nods her head.

"How can I help Mom?"

"You have to talk to her just like you did when you were little. We have to get her to wake up. I'm going to have the nurse wheel your bed down to your mom's so you can talk to her."

Angel cried all the way down to see her mom. When they entered the room, Jake was totally shocked to see them bring Angel in. Dr. Adams just holds up his hands to stop Jake from saying anything.

They slid her bed in beside Kate's. Angel reached over and took Kate's hand.

"Oh, Mommy, why did you do this? Please, Mommy, wake up. I need you. I'm so sorry, Mommy. Please wake up. Don't sleep like you did last time."

Kate hears the voice of her sweet Angel, but Ben calling to her was stronger, and there was no way Kate's eyes would open, and she starts to drift again. This feels right to her, and she has no fears or worries. Ben is there, and she knows she will be safe and happy. She lets herself go.

"CODE BLUE. ICU. STAT."

"CODE BLUE. ICU. STAT."

Next thing Jake knew, the door was flying open and he was being pushed aside. Angel's bed was pulled away, and the three of them watched on in horror.

"Clear!" someone yells, and then he watches Kate's body jump up off the stretcher and then flop back down. Again, he hears "Clear!" He watches after they hit Kate with the paddles again and again. He finds he is leaning up against the wall, and the feeling of nausea came over him.

Angel is now yelling for her mother. It seemed to take forever before he saw Dr. Anderson reach over and hold the hand of the one using the paddles. He saw him shaking his head, and they all turn and look at the straight line that was running on the machine. Then some of them looked down, and others looked at Jake. Dr. Anderson came over and he was talking, but Jake couldn't hear what he was saying. As he walked over to Kate's lifeless body, he knew what had just happened.

He had just lost his best friend: his wife. Angel had just lost her mother and her best friend. The children just lost the grandmother that they will never know. Dr. Adams lost the one person he treated like the daughter he never had. Jake picks Kate up into his arms and pulls her in tight to his body and lets out a scream that was surely heard from one end of the hospital to the other. The cries that came from this man were those of a man whose heart had just been ripped from his chest. All the medical staff watch on until Dr. Anderson nodded for them to leave him so he could be alone with his wife. Dr. Adams holds Angel as she cries with regret.

"Please. I want to give Mom a hug and say good-bye." Dr. Adams pushes her over as close as he could, and Jake picks up Kate and lays her beside Angel so she could give her mother the hug that Kate had dreamed of and wished for over the years that Angel was away. Then Dr. Adams takes Angel back to her room, and they leave Jake alone with his beloved wife and friend.

"I killed my mom."

"No, Angel, you did not. This was Kate's choice. No one could change her mind."

"I don't understand. Mom never came out of surgeries well. Why would she put herself in such danger?"

"You know, Angel. There are none so blind as those who cannot see."

"I don't understand."

"Unconditional love, Angel. Your mother gave that to you right to the end."

"My children will never know their grandma. Where will I go, and what will I do?"

Wrapping Angel in his arms, he says, "You will have to live with your choices and learn to live with your regrets, Angel. You will also have to do the same as your mother did for all those years and learn to love her from a distance."

Chapter One

———•———

D r. Adams stayed with Angel all that night, sleeping in the chair beside her bed and holding her hand. She had woken up several times during the night calling out for Kate then cried herself back to sleep. She had even refused to have anything to do with her son. The nurses understood, and they took care of him. Dr. Adams worried whether this was going to be a long-term thing with Angel or just a couple of days. She now was a small child herself, needing a mother that no longer was available. This made him heavy at heart as he sat and thought about all the wasted time that had gone on between Angel and Kate. Angel had no one but herself to blame. This alone could put Angel on the brink of a breakdown. He knew he was going to have to keep a very close eye on her for some time. He was also counting on Jake's help. Help from the guy she was living with wasn't going to be positive. She looked like she had been run over by a train come morning.

Jake had stayed with Kate all night. This made Dr. Adams think back to the time that Ben had died and how Kate had stayed with him. Guess what goes around comes around.

Jake had gone home in the morning to find Kate's will. He knew where she had it. It was one thing Kate was very adamant about. She had seen too many people lost at a time like this, and she had always said that she would never do that to us. Angel and I would have it as easy as possible when the time came. Kate also had a large angel like the one Emma had. In her wishes, she too was to be cremated and put inside this angel. She had this beautiful string of pearls with a cross on the end that was to be placed around the neck of the angel. The angel was to be placed in her rose garden. She and Emma had decided to do the same thing. They probably bought them at the same time. It was a good idea and a lot cheaper than a funeral home would want. This was not going to look cheap at all. Kate and Emma were not that kind. They were both very classy women.

Kate loved Christmas. Christmas music was what she wanted played at her service. She had a CD of Christmas music done by saxophones; it was beautiful to listen to. Christmas was Kate. It too died when Angel left. Kate never put the effort into Christmas anymore. A simple little tree was all she would do, and she would sit and listen to this CD and watch out the window for Angel.

The day of Kate's service, Angel was let out in a wheelchair just long enough to attend. Her IV pole was on the side with her pain medication, and she was totally numb through it all. Jake, on the other hand, was not numb. He wept out loud, and it made the hearts of all who came reach out to him. He had been great for Kate and gave her and Angel unconditional love and had put life back into both of them. Kate had had the best life anyone could have given her, up to the day Angel walked out of her life. Tearing Kate's heart out at the same time.

Kate never lived again until the time she was able to see Angel and her daughter, even if it was from a distance. Kate believed that they would feel her presence and her love and this would bring Angel around.

Dr. Adams sits beside Jake with Angel and watches Jake's eyes. Never once did Jake look at Angel. Nor did he make any move to console her. He knew Jake was hurting deeply. This was showing him that he would have another bridge to help mend. He couldn't blame Jake for being distant with Angel right now; he only hoped it was something else that would be short-lived. Jake would need time to heal. He knew that Jake was never happy about the fact that Kate moved out of their home just to be near Angel. Even though Jake always knew Angel was Kate's life, he also knew she loved him. She would always tell him: "I am her mother, and I must find her and fix what has been broken." Even though Kate didn't know what was broken or how it had really gotten to this point. She could never fathom the thought of a mother and daughter not communicating.

For Dr. Adams, it was like losing Emma all over again. He didn't feel like he had much left to live for. He was getting up there in age and had hoped, by now, he and Emma would have been living somewhere warm and he would be retired. When Emma died, he saw no reason to stop practicing. With Angel gone and Kate moving away, he felt he had lost everyone that he held dear to his heart. He wasn't really living anymore. He was putting in time. Alex had told Jackie that he had wished so many times that he could have died with Emma that day.

Jackie did not go home until she knew that Alex would not be using the bottle to get by with. He used his work so was hardly ever around. After six months, Jackie went home. She continues to call him every day, just to make sure that he understands just how much she still needs him and how much she loves him. Sometimes she gets the feeling when talking to him, he wished she would just go away. She wasn't granting him that wish today or anytime soon. She loved her brother and they were always close, and so he would just have to get used to the fact that she was always going to be in his face until she takes her last breath. Jackie knew how hard this was on Alex. He had always considered Emma, Kate, and Angel his family. Jackie hurt deeply for Alex and knew that there were no words to console him that time and time alone was going to be the best healer Alex was going to have. So today as she sits beside him to say good-bye to another of his family members, all she could do was hold his hand. She would once again have to watch and make sure Alex didn't turn to the bottle.

When the service was over, Jake said nothing to anyone; he just took Kate's angel and left. He wouldn't even stay around for the lunch and social. He didn't bother to make eye contact with anyone, which was telling Alex that he was some pissed at Angel as well as being deeply hurt.

Alex and Jackie took Angel back to the hospital where the nurses were waiting to get her all settled in so they could bring her son to her.

"Angel, I will be taking you home in a couple of days. I will be staying in town and checking on you every day for the next month. That way, if anything happens, I can get you help right away. Chris had told me he wasn't taking time off work and that he would have your next-door neighbor lady checking in on you. Sorry, but I'm not comfortable with those arrangements, so I will be your doctor."

"I will be okay. You can go home."

"No, I can't. I will do this not only for me or you, but for your mother as well. She has given up her life to save yours, and be damned if I want anything to jeopardize what she has done. To lose you now would be a total waste of Kate's good heart. I want her to be able to rest in peace knowing that you are being cared for, and that someone appreciates her offering."

"Do what you want then, I guess." Angel rolls onto her side away from Alex. Alex wanted to give her a piece of his mind so bad he could taste it. Now was not the time. Maybe tomorrow she will see things a little clearer.

"I'm going to see Jake after I drop Jackie off at the bus. I will be back tomorrow. It will be late in the evening by the time I get back." He leans in and kisses her on top of her head. Yes, his heart aches for Angel, but a lot of this could have been prevented. Angel will just have to learn to live with her choices. He felt she was going to need consoling for some time. He would talk to Angel about it and help set it up.

Dropping Jackie off, he headed for Jake's, and he had no idea what he was going to find there. The three-hour drive gave him a lot of memory time, and he used it well. He relived the years that he had Emma, Kate, and Angel in his life. He thought how lonely and empty once again his life was going to be now.

Pulling up in front of their house gave Alex a feeling of doom. It was early evening, and the sun was still warm. There was no warmth coming from this home now. Would it ever see happiness again? This home that had been so happy a few years ago with a new marriage, a young child, and a dog looks like it has ghosts lurking in every corner. Alex was even looking over his shoulders and didn't know why or what he was looking for.

"Excuse me, sir. May I help you?" an older gentleman asked.

This man looked like he was as old as the house. Perhaps he was the ghost I had been expecting.

"I have come to see Mr. Sanders."

"Oh yes. Mr. Sanders is out back with his Kate. Come, I will show you."

"Thank you. Perhaps I should not disturb him?"

"Mr. Sanders, he just sits and cries and looks at the angel. I think he could use a friend."

"All right then. Take me to him, please."

"Yes, come this way." The old fella shuffles on, and for his age, he was far from being slow. The view of the area he was taking me took my breath away. Weeping birch trees and roses everywhere. They were climbing up all the tree stumps and into the trees. I never saw anything like it. Every color you could think of was here. There in the middle of one of his trees that were covered in red roses stood Kate's Angel. Placed around her neck was a small wreath of red rosebuds. As the older gentleman had said, there sat Jake on the bench with his head in his hands. I could tell he was crying. Going over, I sat down beside him and put my hand on his shoulder.

He nods his head in acknowledgment that I was there. I waited a bit for him to get himself together.

"Jake, I can't tell you how sorry I am for you. There are no words that would express how I feel. I am here for you if you ever want to talk."

"I am so damn mad at Kate right now. I want to scream. I told her I had a bad feeling about this. I wanted her to rethink it through."

"I know you did, Jake. And it wouldn't have mattered if Dr. Anderson had told her that there was a high risk of death. Kate would have still gone through with it to save Angel."

"ANGEL! Seems like she is the only one who comes out of this okay. She got what she needed and can go on. What about the rest of us? I could care less if I ever see her again. She has put Kate through hell for all these years, just for Kate to lose her life for her in the end. How ironic don't you think? Kate had died from the time Angel left. That girl has no consideration of anyone but herself. We had given her everything we could. We were always there for her. Kate didn't deserve this kind of treatment from Angel. Kate was a zombie for a long time. I had thought she would die of a broken heart. Geese do—why wouldn't Kate? Every day when I came home, I was scared of what I would find.

"Her last few weeks there with Angel right across the road gave her more spunk than I had seen in her for a very long time. She was coming home after Angel had the baby, and she knew everything was fine. Coming home. Damn it, Alex. Why? Why Kate? What went wrong? I think if Angel would have talked to Kate the night before instead of turning her away, it would have made a difference in the outcome. She didn't have it in her heart, what it would take to fight and survive."

"Angel thinks she killed her mother, and that will play heavy on her mind and her heart for a very long time, if not for the rest of her life."

"And so it should. She doesn't have to come to me for sympathy because I have none to give her."

"I understand where you are coming from and why. But, Jake, Angel did not ask Kate to do this. Remember she did not know that her mother was her donor. I'm not asking you to take her into your arms as of yet. I understand you have a lot of healing to do. But I am asking you to think of those two little ones that Kate adored. In time,

Angel may come to see you, and I would hope—for the children's sake—you could find room in your heart to let her in."

"Do you know what you are asking me? Angel would be standing here in front of me alive with her mother's kidney while her mother is out here in the rose gardens."

"Yes, Jake, she would be. Once again, I stress to you. It was Kate's choice. Not Angel's.

"Oh god, man. I don't know if I could do it."

"I don't think it will be anytime soon. I only hope that when and if that day arises, you will stand to be the man that we all know you to be." Jake just drops his head back into his hands, and the tears continue to flow. I place my hand on his shoulder one more time in leaving, and again, he just nods in acknowledgment.

Chapter Two

————◆————

A lex had a very tiring drive back to the city. He had thought about staying home but figured he should be there for Angel. He had promised her that he would be back late the following evening, but he knew he wouldn't sleep anyways, so he might as well go back to the city.

He gets to thinking how life can change in such a short time. One day you have a family, and the next day you are alone. He knows he has Jackie and for a sister he couldn't have asked for anyone better. She has been his rock and his shoulder since Emma died. But she was still his sister, not a loved one that you would go home to every day and hold in your arms and share the most of every day. Alex was lonely, and he has had a hard time finding a reason to get up anymore. His practice is just that. Oh, he still cares about tending to his patients, but there was no one that touched his heart and soul as Emma and Kate had done over the years. Although they belonged to someone else, he had always loved them from a distance as well. He was finding that, at his age, he wasn't looking to make a new family with anyone. He hoped that he would be content to live out his days with Emma's memories. Now he would have his memories of Kate to put with her mother's. Maybe someday he would be able to share some of his memories with Angel and her children. His memories may be all that will keep Angel going. The girl should be so full of regret and self-pity that it may take her a long time to live again. He can only hope that her children won't end up paying the price for their mother's mistakes.

Perhaps he should think about moving to the city to be closer to Angel and her children. That way, she wouldn't feel like she had no one to turn to when things got rough. He was feeling like he owed this to Kate and Emma to watch over Angel and her children. After all, what kind of a man would that make him if he were to just walk away? He didn't think there was going to be too much help coming from Jake. He also understood Jake's feeling other than the fact there were two little children who were innocent, and Kate and Emma would expect this of him. Christ, he'd expect it of himself. The pull has always been there with Angel and Kate, so he will see it through. Although she is a mother, she is also a child herself. With no one left to guide her or give advice, Alex felt that this is where he had to step in.

Alex didn't think she would be getting too much help from Chris. He was too much of a controller to worry about someone else's needs. He got under Alex's skin all right, but until Angel opens her eyes, no one will be able to tell her any different.

Getting back into the city late and having a shower just woke Alex up more, and he knew it was going to be a long day but thought he would go in early to see Angel and her son. He could always catch an afternoon snooze if he needed to.

"Knock-knock." Peeking in the door to be careful not to disturb Angel if she were sleeping.

"Hi, Dr. Adams."

"Good morning, Angel. How are my two favorite people today?" That brought a slight smile to her face as Alex bends over and kisses her forehead and that of her son's.

"Okay, I guess. How about you?"

"Well, I think I will survive." He sure didn't want to tell her how he was actually dead inside and lonely. Angel had enough on her plate. "Are you and this little man ready to go home?"

"Dr. Anderson says we might be able to go home this afternoon if my checkup today is like yesterday and better."

"That's what I want to hear. That is music to these old ears."

Angel giggles her little-girl giggle. "You can still make me laugh after all this."

"I'm glad to be of some kind of use to somebody. I will take the good with the bad."

"Dr. Adams, there are a lot of people who need you."

"Yea, you're right, Angel." He didn't want to tell her none of them really mattered anymore. Without Emma in his life. "I'm going to be taking care of you and this little man for a while. You are at the top of my list."

"You don't have to. What about everyone else back home?"

"Don't you worry about them. I have taken care of all of that for the next month. So you and Gregory are stuck with me as your nursemaid whether you like it or not, young lady." He takes the baby from Angel and snuggles into him to get the smell of the baby. To him, there was nothing like the smell of a newborn baby. That is a scent that is so special, and he regrets never having his own to remember, so he must take it from wherever he can.

"Dr. Adams, how was Jake?"

"Honestly, Angel, not good at all. I think losing Kate has almost ended his life. She was everything to him."

"Do you think he will ever forgive me?"

"I can't say for sure. We can only hope he has room left in his heart for you and the children. I have talked to him. Now time will decide. Jake may never get over this, and he has got me concerned. I'm going to keep a close eye on him and help whenever I can. But I can't make him live if he chooses not to."

"It's that bad?"

"Right now, it is. Jake died inside the minute your mom did. Until he heals, there won't be anything we can do. If he chooses not to, then time will take its toll."

Angel breaks down.

"This is all my fault? He will never want me around."

"Angel, the fact that your mother died is not your fault. I want you to understand something. Kate chose to give you her kidney. You didn't know your donor. It wouldn't have mattered if she had been told how dangerous it was. Your mother would still have done what she did."

"Why?" she asks as she chokes back a cry.

"Because, Angel, you were your mother's life. And she knew that there was a good chance of you not getting a donor on time, and you having the two little ones was all she was concerned about. They need their mother."

"I need my mom."

She begins to cry uncontrollably. I sit on the edge of her bed and take her into my arms and rock her along with her son who was sleeping through it all. When I figured she had calmed down some, I began to talk to her.

"The best you have now, Angel, is the memories of what Kate has taught you and to know she loved you more than life itself. You have to draw your strength from that, and you will be just fine. Remember, I will always be here for you."

She nods her head in agreement but finally says, "I love you Dr. Adams, but you're not my mom."

"Well, dear, I'm sorry about that. But I'm all you have left." Saying that sent a horrible feeling through me. Even though it was true, it made me feel like we were the last of our kind. Wondering if the dinosaurs had felt like that.

"I know. I'm going to really miss my mom."

I'm thinking it's now or never. "Well, Angel, I think you are a little late to say that. The one person who wanted to hear that from you is no longer here with us, and you wasted a lot of precious time dodging your mother instead of loving her."

"I always loved my mom."

"You sure had a funny way of showing her. Remember, I was there when she came to see you last. You tore her heart out, Angel, and you didn't even think twice. So please don't lie here and think that pity is something you are going to get from me. Because it is a long way down the line. I'm sorry that you won't get a chance to say that to your mom and that you won't have a grandmother for your children. We get out of life what we put into it. So from here on, I would suggest that you think hard about what it is that you really do want out of this life. You have a second chance, Angel, so do it right. We don't all get second chances. Your grandmother, for one. There wasn't a better person on this earth than her. She should have been one who got a second chance. God saw it in another way. Your mother—she got her second chance when she came out of her coma the first time. To bad it has been short-lived and not all happy for her. Now you—your mother has given you your life again, costing her her own. So I'm here to see that you do right by it, Angel. I hope you can get on track with Jake again. He needs to have you and the children around. I think you need him as well. Yes, I told you I'm here for you. But, Angel, look at me. I'm not a young man anymore. I won't be here much longer, and I would rest easy knowing that you and Jake are family again."

Angel just nods her head, so Alex didn't know whether she really agreed or just what the nod was really all about. Then she said, "Chris won't let me go home. He says I don't need anyone but him."

"Oh really? And where is he today? Where has he been all the rest of the time? I think I've seen him once."

"He is working."

"I understand working, but this wasn't some simple surgery you had. In the end, you lost your mother. He should have been here. And not only that, you just had his son, for christ's sake."

"He didn't want the baby."

"What?"

"Chris never wanted the kids. I did. He won't let me work or have friends. I get lonely real bad, so I wanted the kids so I would have someone I loved close to me."

This made me sick to the stomach.

"Ah, Angel, why the hell do you stay with him? He is killing you."

"He tells me he loves me, and he said he was the only one who loved me."

"Angel, you know that is not true. How could you be so blind? Kate and Jake showed you nothing but love. This guy knows nothing of what love is. You had a very loving and caring family, and you have let him tear it apart. For what? Two babies. Has this guy been rough with you?"

Angel just hung her head.

"I take that as a yes. I want you to get out, Angel. Things don't get any better. In fact, they just keep getting worse, and women end up dead." Angel snaps her head up, and her eyes are big and in disbelief.

"Chris would never do that."

"Oh really. Did you think he would ever slap you? 'Cause he has, hasn't he? Hasn't he, Angel?" Alex raised his voice to her, and she looked scared of him. This tore at his heart; he didn't want Angel ever to be afraid of him. He did want her attention, and he figured he had it now. So he would continue.

"Angel, these men are control freaks that like to control everything you do and say. They get you so you are totally dependent on them. They take away your friends, family, and anything that was you. They strip you down until you are no more than a shell, and you become brain dead and brainwashed from him. Every time, the abuse will get worse, and each time he will have you thinking you deserved what he just did to you. At first, they come back and tell you how sorry they are and that it will never happen again. It will happen again and again until he either has you immobilized or dead. Which one are you choosing? You have two innocent children, Angel, who shouldn't be living like this. The things they will see and hear shape who they will become. In the end, if they don't end up with an abuser, they have become one themselves because that is all they have seen. To them, it is normal and it is a way of life and the cycle starts all over again. So do you want to see your daughter with one of these men, or do you want to see your son growing up to be one of these men? If you stay, you are going to have one or the other.

"The strong ones are the survivors. The ones that are strong enough to run. That is you, Angel. All your life, you have been the strongest little girl I've ever known. You have had some hard times, and you have always bounced back. Now you have two children who might not be able to bounce back. They need friends and family around them the same as you had all the time you were growing up. This is what helped you bounce back all the time. You were loved and cared for by all of us, and you just let us all go because this man said so.

"Your mother never quit loving you, and she waited every day for you. Every day you chose not to call her or go see her, she died a little more with each passing day.

"I watched a woman who loved life—she had become one with no more than a breath. Her life was over until she lived across the road from you and your daughter. She thought that God had guided her there to find you. Perhaps she was right, and he did. Maybe you would still be lying and waiting for your kidney if Kate hadn't made the choices she did. Kate would still be in her home with Jake, and you would be lying in the hospital, waiting. Kate would have had no idea that you were sick or maybe had died in the end if she hadn't had some kind of a guardian angel. Just maybe her angel was her mother, your grandmother. Kate believed that everything happened for a reason.

"So now that your mother has given you a second chance at life again, please don't waste it on someone like Chris.

"I will be more than willing to take you home with me at the end of the month when I know you are healthy and totally out of danger. You have until then to make up your mind. If you choose not to, I hope that you will know when it is time to run. I will go see when your doctor is due in." Kissing her forehead and leaving Angel to do some heavy soul searching.

Chapter Three

---•---

"Well, Miss, looks like I get to take you home. I have your discharge papers and all the orders I need to know. So I can give you the best of care. There will be a nurse come around for the first week just to give me a hand with this little man, and then we will be set to go."

"Dr. Adams, you really don't have to." Putting up my hand to quiet her.

"Yes, I do for more than one reason. The biggest being the fact that I want to do this. So no more word on me not having to do this." I knew it was because of Chris and she was worried about how he was going to take all this news and the fact that I was going to be in his face every day. I was going to be able to see for myself just how controlling this guy was.

We were all packed up and headed for Angel's right after lunch. The nurse had said, now that she had eaten, both she and the baby should be ready for a nap when I got them home. I should have an easy afternoon.

She was right it was an easy afternoon. I had sat in the rocking chair with Gregory for the better part of the afternoon. This was something I never got to do so I would cherish it forever. I wondered if this was how all real grandpas felt. This little boy had me wrapped around his little finger and he didn't even know it. I was glad that

I could see lots of Angel's features in him; it made it easier to love him. Not that I wouldn't have.

"Angel, what would you like for supper?"

"I'm not hungry."

"I know, but Elisabeth will be here soon, and we all have to eat. How about tonight I order chicken, and it will give us time to do some shopping tomorrow."

"Chris doesn't like me ordering meals."

"Too bad for Chris 'cause I'm ordering tonight." I could see the fear come into her face.

"It will be okay. It is just for tonight. Unless he has gone shopping, you don't have anything in here to cook."

"He won't shop. He says that is a woman's job."

"Guess I better put on my dress next time I go to the grocery store."

Angel giggles.

"No such thing as only women shopping for groceries, Angel. There are lots of men out there that have to cook for themselves. I have been one of them for many years."

"Don't you have a maid or something? Or eat out all the time?"

"No, I don't on both accounts. The maid cleaned my house. The rest was up to me. So yes, I can do laundry too. I never knew when I would be home for meals, so I would never ask that of anyone."

"That was nice of you."

"So now I will go order our supper."

"Okay." Angel just lay back on the sofa as if she were in no man's land. It wasn't because of the drugs anymore. They had done a good job of getting her off the heavy pain killers as soon as possible. With Kate's death they had thought maybe Angel would use them as a crutch instead of dealing with the death. I had to say I would have to agree with them. I was just hanging up the phone when I heard.

"MOMMY, MOMMY." Elisabeth came running into the room and right to Angel. I was able to scoop her up just before she made the jump onto the sofa.

"Okay there, little one. You have to be careful. Mommy has a big ow-wee." She pushed herself away from me and had the look of fear in her eyes.

"Elisabeth, this is Dr. Adams. He is here to help Mommy, so you mind what he says, okay?" Elisabeth just nods her head, so I set her down on the end of the sofa. Angel reaches over and pulls her into her side. All I could see were two big blue eyes staring at me. I knew that this little girl had already saw and heard too much. I could tell by the fear written all over her face that she was afraid of men. All I could think of was "that SOB."

"I'm going to go pick up supper. I shouldn't be long. I will push the baby over here so you can reach him while I'm gone. You just give him the soother I will do the rest because you are not to lift anything yet."

"Thank you." I figured Chris should be home by the time I got back. I hoped he would be late so I could be the sounding post for Angel. I knew how nervous she was. Her being upset right now was not a good thing for her it would put to much stress on her kidney. I hurried so I wouldn't leave her on her own to long. When I got back I could see she had been crying and Elisabeth was snuggled as close into her mothers side as the child could get.

"What is wrong, Angel? Did you get up and hurt yourself?"

"No, I'm fine."

"I can see that is BS, so what's up? Why is Elisabeth so damn scared?" Angel hangs her head.

"Chris was home."

"Oh yea, and what of it? Angel, what about Chris? Did he get rough with you?"

"No, he just yelled at me."

"Why was he yelling?"

"Because I didn't have supper made."

"Did you tell him I was buying supper?"

"Yes, I did, and that made him worse."

"Why would that make him so mad?"

"He doesn't want anyone here when he isn't home."

"So where is he now?"

"He said he would go eat downtown."

"Is he going to be home later?"

"I think so."

"That isn't good enough, Angel. You need help with the children, and you can't be alone. Your body could still reject the kidney. You could cause yourself some problems if you try and do too much." She just sits and looks at the floor.

"Do you even care, Angel?"

"Not really."

"What about these babies that you wanted. Who is going to take care of them if you don't?" The tears are trickling down her cheeks.

"Nothing I do is right anymore, and I don't know what to do to make it right."

"With men like this, there is no making it right, Angel. Can't you see that by now? He has had you to himself long enough to show you just what you really mean to him. He should have help here for you or be here himself."

"He says he's not a babysitter."

"Oh, for the love of god. I will get supper set up for you and Elisabeth. Then I will see to having the nurse come in tonight."

"I will be okay, Dr. Adams."

"Fine, then I'm staying." He turns around and goes into the kitchen to make up their plates. While he was doing that, Elisabeth came in and startled him by tugging on his pant leg. He squats down and could see she wasn't quite sure whether she should bother him.

"What is it, Elisabeth?"

"Can I have a drink please?"

"Why, of course you can. Would you like water or milk?"

"Milk please."

"Milk it is." While getting Elisabeth a glass of milk, he wondered if she was afraid of him. So he thought he would ask.

"Here you go, sweetheart. You want to sit up to the table?"

"Yes." Alex helps her up onto the chair. She was as light as a feather. What a petite thing she was.

"Elisabeth, are you afraid of me?" She just looked at him and nodded yes.

"Well, sweetheart, you don't have to be. Okay? I'm here to help Mommy, and you with your baby brother. You can call me *Grandpa*. I have known your mommy all her life, and I love your mommy, so I won't hurt her or you. I hope I can make you believe that all men are not bad."

"Mommy cries."

"I know she does, sweetheart, and I hope to be able to help make Mommy happy again." This is horrible, knowing that this child is so sad. At this age, they should be bouncing with excitement, not trying to hide behind someone or something all the time.

"Let's take Mommy her supper now."

"Okay."

"Here, you bring Mommy's fork and knife." That put a smile on her face. Even though it was a slight one, it was still a smile.

I stayed with Angel and the children for the month. I ended up sleeping on her sofa. Where Chris got to, I couldn't say; and Angel didn't seem to know. If she did, she wasn't saying.

I took Angel in for her checkups, and we were told that all was well with Angel and she could start to do a little more living. That pleased me more than her. She had started to be able to pick her son up, which was nice for both of them to be able to make that bond. All Angel had were her children, and I hoped they would always be close. I would hope that she is learning how to cope with whatever may come her way as a mother. I'm sure Kate was never ready for the fallout that she and Angel had. I hope that Angel will remember all of this and learn to talk to her daughter about what men she should stay away from.

Angel was going to have a very lonely life now without her mother and grandmother. The best she will have is to make things right between her and Jake.

First of all, she has to get out from under this man's spell. I know from my line of work it takes some of these women years to wake up and get the courage to run. Others never survive—either they get beaten to death or they take their own lives. He hoped this wouldn't be Angel. He would make sure that she knew that he would always have room for her and the children. He will get her cell number so he can keep in touch. He had a very bad feeling about the situation that Angel had gotten herself into. Having the two children was going to make it harder for her to feel like she can leave. He knew what he was doing: by getting her pregnant, this would make her more dependent on him. Just what these men like.

The month I have been there with Angel, she never really came out of her shell. I tried to talk to her about all the choices she had, but I felt like it all fell on deaf ears. I tried to point out that the way she was living was not healthy for her or the children.

"Angel, I will be leaving tomorrow. I would like to take you and the children home with me. Once the baby is older, you could look for a job. Even a part-time one just to get you out. I could probably get you on at the clinic filing. The girls are always behind and say they don't have enough time to get it all done in a day."

"Oh, I can't do that."

"And why not?"

"Chris would never let me work."

"Angel, I'm talking about you leaving him. Get out of here while you can and start a new life with just you and the children. I'm sure the clinic job could be arranged whenever you're ready."

"I don't know."

"Well, I want you to keep this in the back of your mind. I want you to keep my phone number handy, and you call me whenever you need to. Even if you just want to talk. Call me."

"I don't have a cell phone anymore. Chris said I didn't need one anymore, and I can't make long-distance calls from here."

"Why doesn't that surprise me? Is that why you never called Kate?"

"Yes. I tried to one time, and Chris caught me."

"Was that the start of the slapping, Angel?"

"Yes. He didn't hit me hard. He said next time he would."

"Oh, nice of him to warn you. You know, Angel, I don't know Chris. But I'm telling you my gut feelings are I don't want to know him, and I want you and the children out of here."

"With Mom gone, it doesn't matter anymore."

"ANGEL!"

She sat up straight and looked like she was ready to run.

"I'm sorry for yelling at you. But it does matter. You are young and have a lot of years left to live, and you have two beautiful children to live for."

"You don't understand."

"I guess I don't, and I can't see that there would be anything that you could tell me to make me understand how your life doesn't matter. How the lives of your children don't matter."

"Don't worry about us. We will be fine, Dr. Adams."

"I can see that, Angel, with my own eyes. I hope that you will think about what you are doing before it is too late. Please remember I'm there for you. I promised Emma a long time ago that I would watch out for her girls, and be damned if I will just turn my back on you and the children. If that SOB so much as raises a hand to you, you call me and I'm coming to get you and the children. Angel, please promise me you will. If this ever happens to you again."

Angel nods her head.

"Angel, look at me and promise me that. ANGEL."

She jumps and says, "I promise."

I hate the way she goes into outer space. I know she is doing it to block everything out that hurts her. This does not sit well with me as she has two children to tend to. Making a mental note to myself to talk to the neighbor lady as soon as possible.

Chapter Four

———— • ————

Alex got up early. There were some things he was wanting to get done before he was to leave Angel's. One of the things was to make arrangements for the lady next door to help Angel and to stay as close to her as possible. When Alex went over to meet this woman, he found out that she was a retired RN, thinking he couldn't have been any luckier. He was going to pay her very well for doing this. He wanted her to become Angel's mother and the grandmother of the children, if that's what it took. He said he would call her every night to check on Angel and had told her of the suspicions that he had about Chris. She had told him that she never liked the man. He was never friendly. Alex hoped that this wasn't putting the neighbor in danger. She told him not to worry; she could take care of herself. She knew how to call the police. Alex was leaving her place feeling like he just put Angel into the hands of a sergeant. This might just be what Chris had to come up against to see that not all women are intimidated by him. He got the feeling that Tracy Bloom was ready to battle with Chris.

Hugging Angel good-bye and slipping a cell phone with his number programmed into it. Into her pocket. "Keep that hidden and use it whenever you have to, day or night. I don't want you ever to wait because of the time. If something is wrong, don't hesitate to call me. Do you understand, Angel? There is a bank account at the Royal in your name, so when you need money to get out, use it." He takes her face in his hands and lifts it so she has to look into his eyes.

"Do you understand, Angel? I'm worried about you, and I will be every day that you are still here with him."

She goes to drop her head again, and Alex just lifts it back up.

"Look at me, Angel, and promise me that you will hide this phone. You don't have to worry about anyone calling you and giving it away. But you will have it to get help when you need it."

"I promise. Thank you."

Hugging Elisabeth and going back to Angel and Gregory, he says to her, "Angel, I hope that you will know when it's time to run."

She just nods her head as he gets into his car and drives away. All the way home, he couldn't help feel that he should have just packed Angel and the children up and brought them home with him. Except he has seen enough of these women that aren't ready to get out just turn around and go right back into the same situation as they were just taken out of. So until they are ready, it would just be a waste of time. It always ends up making their life worse when they go back, but they can't see that. Some try two or three times before they are free. Others end up dead. In this situation, only the strong survive. All Alex could do was to pray and wait for the day that Angel would call. He believed that Angel would be one of the strong, and she would survive even if it is by the skin of her teeth. Looking up, he decided to talk to Emma.

"OH, Emma. What the hell do I do now? Your granddaughter is in way over her head. I feel it is up to me to see her safe, but I really have no right to pry or push my way in. But goddamn it, Emma. After all these years, I can't just walk away. I know that's what Angel thinks she wants, but it's not happening. She is like my own flesh and blood, and I don't want to let you down. I know that you would expect me to see to Angel and her children's safety while I still had any kind of breath in me.

I will do my damnedest to see her get free. You and Kate can rest assured that this is one promise I aim to keep."

Alex wasn't looking forward to going into his empty house. He knew it would be clean and warm and inviting, except it would be empty. On the times that Emma would visit, he loved coming home anytime. Her presence always made his home feel welcoming to whoever came through those doors. There will be no more warm welcoming in his home, and that gave him a heavy heart.

"Oh, Emma, my dear. I miss you so." He was right; his house was warm and clean. The quietness of it was eerie. His housekeeper had long gone home and would be back in two days. He felt every two days was enough for her. He wasn't home much to mess things up. But having Gail come in and put a woman's touch on the place made a big difference. Gail had been doing this for him now going on ten years. He had also set up a bank account for her. She said she didn't need it—that the money he paid her was plenty. He had told her, "I don't have anyone else to leave it to, so you may as well have some of it."

Gail was now in her early forties, and she had three children that she was raising alone. He had met her through the clinic when one of her children was sick and she had no money to buy the medication that she needed. He offered to buy her the medication in place of the job, and she has been with him ever since. He felt good that he had made a difference in a young family's life. He also played Santa Claus each year, and he never knew if Gail figured out who would leave all the gifts on their step every Christmas Eve. If she knew, she never let on. Some of that, of course, could be her pride. Alex also made arrangements for money to be available for her children when they wanted to further their education. He knew the second boy wanted to be a doctor. He had firsthand experience on what that cost was, so he had no problem seeing that the money would be there for him.

He had always thought he would do the same for Angel, but then Jake came into the picture and could give Angel whatever schooling she wanted. Although Alex has left Angel well provided for when he will no longer need the money. Until then, Alex just backed off until now because he didn't think there would be any money or help of any kind coming from Jake for Angel for some time to come. Alex tried to keep an open mind about this and understand why Jake has become so cold towards Angel. It was not Angel's fault that Kate died. Maybe Angel would not have allowed her mother to be her donor, and Kate may still be alive if the two had been talking like mothers and daughters should be. There still was the chance that Kate would have gone behind Angel's back and been her donor anyway. Kate was a strong-minded person, and knowing that her daughter's life was at stake, there would have been no stopping her. So both Angel and Jake had both forgiving and healing to do. Alex hoped that they have seen what holding a grudge does and that time will not stand still waiting for you to get your ducks in a row. He knew he would be playing middleman for some time. He knew Angel was going to be easier than Jake to deal with. Alex actually thinks there is a chance that Jake won't live long now that Kate is gone. Jake has himself believing that, without Kate, there is no life. Alex, for one, knows that feeling. It has been a long, lonely road without his Emma. There is always someone needing his help, so it has helped Alex to move on slowly. Whereas, with Jake, he has no one. But Angel and the children and they could bring him many years of happiness if he would only open his heart and work with him.

Alex hopes in time that Jake may think about how Kate would want him to react to this. That she would want him to be there for their grandchildren and her daughter. His daughter—the one she so gladly signed over to him when she was just a little girl. The little girl who fell in love with him and asked him to be her daddy so many years ago. Will that thought ever come to mind for Jake, or will he just become a lonely old man and die with a broken heart?

Alex was going to do all he could to see that this would not happen. He also knew there was only so much a person could do to help. He has learned in his practice and through life that you can't help those who aren't willing to help themselves. This made him sick at heart to know that there would be four wasted souls. He himself was going to try and make the best of what time he might have left to enjoy Angel and her children. Yes, he was now seventy but still in good health and hoped to have another twenty-five years or so. He hoped he wasn't the lucky one and would outlive the rest. He knew he would have a lot of praying to do for both Angel and Jake.

Tracy thought she should slip on over to meet Angel before that fool showed up. She figured the children would be getting ready for their afternoon nap and maybe Angel could use a helping hand. Ringing the doorbell a couple of times and after waiting a little longer she was about to turn away when the door opened just slightly. All she could see were these two big blue eyes looking back at her.

"Hi, sweetie. Is your mommy home?"

The eyes move up and down. She knew the little girl was nodding yes.

"My name is Mrs. Bloom. Do you think I could come in and see your mommy and baby brother?"

Her eyes go up and down again, but she wasn't moving to open the door. Then I hear "Who is it, Elisabeth?" Then the door gets pulled open.

"Hi, I'm Tracy Bloom. Alex asked me to help you."

"That was nice of Dr. Adams, but I don't really need any help anymore."

"May I come in a bit? Gets lonely sitting over there by myself." I take a step inward. I knew this was being a little more pushier than I should be. Angel steps back and allows me to come in.

"Are you putting the wee ones down for their naps?"

"Yes, I am."

"May I make us a cup of tea while you do that then?"

"Oh, there is no need for that. I will be fine."

"It's no problem, Angel. I don't mind, then we can chat a bit and get to know each other. After all, we are neighbors and we should know each other." I say that as I walk past her to the kitchen. I did know where that was because I knew the people who had lived here before. Alice and I used to visit back and forth. Then I took care of her when she got sick with cancer. So knowing the layout of the house wasn't a problem.

"Okay then. I will just go put the children down."

"That will be fine, Angel. I will have everything ready when you are done." Angel nods her head and walks away. Tracy could tell Angel was used to taking orders. This would make it easier for Tracy to work her way in because she knew that Angel wouldn't have the strength to tell her off or throw her out. Yes, she was going to take advantage of the fact that Angel is being manipulated and controlled by the fool she is living with. The difference being, Tracy wasn't there to hurt her or the children. In time, she hopes to be Angel's strength. Maybe her getaway. Only time will tell. Tracy herself was once a victim of abuse. She knows how hard it is to take the final step. Once you do, there is no turning back, and nothing but brighter skies lay ahead of you. She is hoping to be able to tell Angel her story, and maybe it will give her the boost that she will need. It won't be today, but soon. She must win Angel's confidence first. If Angel trusts her, then it will be easier to make her see that it is time to get out. With that thought, Angel came into the kitchen.

"Here you go, my dear. Tea is ready, and I found some tea cookies to go with it."

"Thank you, Tracy. But you really didn't have to."

"Like I said, it is about time I got to meet you and the children. Life does get lonely when you have no one around. For me it is a good thing I have a phone, or I would go crazy. Guess us old women just like to babble lots. We always seem to have a lot to say each morning. Someone always has news to tell. How about you, Angel? You and your friends phoneaholics too?"

"No, I don't have a phone."

"Oh, my girl, how do you get by today without a phone? I would go crazy if I didn't have mine."

"Chris has his for work. That is all we need."

"I see. What if you needed help, then what?"

"He said I have to wait until he is home."

"That is the craziest thing I've ever heard. Especially when you have small children, anything can happen at any given time."

"We are fine."

"Angel, you just had one of the biggest operations a person can have. You should have a phone. I will call Alex and tell him so too."

"OH please! Don't bother Dr. Adams. He has done enough already." She hangs her head.

"Angel, are you okay? I'm a good listener."

In a whisper she says, "Dr. Adams got me a cell phone to use, so if I need help, Chris doesn't know it. I am to keep it hidden away."

"Well, that is great. Now I won't worry so much. Angel, I won't tell Chris you have a phone, so relax." I reach over and place my hand on top of hers. A lone tear rolls down her cheek. This girl was so very sad, and it was heartbreaking not to be able to do something.

"Like I said, I listen well. I am an RN by trade, and I have heard a lot of stories. You don't have to be ashamed nor afraid that I would use you for gossip. That is not what I meant by the phone."

"I know you didn't. I also know you must be a very good person or Dr. Adams wouldn't have ask you to do this."

"You knew, about the arrangement?"

"Not really. I saw him over there before he left. He thought I was still sleeping."

"I'm sorry, Angel. I didn't mean to mislead you."

"That is okay. You didn't. I know he is worried about me and the kids."

"Has he just cause to worry, Angel?" She just raises her shoulder and didn't really answer, so I let it go. She wasn't ready yet to divulge that information.

Chapter Five

———◆———

Over the next three hours we had talked about several different things. I guess I did most of the talking. I let her know I was an RN and how many years I put in at the hospital and some of the things I saw that came through there. Some were pretty funny and others were not. But all in all I had enjoyed my job and took early retirement. God, I don't know why I did. Haven't done much in the way of traveling, so I still haven't seen any of my family that I wanted to see. Something always came up. I was hoping to see them this coming summer. That was my plan anyway. By the time I had gotten this far, Angel was starting to come around, and that is where I wanted to leave it. I wanted her to want to talk to me so next visit, perhaps, she will tell all—or some.

"Must be going, Angel. I have to meet up with the ladies for bowling. We're not good at this, but it sure is fun. Once you are in what they call the golden years, everything is to be fun, but we are so rustic that we need WD40 to be able to move around. Whoever came up with the saying of the golden years should be shot. By the time we get here, we are so worn out and the government decides on how much money you need to squeak by. So you don't dare sneeze and put a hole in anything 'cause there isn't enough money to fix it or replace it." Giving Angel a hug and holding her a little longer than need be, hoping that she would feel that I cared and she could trust me.

"Thank you, Tracy, for coming over. I really enjoyed the company."

"Your welcome sweetheart and take care. I will pop in tomorrow about the same time if that is okay with you. I would like to check over your surgery as well. Dr. Adams will be wanting an update on how it is healing."

"Yes, that will be fine." The door opens and in walks Chris. Tracy could tell by the look on his face that her presence is not what he wanted to see. So she thought she best speak up before Angel paid the price.

"Hello. I'm Tracy, a register RN. I'm here to check up on Angel's surgery. She will still be some time recuperating. So I am to help out where ever else she needs me to."

"I'm sure she can do fine on her own."

"NO, she cannot. Too much chance of tearing things apart inside. She should not be lifting anything yet, the baby is still more than she should be doing on a long term base."

"Thank you for your concern, but we will manage," he says as he sort of pushes me out the door and slams it shut. Under my breath, I say "jerk." Then I heard a slap, and I knew he had just hit Angel. Putting my hand over my mouth and standing there wondering what I should do. Then I hear him yell at her.

"How many times have I told you not to have people over? This is my home. It has taken long enough for the good doctor to leave. I want to be able to sleep in my own bed tonight. He wasn't about to tell her that he had been sleeping in his truck just down the road, waiting for Alex to leave. The one time he had to talk to Alex, he had told him that he would be out of town for a while. That was one of the reasons Alex stayed as long as he had. When I come home, I don't want some nosy busybody in here thinking she knows what's best. Do you understand, Angel?" Tracy could picture Angel standing with her head hung and nodding with her hand on her face. There were no more sounds coming from the house, so I left. Sick as I may be to the stomach. I also know that going back in was not going to help Angel out at all. I will make a note of this in my diary. Tracy also knew that she would be letting Alex know that his fears were warranted. She also knew that she too would be going back to Angel's tomorrow, come hell or high water. Tracy hoped that a slap was all Angel was going to get as she isn't strong enough yet to take much knocking around. Her kidneys will always be weak for the rest of her life. She has to know that she has to take care of them because next time she won't be as quick to get a donor. Her age will also be against her.

Tracy gets home and makes a note in her diary about today and then waits for Alex to call. He said he would call between his afternoon shift and evening. She knew he would be true to his word. He loved Angel and her children as though they were his, and he would keep an eye on them even from a distance.

Tracy opened her blinds just so she could see if the fool across the street would leave. Then she would go over and check on Angel and the children. Men like him got under her skin pretty deep. She herself, having been in that situation once and not having anyone there waiting for her to get free, made it a little harder than for someone who has got a place to run to and people who love them and are willing to do whatever it takes to get her free. It is a very painful experience to live through, and I guess for us who live through it, we should be grateful.

It takes a long time to get your self-esteem back, and to think for yourself has become almost impossible. It is a long road back, and for some, they never make it all the way back. They go through the rest of their life looking over their shoulders and always second-guessing themselves. Not knowing the choices you have made at the time would ever bring you to this.

Being scared of society becomes a way of life instead of enjoyment. When you start mistrusting everyone and see nothing but evil in anyone you meet, you know that your brain has become that of your abuser. They too don't trust, and that is why they like to have the upper hand at all times.

Some scars heal and others just get a fine scab over them that will tear away at any given time. To be able to heal from deep within is not an easy road or a short one. After all, some have taken this abuse for years, and for some others a lifetime. To come out of an abusive situation and live your life to the fullest is remarkable for the ones who have been strong enough to face their demons and win. So any helping hand along the way for some was more than an answered prayer. Especially for those who have walked that road alone. When you walk this road alone, it is a long lonely one, and there never seems to be a light at the end of the tunnel. It almost takes a train running you over before you wake up and smell the coffee or, in this case, see the light.

Angel has been given lifelines, and now she must choose the time when it's right for her to run or else she will not stay away. The abusers can always convince them that they should go back if they don't leave on their own accord. I pray that Angel wakes up before she has wasted many years and the scarring gets deeper. With that thought in mind, the phone rings, making me almost jump out of my skin as my past has been haunting me with the thoughts of Angel and the situation she has gotten herself into.

"Hello."

"Hello, Tracy. This is Alex."

"Yes. Hello, Mr. Alex."

"How did things go today, Tracy, with you and Angel?"

"OH, Mr. Alex, all went fine until I didn't get out early enough and he came home and almost threw me out. Then when I was standing on their step, I heard him slap her because I was there."

"Oh. That bastard. Excuse my language."

"I feel the same way, Mr. Alex."

"That guy makes my blood boil."

"He makes the hair on my neck stand up. I don't like that feeling. If I were a dog, I would have bitten him, except he would have left a foul taste in my mouth."

"That is so true, Tracy. Would you please check on her first thing in the morning? I hope a slap is all she got. He knows how fragile her body will be right now, but I don't know how far he is willing to go. 'Cause he could get big charges out of this if he puts her back into the hospital causing any problems with her kidneys."

"That might be a good thing then."

"It could be depending on how much damage he does to Angel. In the meantime, she has to be careful. She has no more donors that are related to her, so she could be on the list for a very long time."

"Was that not her father that was living across the road with her mother?"

"Oh no. Ben died many years ago when Angel was just a little girl. They were both in the accident, but Angel got nothing more than a broken leg."

"Oh, that poor girl. She has seen enough tears in her short lifetime."

"She sure has, Tracy. Her stepfather loved her too. He would have given her the world. Until her mother died."

"Does he blame Angel for her mother's death, Mr. Alex?"

"Yes. In some ways, he does. I have talked to him, but whether or not he will come to the understanding that Angel didn't have anything to do with it other than being Kate's daughter, we will have to wait and see."

"What about Angel? Does she believe that she also is to blame?"

"She does believe she killed her mother."

"Oh, Mr. Alex. How will that child get through all this with that horrible man?"

"That is why I need you, Tracy, to be there as much as you can. We have to let her know we care. She has to know that all she has to do is decide. I will be down every weekend to see her and the children."

"Did you tell him that?"

"NO, I don't plan on giving him any warnings. I would sooner catch him in the act of abusing her. Not only will it give me a reason to knock his head off. It will also give her a witness if she needs one."

"Oh, me too, Mr. Alex. I will be a witness for her. I am watching to see if he leaves to go out. I wanted to go and make sure she was okay before I go to bed."

"Thank you, Tracy, for helping me. I know Emma guided me to you."

"Emma?"

"Yes. Emma was Angel's grandmother and my friend."

"Oh. I see, Mr. Alex."

"You call me in the morning if things get out of hand. You can call me at any time things aren't looking like what they should."

"Yes, Mr. Alex. I sure will."

"Goodnight, Tracy."

"Goodnight, Mr. Alex."

Tracy didn't sleep well. She hadn't been around anyone in an abusive situation for some time. This brought back nightmares that she thought had died a very long time ago. Getting up and making herself some hot chocolate and sitting by the window looking out towards Angel's. She had had to turn her chair so she could see better. Tracy had lost the sight of one eye due to a beating that she got before she had finally gotten brave enough to leave. The doctors had hoped that when the swelling went down and the bleeding in around the eye stopped that her eyesight would return. After a month, there still was nothing, and today she has got like a white cloud over her eye. She hopes to be able to explain and show Angel just how bad it can get.

Tracy sat at her window all night. No one left from across the street until around 6:30 a.m. Tracy knew that with two little ones, Angel wouldn't be sleeping long either. She would wait until 8:00 a.m. This gave her time to put some laundry in and prepare what she wanted for supper. It was such a blessing when they came out with the slow cooker. This was one cooking invention that Tracy loved and used almost every day when she was still nursing. Her husband then wanted meals on the table as soon he came through the door. He complained about the slow cooker but was happy to have his meals made for him when she was working the shifts that took her through mealtimes. He knew his meals would be ready, and he could eat as soon as he got home. Now she doesn't use it as much as she settles on soup and a sandwich most days. When you are alone, you don't cook big meals. It always seems like a waste of time and a big mess for what. When a sandwich and a bowl of soup does the same thing and is also healthy for us. Today was a day she would use the slow cooker so she could spend more time with Angel.

Once she had her laundry done and her house tidied up to where she was happy with it, she headed for Angel's. When she got up to Angel's steps, she could hear the little girl and the baby crying. The little girl wasn't crying any normal cry, but a cry of fear. I could hear Angel talking to her, but the child was not calming down. So I knocked and at the same time opened the door. I usually wait for the person to answer their door, but I figured Angel had her hands full already this morning. Pushing the door open and stepping inside, I had walked into a war zone. Stepping over things and going around things, I finally got over to Angel. She was sitting on the floor, holding the baby and trying to calm Elisabeth down.

"What the hell happened?" As I squatted down in front of her. I reach out to take the baby and then and only then she looked up at me.

"OH MY GOD, ANGEL. WHY?" My stomach wrenched with memories at the sight of Angel. She could not see out of the left eye, and there was blood all over her face and in her hair from the split lip she had and, obviously, a nosebleed. Taking the baby from her I then said.

"I will watch the children, Angel. You go have a shower. It will ease some of the pain and take away some of your daughter's fear." I help her up off the floor, having taken the baby from her. He started to calm down right away. Up until now Angel has not said a word.

I gather her mouth hurt too much to say anything. She just dropped her head and went to the bathroom. Elisabeth is not crying as hard now but is still hiding behind the end of the sofa. I sit on the sofa and start talking to her.

"Elisabeth, would you like to come and sit beside me? Come here, sweetheart. I won't hurt you." Her eyes told me she had seen too much already and believing me was the last thing on her mind.

"Elisabeth, would you like to help me make some coffee for Mommy? Maybe I can get you something to eat. Are you hungry, sweetheart?"

She just nods her head. I put my hand out for her to take. It took her a couple of minutes before she came out from behind the sofa to take my hand. We walk slowly to the kitchen, moving in and around the furniture that had been thrown around.

Putting the baby in the swing chair and setting Elisabeth up to the table, I then get the coffee on and get the frightened child some cereal. I sit and talk to her about shows I think she might have watched on TV. She would nod her head yes or no, and that was all I was getting out of her. Looking up, I see Angel coming in. I get up and get her a cup of coffee and put some toast on. There was no reason to ask because I know she would just say no.

"Did you take something for pain, Angel?"

"Yes."

"Angel, you need to have your lip stitched up. That is too big of a cut to leave open like that. It won't heal right, and you could get an infection. Having a cut like that around the mouth is not good."

"NO!"

"Angel, you have to, and I'm going to take you as soon as you have had your coffee and toast."

"You can't stay," she says with tears in her eyes.

"This was all over me being here?"

"Yes."

I knew some of it was, but I had no idea how long this had been going on.

"Angel, has this been happening a lot?"

"NO! He used to yell a lot. Since Mom died, he has gotten to be like this."

"That's because he thinks you have nowhere to go, Angel, and he is wrong. You know that, right?"

"Jake don't love me anymore. He won't let me go home."

"Mr. Alex would take you and the children in a minute."

Chapter Six

"This Jake I do not know."

"Dr. Adams is not family. I can't ask him for any more help than he has already given."

"Mr. Alex, he thinks of you as his family."

"We have known him for a very long time."

"That is what he said, and you are to call him whenever you need help of any kind."

"I know. He gave me a cell phone before he left."

"You use it too. Now finish up, and I will take you to the hospital to get stitches."

"I really can't do that."

"You have no choice. If you think I'm scared of Chris, think again. And you better not be either. You can stop this, Angel, and you know it. Things won't get any prettier by staying. And when they start this, it only gets worse."

"NO. Chris loves me."

"Bull, Angel. There is nothing about love in this, it is all about control. Look at me. NO, really look at me. What do you see?"

"Nothing, Tracy."

"Then look again." And I get right in her face.

"See the scares on my face?" I ask as I pull my hair back.

"Look at my eyes, Angel. Do they look the same to you? This one I can't see out of because I got a beating like you have from my husband. He also told me he loved me. These men don't know what real love is. I hope when the swelling has gone down you will be able to see. This has to be reported."

"No. It was my fault."

"Like hell it was, Angel. It was all over me being in his home. I heard him when I left. You did nothing to deserve this. Or to have your furniture destroyed like that." Tracy waves her hand to the living room.

"How much of this did your daughter see?"

"All of it."

"You're lucky, Angel. He turned on the furniture or you could be dead by now—if you took the same beating as your furniture."

"Chris would never do that."

"OH really! Did you think he would ever do this to you, Angel? Did you?"

"NO."

"I never had any children to see this happen to me, and you had better think about what impact this has on them for the rest of their lives. Did you live through this kind of life at home?"

"No. My dad was a good dad."

"What about Jake?"

"No, he was a good man too."

"So you know there are good men out there. Why would you settle for this? Did you love your father, Angel?"

"OH YES!"

"Then think about how he would feel if he knew his daughter was being beaten by the man she lives with and has had two children with him."

"Dad would be very angry, and he would probably beat Chris up."

"Well, I think there are a few of us who would like to do the same thing now. This is not human, Angel, nor is it legal. You can charge him for this. I don't recommend it if you don't leave because it will be nasty for you and the children to stay afterwards. It would only add fuel to his fire."

"I don't want to charge him."

"No, of course you don't." I say this with a bad taste in my mouth. I had a feeling that Angel was going to be around for a few more beatings. She wasn't ready to open her eyes. He had her pretty well brainwashed to his way of thinking. Every time he beats her, it will be her fault. This is hard to convince yourself of anything different. Unless there is someone else strong enough to keep putting it into her head that she did nothing wrong to deserve such treatment.

We get to the hospital and, of course, their first concern was that Angel wasn't having trouble with her kidneys that would have made her dizzy and cause her to take this fall. After she had assured them that her kidneys were fine, all the routine questions were asked, and all the normal lies were told. I had worked there for too many years, and the head nurse was looking at me for the right answers. It wasn't up to me to play God. Angel had to come clean on her own. Angel has no idea how much better she will feel when she finally admits that Chris did this to her, and to keep her and the children safe, she must know when it is time to run.

It took six stitches to her lip and side of the face. The stitching was done on the inside, and butterfly tape was put on the outside to help prevent as much scarring on her face as possible.

"Sorry, I can't promise no scarring. I can say it will be small. You do have to watch for infection. Wounds around the mouth are prone to infections."

Angel just nods her head. She refuses to look the nurse in the eye.

"If you fall again, I think I would be removing the coffee table. This is a pretty nasty bang you took. We will want to check your eye after the swelling has gone down. You know what signs to watch for—for concussion, I mean?"

"I will keep an eye on her. I am helping Angel for a while."

"That is good. You may have a headache for a few days. You let Tracy know if you get sick to the stomach or anything changes."

Again, all Angel did was nod her head. Elisabeth sat watching with big eyes. I'm sure she wondered what was to come next. Not once did she move or say a word. Gregory slept through it all. On the whole, Angel had pretty well-behaved children. Probably scared into behaving. The sadness in the little girl's eyes would rip the heart out of any loving human being.

The nurse pulls me to the side as we were getting ready to leave.

"I sure hope you can wake this girl up before it is too late."

"You know there is nothing anyone can do until she is ready. She will have to hit rock bottom before she sees the light."

"The way it is going, she won't be seeing much for too long, never mind the light."

"I plan to work on her and being her ally when need be."

"That little girl saw it all, didn't she?"

"Yes, I'm afraid so."

"You can tell just by watching her. The child is going to have nightmares."

"She will be another one lying on someone's couch when she gets older if it doesn't come to a stop quickly."

"I wish you luck, and them." As she tilts her head towards Angel and her children.

We leave and go back to Angel's. She puts the children down for their naps, and I start to clean up.

"Oh, Tracy, you don't have to do that."

"You're right, I don't. But I'm going to help you, Angel. Do you want your friends to see this?"

She hangs her head as she says, "I don't have any friends anymore. Chris didn't like them, so I couldn't hang out with them, and they quit coming around."

I already knew what her answer would be before she said anything. That is how these guys operate. They take away everything that is you and anyone that knows you and could make you see what he is up to. They do it so subtly that it is all done before you know what hits you. Your family is the last they take away because, by then, they have convinced you of how right they were about your friends and coworkers that you believe whatever they tell you about your family. At first, there might be some hesitation in your mind because of the closeness you have had with your family, but it doesn't stay long because they know how to manipulate.

As we clean up, Angel tells me a little more about herself. She had a very happy childhood until her father died, and then again after her mother had remarried. She told about a baby brother that she never got to see, how she and her mother were on their own then and wanted the baby so much.

"You know, I don't think my mom was the same after my dad died and after she lost the baby."

"I could see why she wouldn't be. That would have been a big loss for her. The baby was going to be the healing point for her since your father died. With her losing the baby, the healing never came."

"But she married Jake and seemed very happy then."

"She might have been happy to you on the outside, but inside she hurt like hell."

"You really think so?"

"Yes. When people don't heal from a loss, they don't ever find happiness. It is a door that has to be closed before you can open another. In the end, it will eat you alive."

"I had not talked to my mom in a very long time. And when she came to see me, I chased her away."

"When did she come to see you?"

"The night before my surgery."

"OH, Angel. I'm sorry."

"Not as sorry as I am. I loved my mom with all my heart."

"Then why did you quit talking to her?"

"I don't remember why in the beginning, but Chris told me I didn't need them. She never called or came around to see me."

"Why do you think that was?"

"I don't know. I sent Mom my new address when we moved."

"YOU DID?"

"Yes. When she never came around, then Chris started to point out that she didn't love me as much as she loved Jake. That she didn't need me anymore, that I was just a thorn in her side. She had all she needed and was happy now. After a year and I never heard from her, I took it to be true."

"Do you still believe that, Angel?"

"I don't know."

"Come on, Angel. If anyone knows their mother, it would be her daughter. Do you think that is how your mother felt?"

"No, not really. But why didn't she come and see me?"

"That is something you might have to ask Chris or figure out on your own. You know, Angel, if your mother didn't love you more than her husband, do you think she really would have put her life on the line to give you one of her kidneys?"

"You know about that?"

"Yes, Mr. Alex told me what happened. It was a very grand thing she did for someone she didn't really love. Wouldn't you say?" Angel sits down on the closest chair and cries. I gave her the time she needed, and I went ahead and cleaned the blood out of her throw rug. I thought it was going to be a throw away rug but it came clean enough. The broken furniture I hauled out to the dumpster in the back, no one was going to be able to fix it anyways. Coming back in Angel had gone into the kitchen and put on some coffee. So I continued to pick up. There were books from one end of the room to the other. They were some kind of mechanic books. Looked like Chris was or wanted to be a mechanic. I wasn't asking. I stood the book shelf back up and started to put his books back in place. I would have rather taken them out to the dumpster as well but that would get Angel another beating for sure. As I lifted this one book up, it fell open and a card fell to the floor. Picking it up and turning it over, I see it was a change-of-address card. "OH my god," I say as I put my hand over my mouth. I continue to read, and it was the card Angel had written out for her mother. There was even a stamp on it. Now why was it in this book? Did Angel put it in there and then forget to send it? Or did he? My bets were all on him. I tuck it into my pocket and continue to put books up. I figured I would show her when we had our coffee.

The room was starting to look half-ass clean but a little short on furniture. The lamps had been smashed as well, so we would have to vacuum once the little ones were awake. This guy must have really lost it at one point, and all I could keep thinking was how lucky Angel was that he took more of it out on the furniture than her. Although there is no doubt in my mind that she got a beating.

"Tracy, our coffee is ready."

"Okay, I will be right there." Going on into the kitchen and seeing Angel's beautiful face changing to all these horrible colors, I decided right then. I was going to tell her what happened to me. I waited until we were seated and halfway though our first coffee. Just out of the blue, I decided to hit her with it.

"You know, Angel, my husband didn't destroy anything but me. Guess he felt everything else was too costly to replace.

"I was a runaway from home, so he also knew I had no place to go. I met him waiting on tables. He had become one of my steady customers and was a big tipper. In the end, I knew why, and it was all part of a bigger plan for him. He had no respect for women at all. His mother used to hook for a living. Being a single mother, she thought it was good money, and in the end all she did was destroy her son's belief in women and what they really were.

"He used to treat me like a hooker after we were married. Never once did he lay a hand on me until we were married. To abuse me or for sex. I thought I had found a real winner, a gentleman. My boss had told me then, 'Make sure you hang on to that one, there aren't many out there like him.' It only took three months before all hell broke lose. I had no idea what I did to provoke it the first time or any other time after that. He did start accusing me of seeing other men at work. It was all in his head no matter what I tried to tell him. He would tell me I was just like his mother. My first day back to work after the first time was easy to lie about because they never expected this of him. When the fourth time came around and then they were getting closer and closer together, my boss finally caught on. Because of them, I finally got out. I had hit rock bottom after a year and a half of the beating and being blinded in one eye.

"Lillian and Bill knew I was saving up to go to nursing school. So one day when I went to work, I never went back home. They had put me on a bus and sent me out to nursing school. I owed those people my life."

Angel's mouth dropped open as I continued after pouring us a second cup of coffee.

"Did your husband ever find you?"

"No, I don't think he even tried. I can't be sure of that. I lived looking over my shoulder for a year."

"Where is your husband now? Do you know?"

"I can't really say. I never went back. There was no need to. I filed for divorce two years later, and my address was never divulged due to my safety. There was enough evidence on the case that no one was telling him where I was. Lillian and Bill came to visit me every year up until they passed away. They never had any children and left what they had to me. There was plenty for me to have a good life along with my nursing. It was because of them that I could retire early. I had a lawyer sell whatever could be sold and, in turn, I opened up a trust fund to help out other girls that would end up in a crisis center to get their nursing if that was what they were wanting. This is called pay forward.

"I myself believe in what goes around comes around."

Chapter Seven

---◆---

I could see Angel was thinking very deeply. I did not pry, nor did I want to push her into defending what Chris had done to her. A little push at a time will be better than nothing. I only hope that we had time to play the waiting game. I left Angel to think about what I had said. I went back to picking up the books. I had no idea how long the little ones would sleep. Angel's home had a very eerie silence to it. No music playing softly in the background, no humming of a washing machine or dishwasher—just silence. Some people say silence is golden; in this case, silence is deafening. It is as though there is no one else around but Angel and myself. There is no outside world when you live like this. The outside world is what we have learnt that kills us. So you learn to stay tucked away within your own four walls. It becomes your safe haven, to a point. You are better off not knowing anything when he comes home. That way, he feels he still has total control. He does have total control, and it is a horrible way to live. To these men, women are nothing more than a sex stick and someone to tend to their every whim. By them beating on their women, it makes them feel powerful.

There have been cases of where the man got physical once and he felt like such a heel, it never did happen again. There are breaking points for everyone; some get it into check before it gets ahold of them. Others, it is a sickness, and they need professional help.

The baby woke up and put some life into the house. As Angel was feeding him, I had noticed she didn't really care if she fed the baby or not. So I thought I would have a chat to see what was up.

"You have a great-looking son, Angel. He's so adorable."

She sort of nods her head, so I pull up a chair beside her.

"Angel, did you not want the baby?"

"Yes."

"Then why do you look so sad?"

"I had hoped that when Chris had a son, he would be happy and change."

"Did Chris want the children?"

"NO."

"Oh, Angel, that never works. It only adds fuel to their fire. 'Cause now he has three to control instead of one. Is that why you got pregnant again?"

"Yes, and my babies are all I have. They are my family now."

"Yes, they are. And it is up to you to see that they are safe, Angel, and well cared for. They have no way of knowing how to deal with their father when he goes on these rampages, and they are usually the ones who get hurt the worst. 'Cause they will never say to him what he wants to hear. He takes that as disobeying him. He will punish them the way he sees fit. Are you willing to stand by and watch this, Angel? You are all these two darling little children have to keep them out of harm's way."

"Chris would never hurt the children."

"Oh god, Angel, what will it take to open your eyes? When he gets mad, he won't care that they're little children. Children he never wanted, and you are going to hear about that."

"I already have." A silent tear rolls down her check.

"Aw, Angel, why are you staying?" I reach into my pocket for a tissue, and my hand makes contact with the card I had picked up. Looking at Angel and wondering if this was a good time then choosing to lay it all on the table for her, I just slide it on the table in front of her.

At first, I didn't think she saw what it was. Then a frown came upon her face. She looked like she was trying to place this card, as she looked up at me and says, "Where did you get this?"

"It fell out of a mechanic book when I was picking them up." She moans a horrible sound and holds the card to her chest. Shaking her head back and forth in total despair.

"All this time, I thought she wanted nothing to do with me because I left with Chris. This is why she never answered. She never got her mail. So this must mean that Mom never go anything I sent her."

"Did you not go to the mail, Angel?"

"No. Chris said he would get the mail and send it as he always had papers from work that had to be sent out or picked up. He said there was no need in two of us spending gas money on tending to the mail. I didn't see anything wrong with that."

"So you never got anything from your mom since you left?"

'No, nothing. I thought all this time she had disowned me, that Mom never loved me anymore. I missed my mom so much, most days I couldn't think straight. If Chris caught me crying 'cause I missed her, he would say, 'Well, she can't love you or miss you. You never hear from her.'"

"Why didn't you call her? You knew her number?"

"Chris said I couldn't call long distance. So I waited for her to call me." As she lays the card back down on the table saying.

"But I guess she never got the number. I wrote it on this card."

"Oh, Angel, all those wasted years. Your mother must have been heartbroken."

"Yea, me too. I was so angry at her when she came to the hospital, and it wasn't even her fault. Aw, Mommy. I'm so, so sorry," Angel says as she rocks back and forth on her chair.

"Angel, Chris has taken a lot from you, and it is time to get out. You have lost the last years with your mother, and your children will never know their grandmother because of him. Your stepfather is all you have left and the only grandfather your children will know. You have to take your children and go to him, Angel."

"Jake won't want us. He thinks I killed Mom."

"He will understand if you show him this." Tracy hands the card back to her.

"Put this where it is safe so you will have it to explain to your stepfather."

"Should I tell Chris we found it?"

"Just keep the info to yourself until you need to use it. He may just get mad and slap you around for it. It was in his books, so he will accuse you of snooping in his things."

"But it fell out of a book."

"That won't matter to him. It is not how he is going to see it. Believe me on that."

"All right." She tucks it into her pocket just as the doorbell rang. Angel looked so startled.

"It's okay. I will get the door." Boy, has this guy got her number. Opening the door to a nice surprise.

"Well hello, Mr. Alex. How are you?"

"Hello, Tracy. I'm fine, how about you?" he says as he steps in. "What the hell happened here? Where is Angel and the children?"

"They are okay, sir. They are here. I was just helping Angel get her house back in order." He goes hurrying off to the kitchen when he heard the baby cry. When he saw Angel, he lost it.

"Angel! My god, child. Where is that bastard now?"

"At work."

"You and the children are coming home with me."

"No, Dr. Adams, we can't."

"Why the hell not?"

"We belong here."

"Bull you do, Angel. You are no man's beating post. This is no way for you and the children to live. Are you not scared every day?"

"Yes. But I just have to be careful of what I do or say."

"You have quit living, Angel. These children have to be able to live in a happy home. Not one where they get to see their mom as a punching bag or whatever else he decides for you that day. This is no way to live, Angel. Now you get some clothes packed, I'm taking you home."

Angel hands him the card that she had in her pocket.

"What is this?"

After he read it, he still didn't understand.

"Angel, what is this to mean?"

"It was my change of address card with my phone number on. It was supposed to be sent to Mom."

"So why didn't you send it?"

"Chris said he did. But he didn't."

"Is that what the mess is all about?"

"No, the mess is because of Tracy being here. This fell out of one of his books when she was picking them up."

"Angel, this is horrible. Your mother waited a long time to hear from you. She thought that you had quit loving her."

"I waited to hear from her too. I was feeling the same way—that is why I was so mad at her when she came to the hospital. It wasn't even her fault."

"No, and he knew what he was doing. This is why he stayed away while you and your mother were in the hospital. Chris thought this would all come out before it has. He probably would have just disappeared. When your mother passed away, it just gave him more ground. You know he wanted you to find this, that is why it was put into the book. It is just a way of letting you know he controls you and everything you do." Angel starts to vibrate.

"Are you cold, Angel?"

"No, but I can't stop shaking."

"You are having an anxiety attack. You are on overload right now, and your body doesn't know how to handle it. Tracy, will you take the baby, please? I will go get her something for this, and we will wrap her in a warm blanket. I want to put one in the dryer to warm up. It will work the fastest."

He leaves as Tracy is taking the baby from Angel. Guess once a doctor, always a doctor. They carry their bag with them all the time.

Just like when the doctors used to make house calls. Not many do today. There are a handful that still make house calls, and we were so lucky to have one on hand. Laying the baby down and getting a blanket into the dryer was like working in the hospital. You always had so many things to tend to, and I hadn't had much in the way of responsibilities for a while. So I was enjoying this. It was only too bad that Angel had paid the price for my enjoyment.

"Mommy, Mommy."

"Come here, sweetheart. Mommy doesn't feel good. Mommy is going to be lying down on the sofa. Come, I will take you to her."

Poor little thing was still scared. She didn't know what to expect. She came and took my hand. What a little doll she is. Yet to be so sad when her eyes should be sparkling with happiness. A child at this age should not know fear at this level.

"Here, Angel. I want you to take these pills, and we will wrap you up in a blanket."

Mr. Alex handed Angel the pills, and she did what she was told as I brought the warm blanket out to her. I had thrown in another so we could just keep changing them out. Elisabeth climbed up beside her mom. She snuggled in so close, you couldn't hardly tell she was there.

"Tracy, could you get some clothes together for the children? Angel will help you get her own clothes together once she has calmed down."

"Yes, Mr. Alex. I can do that."

"Please, Dr. Adams. I can't live with you. Thank you for your help, but we will stay here."

"No, Angel, you are not staying here with this fool. Your mother and your grandmother would want me to get you and your children out of here. You don't have to live with me. I will get you your own apartment. But you are not living like this, do you understand? You are not married to this fool, and these children are not to see any more of this. If you are lucky, Elisabeth will forget this episode. If you keep them in this situation, you will only cause them mental disorders down the road. Is that what you want hanging over your head? To know your children are not right in the head and are not able to handle society, and it is all because of your bad choices. Think about it, Angel, before you throw your children to the wolf."

Alex turns around and heads for the kitchen. You could tell he was disgusted with Angel right now, and he needed time to get his temper under control. One man out of control is all anyone can handle.

Tracy had gone off and done as Mr. Alex asked and had gotten clothes packed up for the children. Angel didn't have much for the children, so Tracy was able to get everything into two suitcases that Angel had under the crib. No doubt, Chris would not be giving her money to spend on children that he never wanted. Tracy must remember to get her address so she could send her things that she would be needing for the children, or if she buys something that catches her eyes, she will buy it for these two little darlings who have no one to spoil them. She will play grandma and enjoy it.

Tracy found a large box and put a lot of Angel's clothes in it. Angel too had very little to her name. Her underwear drawer she packed into an overnight bag. By the look of some of the things that were in it, it was the bag she had at the hospital. It was plenty large enough for that drawer of clothes. Tracy knew there were clothes to be washed so she headed that way. Going though the kitchen she stopped to ask Alex.

"What time are you wanting to leave with Angel and the children?"

"We will leave whenever we have things all tended to."

"Why are you asking?"

"Angel doesn't have much for clothing for her or the children. I was just going to make sure the laundry was all done up so she wouldn't be short handed."

"That will be fine, Tracy. I don't care what she takes because I will make sure she has more than enough when I get her settled back home. I will have her bank account switched to there, and she can use the money for whatever she needs or just wants. You may continue until Angel has a rest and is up to leaving."

"You know she may not want to leave after she feels better."

"I know, and it is too bad for her. If he can bully her, so can I for a good cause. She is coming back with me."

"She is lucky to have you in her life, Mr. Alex."

"Let's hope she will feel the same way."

"I will miss them. Now I know it hasn't been long, but Angel and the children are so easy to love."

"That is so true. The first time Kate brought Angel to me after she was about two, her big brown eyes took my heart away. She was always a beautiful baby, but as she got older, she got more of a personality. She won people's hearts wherever she went. She was so happy all the time. The death of her father was very hard on Angel. She and Ben were very close. But she bounced back like the little trooper they knew she was."

"I hope she bounces back from all of this. Losing her mother and now this. It could break her spirit."

"Yes, it could. I'm hoping that once she is back home, Jake and I can rebuild her spirit."

"I wish I could help, Mr. Alex. That girl needs a woman in her life."

"So why don't you?"

"Why don't I what, Mr. Alex?"

"Why don't you move back with her and the children? What is keeping you here? You told me you have no family."

"Are you serious, Mr. Alex?"

"Yes, Tracy Bloom, I am. I will make sure she gets a place big enough for you too. It would do Angel good to have you there. I know you won't let her sit by and die. I will pay you the same as you are getting now. With a raise to come."

"Oh, Mr. Alex, you pay me plenty. I don't need a raise."

"Everyone deserves a raise, Tracy."

"Do you think Angel would mind?"

"Well, why don't we ask her when she wakes up?"

Chapter Eight

———◆———

"What are you wanting to ask me?" Angel says in a groggy voice as she staggers to the fridge and gets a glass of water.

"Well, Angel, Tracy has a proposition to make you."

"I do?"

"Yes, you were just telling me about wanting to move." Alex thought he would help Tracy get to the point.

"Yes I do, Angel, and I thought I could move close by you and the children so I could still help out. That way if you want to get a job, I would still be there for the children.

"Angel, you know you can have a job as soon as you want. I already saw to that." Alex tells her.

"I don't want to work yet. Gregory is too young."

"Part time would not hurt you or the baby. In fact, it would do you both good. Seeing how you would have help from someone you can trust with the children, you would be a fool not to take it. It is a very good opportunity for you. It would help you get your life back on track."

"Thanks, Dr. Adams. I will take this one step at a time."

Alex knew that her grieving for her mother is going to be long-term as she is so ridden with guilt. A year won't be long enough, and she is going to be somewhat lonely over the years. They could only hope that when her children grow up to be more company than work, it will help Angel move on. There was no doubt in Alex's mind that Angel would need professional help along the way. He would get that all set up so when she was ready, it would be only a phone call away. In the meantime, they would have to stay strong and focused for her. Angel no doubt will be a zombie for a while yet. Alex would pull out all his resources to get her help. He knew she would need the best of physiologists that money could buy. Right now he is thinking, *Boy I'm glad my father was a wise investor.* Although he had more money than he would spend. He wanted to make sure he could leave Angel and her children well provided for. He also had it set up so it did not matter what man came into her life; he would not be able to get one penny of her inheritance.

"All right, Angel, you're right. We will get you moved first. Then worry about the finer details later. You can stay with me until we get you something that has plenty of room for all of you, and the children can have a large yard to play in."

Angel just nods her head and goes to her room.

"I will get my place in order, Mr. Alex, and will be there in two or three days. That girl should not be alone in her state of mind."

"Thank you, Tracy, I totally agree with you. It won't take me long to find a place. I have one in mind, and it is close to the clinic and hospital. It had belonged to a doctor who had retired and moved away. It has been empty for a couple of years now. It would be perfect for Angel. It is back against the park, so the children would have plenty of room to run. Angel could see them for the most part without leaving her house."

"Sounds like a dream come true, Mr. Alex."

"I will start putting the children's bags in my truck."

"I will go see if I can help Angel. Gregory should be waking up soon. I will get Elisabeth fed. Then they will be ready to go."

"Thank you for your help, Tracy."

"Oh, no need to thank me, Mr. Alex. It is my pleasure to be able to help." She goes off and finds Angel lying on her bed, weeping.

Going over and sitting on the side of the bed, she starts to rub Angel's back.

"Come now, dear, tell me what the tears are for. Are you hurting somewhere, Angel?"

She didn't answer at first. Then she sits up a little and says, "I have made such a mess of my life. Now I have two babies to take care of, and I don't have my mom. I can't do this without her."

Tracy pulls her into her embrace and starts to rock, saying, "Angel, do you remember the things your mother has taught you?"

She sniffles and says, "Yes."

"Then you will always have your mom with you. Whenever you are in doubt. Just take the time to remember your mom and think. What would Mom tell me? The answers will come to you. She will relay them to you through memory. Her guidance will always be there, you just have to learn how to use it."

"It won't be the same as talking to her."

"No, it will not, but it will be better than nothing. While thinking about how or what she would do, share it with the children. This will help keep you close to your mom."

"What do you mean, Tracy?"

"Well, say things like 'You know, Elisabeth, your grandma Kate would say do it this way or this way.' You will work out the answers and, at the same time, you are helping your children get to know what their grandma Kate was like. What she liked and didn't like. They will learn of the things Grandma used to do because she has taught you how to do the same things.

"When we get all settled in, we will put pictures up of your mom all over the house. Nice big pictures so it will be like she is still here. The children will get to know her face. They are young, and to them, her face will be etched into their minds as though they grew up with her."

"I don't have any pictures of my mom."

"Are you joking?"

"No, they were all at Mom and Dad's when I left. I only took my clothes."

"Well then, we will have to see what we can do. This will be fun, Angel, to go picture hunting. I'm sure your stepfather will have pictures. I too will learn about your mom. Over the years, there should have been great pictures taken."

"At Christmas and Easter, all those special holidays. I think the best ones will be when Grandma and Mom and I went to Australia. We had fun there. We played Grandma out."

"See, there you go. Those are the pictures we want and we will make your memories happy ones Angel. It is time to leave all your sadness behind you. It's time to move on for you and your children. Do you think you can do this?"

"It won't be the same, Tracy, as having Mom here."

"No, it won't. But it is the best we can do, and by god, we are going to make it a happy one. In time, you will see what pleasure it will bring you just by having your mom's picture hanging around the house. Talking about her as if she had just done something or had just been for a visit. We want to have her in every room. That way, she can do your housework with us."

That got a chuckle out of Angel.

"Mom would say, 'I missed a spot.'"

Taking her back into my arms and smiling, I tell her, "That is what I want to hear. Share your mom with me, and your grandma. Do you think you can, Angel?"

Angel smiles and nods her head.

"Good. Now let's get you packed up so we can get started on this new life of yours. What do you say?"

"Okay. Thank you, Tracy."

"You're welcome, Angel."

It didn't take us long to get her clothes together, or her personal belongings. This girl didn't have much to her name. Some things I thought she should take but she said no, she didn't want it. I gathered they were things that maybe Chris had bought for her at one time. The crib was the only bed that was taken. Mr. Alex told her he would make sure she had all she needed and then some. All she had to do was let him know what it was she would be wanting or needing. That money wasn't a problem. I could only shake my head and think. How lucky this girl was. But then I had been lucky to have help when I needed it as well. It was there. There are many girls out there that are not lucky. They live a life of hell until the day they die. Unfortunately, these men prey on weak women and ones who don't have family to turn to. So getting help is not something all these women living in these dreadful relationships have access to. It is left to the grace of God to see them through.

By four thirty they were all packed up and ready to roll. Hugging and kissing each of the children made me sad to know they no longer will be living next door. On the brighter side of things, it was all such a good feeling to know that in a couple of days I too would embark on a new life and will have a role to play in Angel's future.

Not having children of my own I could put my whole heart into this without the worry of upsetting anyone. There would be no one to feel like I'm spending more time with her then I am with them. I had heard how that is a big problem in many families. It doesn't matter if there are two children or four, the outcome is always the same. Whether it is justified or not, there will always be one child that has that feeling of being left out. Money alone does not fix this. Some of it is because the children have grown selfish and can't see for anything but for themselves. It is all about them and only them. My only hope is that, maybe together, Angel and I can see to it that neither of her children feels this way. I get to be a nanny and a grandma all in one, and it is a little overwhelming, but I'm sure I can do it. If nothing else, I look forward to the challenge and the experience.

It was nine thirty that evening when Angel called and said they had just finished putting up the crib. She had some joy in her voice. It wasn't there long after she had asked, "Tracy, did you see if Chris came home?"

"Yes, I saw him come home. He wasn't in the house long."

"Really?" I could hear the fear in her voice.

"Angel, listen to me. You will be safe. He doesn't know where you are. He has no idea where Mr. Alex lives. So don't going getting yourself all worked up over nothing. Mr. Alex won't let him hurt you."

"Tracy, Dr. Adams is too old to have to fight with Chris. Maybe I should go back so he won't come here and hurt Dr. Adams?"

"Don't you talk foolish now, girl. You stay put, you hear me? I will be there in two days. Mr. Alex, he will call the cops if Chris shows up on his doorstep. He told me his place has very good security."

"Yes, he does. It is almost like a jail here."

"Good, now don't worry."

"There are other people around when Mr. Alex is gone to work."

"Yes. He has a housekeeper come in. There is also a groundskeeper."

"See? So no need to worry, Angel. Just relax. You can call me anytime. Remember, I will be there in two days."

"All right, Tracy. Thank you."

"You're welcome, my dear girl. Now get some sleep, and I will chat with you tomorrow. Unless you need me through the night. Just call."

"Goodnight, Tracy."

"Goodnight, Angel."

Tracy knew that she had better keep her promise and be there in two days. She could see Angel coming back just to protect Mr. Alex. Tracy also knew that Mr. Alex would take no bull from Chris, and the fact that he would be well-known in his town. It won't take him long to get help. That is also a benefit to being a doctor.

Sleep didn't come easy as I was too excited about moving, and I wanted it to happen as quickly as possible. Finding a storage that would have enough room to hold my belongings until I knew whether I would be needing any of it or not might not be that easy, especially if I want it all in one place. Guess if I have to split it up then I will. I could just put it all for sale in the secondhand store and maybe just buy new. The personal pieces that I have that belong to

Lillian and Bill I would keep. Now I will have Angel to pas them down to. Yes, that is what I will do.

So Tracy headed out to the secondhand stores to see who would be interested. Stopping along the way to find a small storage unit for what she would be keeping and someone to move her belongings over. Feeling good about her decisions and now that the plans were all made she headed home to separate what was going where. There was going to be a small box of trinkets she would take with her to make her room, her room. Deep in thought and excited about her move after all these years Tracy did not hear the doorbell the first time then there was a pounding on the door with the doorbell.

"All right, all right, I'm coming. You guys are—" She was stunned to see Chris standing on her step.

"Where is Angel?"

"Nice to see you too, Chris, and I don't know."

"Don't bullshit me. I know you had something to do with her leaving. She wouldn't have the balls to do it on her own."

"Well, as you say. But I'm glad she got balls and left you." With that, he made a step towards me, and I could see the fire in his eyes. I didn't budge. He looked like he was going to either slap me or push me.

"Go ahead, I'm not Angel. And I will have your ass in jail so damn fast you won't know what hit you." He stopped dead in his tracks.

"That's right. I lived with an asshole like you once, so I'm not scared of any of you. I do know how to call the police, so either you leave now on your own or they can take you out." With that said, one of the moving trucks pulled up out front. I have to say I was pleased to see them although I didn't want to show him I was scared of him. I was terrified; my heart felt like it was going to jump right out of my chest. I saw what he had done to Angel, so I know it wouldn't take much to push him to that point.

"Is this Tracy Bloom's house?" the man on the passenger side yelled out his window.

"Yes, it is. Come on in. You mind moving your truck?" I say to Chris.

"Going somewhere?"

"It's none of your business, but yea. I can't stand who I have for neighbors."

"Too bad you didn't learn to mind your own business before now," Chris says as he turned around and kicked the garbage can off my deck.

"Tough guy you are. Glad to be moving," the guy with the name tag Jessie said.

"Is there a problem, Madam?"

"No sir, just getting rid of some scum." I go back on into the house, and I find the closest chair and sit down. I had the shakes so bad, when Jessie came in he noticed it right away.

"Madam, are you all right?"

"I will be in a bit."

"Who was that guy?"

"Just an unliked neighbor."

"Seems like it was more than that. Will he be coming back?"

"Hope not."

"Should we call someone for you in case?"

"If he comes back, I will call the police. The door won't get unlocked and opened to him again."

"You sure you don't want us to call someone else?"

"No, I will be fine. Thank you for your concern."

"May I get you some water or something?"

"Yes, you may. Thank you." Jessie goes to bring me water, and I got to thinking. How far would Chris have gone if these guys hadn't shown up yet. Would they have found me beaten and lying dead or close to dead? Would Chris have just backed away with his tail between his legs? Somehow, Tracy doubted it. Chris had his taste of power over women, and he will thrive on it until someone stops him or until the day he dies. Which was a real waste. He was a very good-looking man. Too bad that was all he had going for him.

"Here, madam, is your water."

"Thank you, Jessie."

"Are you going to be okay now?"

"Yes, Jessie. I will be just fine."

"All right then, madam. We will start to load up the truck if you are up to telling us what you are wanting us to take."

Taking another drink of water and a couple deep breaths, I head on into the living room. In no time at all, the boys had loaded what I wanted out of the living room and was bringing the stuff out of the bedroom. It was a good thing for them that I had no stairs. I saw the relief on their faces when they looked over the house to see what they would be taking out.

By the end of the day, my house was empty. It gave me a lonely feeling as I had lived here for the bigger part of my life. Now it was time to move on. I do believe that everything happens for a reason. Meeting Angel was in my cards a long time ago. There was this draw to her, but I never felt anything warm coming from her as an invite to get to know her. I am ashamed of myself now because I should have known the signs. I suppose I have been away from it for too long. It just didn't ring a bell.

My empty house was going up for sale and I knew I couldn't stand here and watch it go, so it was going to be better that I be away while they sold it to another. Tonight I would take what little bit I kept and go get a room. In the morning, I will sign whatever papers I need to, close my bank account, and by tomorrow night, I should be back with Angel and the children. Funny—it hasn't been long, but I am sure lost without them.

Chapter Nine

———————•———————

The morning came fast, and before I knew it, it was noon and all arrangements were taken care of. I was going to have lunch at one of the local fast food joints and then hit the road. I was so very eager to see Angel and the children.

It was late when I pulled into Samson's Hill. So I had decided to once again get a room, then I would go to the hospital in the morning and find Mr. Alex. I had understood that if he wasn't there they would call him and he would be there within minutes. I was not going to do that tonight incase he was finally home enjoying time with Angel and her children. He was a lonely man so she didn't want to intrude on his private time.

Angel is curled up in the big chair by the fire. Alex thought now would be a good time to have a heart to heart talk.

"Angel are you wanting to start work this week?"

"I would like to wait until Tracy gets here. I don't know anyone I would want to leave the children with even if it is only three days a week."

"I understand. I will let the girls know that, come Monday, you will be in around 9:00 a.m. How does that sound?"

"That will be great. Thank you, Dr. Adams."

"You don't have to thank me. Just knowing in here"—he places his hand over his heart—"that both your mother and grandmother will be happy."

"You really think so?"

"Oh, believe me. I know those two are watching over us, and I had better toe the line."

"Dr. Adams, may I ask you something personal?"

"You sure may."

"Why did you never date Grandma?" Alex got that deep faraway look in his eyes. He wondered if he had the right to say anything. If he did, would it be breaking Emma's trust in him after all these years?

"I'm sorry. I should not have asked."

"No, it's okay that you did. You know, Angel, I'm going to share something with you that as far as I know even your mother never knew."

"Oh, you don't have to do that, Dr. Adams."

"Yea, I think it is time. It won't hurt anyone."

"All right. If you don't want me to say anything to anyone, I won't. Besides, who would I tell? Mom isn't here anymore."

"Well, Angel, I and your grandmother did date at one time."

"YOU DID?"

"It was a very long time ago. I was just accepted into medical school. We were happy and carefree then, and we had these big dreams, Emma and I. So I moved to the big city so I could go for my internship. Your grandma was still in college as well, so she would come and visit me whenever she could. Things were great between us, and we thought we would be together forever.

"I guess all my hours that I had to put in at the hospital put too much strain on our relationship, and your grandma wanted to be a model. For her to get this, it took her in a different direction then where we were. She had gone to New York. She was so excited when she got the letter saying they had accepted her. I couldn't do anything but be happy for her as she had been for me when I got accepted into medical school.

"Although it was tearing me apart inside, and I knew it was doing the same to her. I was scared that I would lose her, and I had told her that I would give up my internship before I would let that happen. We talked it over, and we thought we had it all figured out. There was no way she would let me consider giving up my dream. She had felt that once we both had what we wanted, we could go anywhere in this world together. We laughed a lot and we cried a lot about it, and in the end, we felt we had made the right choices and that our relationship would survive the distance that was going to come between us. For the first three months, it seemed to work out just fine. Then they started to send her all over the world with her modeling. When Emma would call me, she was sad that it was keeping us apart. But I could hear the excitement in her voice about the upcoming shots that she had, and all I could do was encourage her to go for her dream as she did me for mine.

"We had really thought that we would get together for that Christmas, but it never happened. Then again for the spring. Time went by so fast, and I guess we both got lonely and we allowed others to get into our hearts.

"My marriage was never a great one, and it should never have happened. In the back of my mind, I always waited for your grandma to come back. She was my true love and would be until I died. So there had been no real commitment on my part as far as making our marriage work. I just spent most of my time at the hospital, and finally, my wife had enough and she wanted a divorce. I didn't fight her for anything. I couldn't blame her for leaving. I didn't think she would clean me out like she did. But she felt I owed it to her, as I was never really a husband. She was right again, so I just paid my dues and we went our merry ways."

"Did Grandma come back then?"

"Unfortunately, no. Emma ended up in Paris the last I had heard, and she married an older gentleman over there. He was her manager in the beginning, and that was how she ended up in Paris in the first place. He knew the right strings to pull to get her sent there."

"How sad is this?"

"No, I was happy to hear she had gone to Paris to model. It was all young models dreamed of, and your grandmother was living her dream as I was living mine."

"Do you think Grandma missed you?"

"Yes, your grandmother missed me. I did get to Paris to see her once on a shoot, and she was still as beautiful as the first day I met her. She still loved me as I loved her, but she had made a commitment to someone else and she would see it through. That is the kind of woman your grandmother was. After that visit, we never saw each other again until her husband passed away and she moved back here to be closer to her mom and dad. They were both getting up in age, and they needed some home care help. This was when we had met again. It was ironic because I was her parents' doctor in the end."

"This is such a sad story."

"No. We picked up our friendship again, and it was great to get to know each other all over. Except she had Kate now, and she put Kate first over everything. The first time I saw Kate, it blew my mind that two people could look so much alike. To me, it was like looking at Emma when she was younger."

"People said that about Mom and me."

"Yes, the three of you were like angels all woven into one."

"So why didn't you get married once you found each other again?"

"You know, Angel, I can't honestly answer that. The question was always on my mind to ask Emma for her hand. There just never seemed to be a right moment. At first, she was so busy with her parents, and I was still busy with my practice. We fell into this routine that we both seemed to be comfortable with, and before we knew it, the years had gone by. And then . . ." Alex got very quiet.

"Then Grandma got sick."

"Yea, then she got sick, and I felt like a real heel for never getting off my butt and marrying the only woman I have truly loved. They say there is only one true love in a lifetime for each person, and I totally agree."

"If that is true, why do so many people get married?"

"Lust is a wonderful thing when it is new."

"Lust."

"Yes, Angel, lust is the common cause of most marriages. And when that dies, so does the marriage. That is why the divorce rates are so high."

"Did you and Grandma ever?"

"Have a lustful relationship?"

"Sorry, I shouldn't have asked."

"That's okay, no harm done."

"Yes, we got caught up in the heat of the moment once, before she left for modeling school. We both felt guilty after because we had promised each other that we would wait until our wedding night."

"Good thing you didn't wait."

"Yes and no." I think we had lost some respect for each other because of it. I know Emma was very upset with herself, I tried to make what we had done okay because we were going to be apart for so long. Bottom line was we had promised each other, and if we couldn't keep that promise, how many more would we break?"

"That's not the same."

"To Emma, it was. A promise is a promise, and if you don't intend to keep it, then you shouldn't be promising. I have thought that maybe that was what stood between us from ever getting married. I had already broken a promise to her and one to my wife. So I just couldn't bring myself to hurting Emma again. I think she was afraid I would ask her to marry me because then she too would be worried about broken promises. The way we lived, there were no promises made to be broken. We just lived for each other and any day we could share. Each day to us was a pleasure that we enjoyed to the fullest. Nowadays, people don't have to get married to be a couple, and I guess Emma and I just felt that we were a couple from the first time we met. The other people who came into our lives along the way were just stepping stones to our happiness."

"So you were really happy living like that?"

"Yes. When we were reunited, I knew I still loved your grandmother as much then as I did when we got separated. And she loved me, there was never any doubt about that. The love we had for each other was all that counted. She never once complained about the hours I put in at the hospital or made me feel guilty for doing so."

"Do you think Grandma was happy living that way?"

"I believe she was. She never said anything to make me believe otherwise. When she got sick, I had wished we would have married."

"Why then?"

"Out of respect for her and the fact that she was going to meet our Maker, I wanted her to go to heaven with a clean slate."

"I don't think God looks at us that way."

"Emma didn't either, and she said she was fine dying as who she was."

"Didn't you ever want kids of your own?"

"Oh yes, but I wanted them with Emma and no one else. My wife told me after we were married that she never wanted any, and that was fine with me."

"So you and Grandma should have had a baby after you met again."

"No. Emma was happy just having Kate, and I think it was because she was also the only child. We had already passed our prime for bearing children when we rebuilt our relationship."

"But you would have someone to share your life with now."

"I do, Angel. I have you and the children and Jake."

"Do you see much of Jake?"

"Not as much as I should. I try to keep myself as busy as possible."

"That is not enjoying life."

"This is coming from someone who was a prisoner in her own home."

"It didn't start out that way. Then before I knew what was happening, everything had changed. I didn't know who Chris was anymore. Hell, I didn't know who I was anymore."

"Do you, now?"

"Yes. I am a person without a mother or father. I am now a single mother who has nothing or anyone but my children who I have let down badly."

"You and only you can turn that around, Angel. If you work at it hard enough Elisabeth probably won't remember anything she has seen or heard. Maybe if she sees something or hears something it might trigger a memory, at that point she will just think of it as a bad dream she has had at sometime."

"If I could only be so lucky."

"She is pretty young not to forget. Some children remember for a lifetime, and others can't remember tomorrow what happened today.

"We could get her in to see a counselor, and they would be able to tell you how dramatic it was and if it will scar her for life."

"I think I will do that. I never wanted to hurt my children."

"Of course not, Angel. No one wants to hurt their children. You got so wrapped up in what was going on around you and what Chris was wanting from you that you couldn't set things straight in your mind."

"At first, I did. He would leave, and I would think about what he had said to me and would have it straight in my mind to tell him that night when he got home that he was wrong. Then when he would come home and start saying all those mean things to me again. He made me feel like I had really done something wrong, and he would have me convinced that I was wrong."

"These men know how to play this game better than anyone. Now that you are out of there, you can get your life back and move on. Make plans for the future and work on your dreams."

"It is going to be hard to move on without Mom."

"I understand that, but think about what your mom would want you to do. Would she let you sit around and feel sorry for yourself and wallow in self-pity? To mourn her is one thing, and you have the right to do so. Just remember there is a time when you say, 'Okay, Mom, I have to move on now. It doesn't mean that I won't love you or that I will forget you, but my children need me as I needed you.'

"She will understand, and she will be there to guide you if you reach out to her. Your grandmother used to always tell me, 'If you are tuned into your body, you can communicate with the dead. There will be signs, and you will know they are coming from either your mom or your grandmother. Just relax and let it happen. Talking to the dead does not mean you're crazy.'"

"I talked to Daddy lots when I was little, and I remember Mom talking to him too. Sometimes she didn't know I could hear her. She cried lots at night for Daddy for a very long time. After she lost the baby, I thought Mom would go crazy. I think Daddy knew that, and he sent Jake to meet Mom and me. It was like we were all alone one day and a family with Jake the next."

"Jake was a welcome surprise, that is for sure. I too was worried about your mom. I didn't know how much more she could take. Then."

"Then I walked out of Mom's life."

"Yes, we all told her you wouldn't be gone long. As the time went by and she didn't hear from you, she then went into her cocoon. We talked to her, but it went in one ear and out the other. There was nothing on her mind but you. She wasn't eating enough to keep a mouse alive. Jake came to me many times for help. All I could say was 'give her time' because Kate was mourning you. Jake did, and he stood at her side and never complained. He came to me when she left to find you. He was worried that she wouldn't be back."

"Oh god, he was so right." Tears started to flow.

"Now, now, Angel. No one knows what lies ahead of us. Your mother believed as her mother did, that everything happens for a reason. If she were here today, she'd tell you that it was her time. Otherwise, God would not have led her down that road that day. She died helping you instead of being hit by a car. Nodding and sitting quietly and watching the fire, Angel fell asleep in the big chair. Alex covered her up with the throw that was there and went back to the hospital to check on a patient that was also on his last days.

Chapter Ten

———————◆———————

Lately, it seemed like there were a lot of people passing on. Alex had wondered a few times when his number would be pulled as he was lonely still for Emma.

Tracy found him asleep in the doctors' lounge at 5:30 a.m. She had checked the night before and was told that he would be in around that time. No one knew he would be back that evening to check on a patient; otherwise, they would have called him for her.

Wiping the sleep from his eyes, he couldn't figure out how Tracy got there at first. It was like one minute he was dreaming about her and Angel with the children, and the next minute, she was shaking his shoulder.

"I'm sorry, Tracy. I'm not with it yet."

"Oh no, Mr. Alex. I'm the one that is sorry to have awoken you. You had a long night again?"

"Yes, I did. It seems to me like that's all there is anymore. Long nights."

"I will get you a coffee, Mr. Alex."

"No need to do that, Tracy. We can go down together and get caught up before I take you to the house."

"All right. I would love to." So, sitting over a cup of fresh hot coffee, Tracy started by asking about the children and Angel.

"Are Angel and the children doing okay?"

"They will come around, but it is going to be a very slow process. Especially for Angel. I hope Elisabeth hasn't seen so much that it has already scarred her deep."

"I was so worried about maybe he would come and get Angel."

"I don't know if we are clear of that happening yet. It might still be to early. I hold my breath each day when I go home hoping that she hasn't decided that she was wrong and I go home to find a note and no Angel and kids."

"Has she heard from him at all?"

"Not that I know off, Surely she wouldn't call him when I'm not at home."

"One can only pray that she doesn't."

"At this point, I'm sure if that SOB comes around, I wouldn't have a problem putting him in the hospital."

"Oh, Mr. Alex, that would not be good. And it could be dangerous for you."

"Maybe so. But someone will have to stop him. Seeing how I'm all Angel has left that is close to family, it would be up to me."

"Well, I'm here to tell you that I won't take no guff from him."

"Now, Tracy, I want you to promise me that if he ever comes around, you will call the police right away. Don't even let him in the door. In fact, don't ever open the door to him."

"Oh, Mr. Alex. I have already learned to use the peephole before I open my doors. One run-in with him was quite enough, thank you."

"Chris was at your home?"

"Yes. He came over to find out where Angel had gone. He was some upset when I told him I didn't know. The moving men came along right at the time that he was getting angry, so I was safe. But I have to say he had me shaking something fierce. The moving men were good about watching over me. When they left, I was ready to leave the house as well. I went and got myself a room so I wouldn't have to worry about having another encounter with him. But I don't mind saying that he had me scared out of my mind. I didn't back down. I wasn't going to give him the satisfaction of knowing he could scare me. Men like him thrive on that kind of power."

"You are so right, Tracy, and I want you to be very careful if he comes around. We already saw what he did to Angel, and I don't think he would think twice of doing the same to you. Especially if he thinks you are the cause of her leaving him. I will make it plain to him if I come across him that I was the one who took her away and not you."

"Thanks, Mr. Alex. I don't care if he thinks I got her out of there."

"I know you don't, Tracy. But I do believe it would be safer for you if he knew the truth."

"All right, Mr. Alex."

"Now come and I will take you home to Angel and the children."

Tracy puts her hand over her heart and says, "Aw, please do. I have missed them."

"I think Angel has missed having you around." A big smile comes across Tracy's face as she gets up quickly to follow Alex out to their vehicles.

Tracy felt like she had just gotten her second wind and she also felt like she found where she belonged. After all these years of being alone she now has a family. Once her and Alex got to the main floor they would have to separate.

"Tracy, we park in the parkade, so I will go get my truck and come around front to guide you home."

"All right, Mr. Alex. I will be waiting in my car."

"I will only be a few minutes."

"That's fine no hurry." She turns and walks out to her car. The hair on the back of her neck stands up and she gets goose bumps all over. She was not going to look behind but she was scanning in front of her to see if someone was close by. It was early morning and there were people coming and going so she didn't feel like she had anything to worry about. She did pick up the speed in her walk and when she got into her car she made sure the first thing she did was lock her doors. She didn't look all around, but she did glance in the mirror and looked out in front for anyone who may just be standing around. Of course Chris was on her mind. Who else would make her feel that kind of fear. She had not felt like that since her husband. Again she would not show him she was nervous so she turned on her radio and sat and waited for Mr. Alex to come. Not seeing anyone or anything out of the ordinary she began to think just maybe her mind was playing tricks on her and making her jumpy because of the talk that her and Mr. Alex had just had. Just then, Mr. Alex's truck came into view and she said, *"Thank you, Lord."*

Following Mr. Alex home did not take long at all. His home looked well kept from the outside, and he had a lot of huge overhanging trees. Going inside, we found Angel just putting Gregory down from his morning feeding. I stood off to the side and waited as Angel turned around. The look on her face was all I needed to see to know I had made the right choice. She almost ran me over.

"Ms. Bloom," She says as she throws herself into my arms.

"Hello, dear, how are you?"

"So much better now that you are here." Looking at Alex and saying, "I'm sorry, not that I don't like your company. I just need—"

Angel got quiet as Tracy just pulled her in even closer.

"It's quite okay, Angel. I know what you mean, and I am not offended by it." Alex knew that she was needing a mother around, and Tracy was the closest person around that could provide such a comfort.

"I thought maybe you would change your mind and not come."

"Are you kidding? I missed you and your babies before you were even out of my eyesight that day. I'm afraid you are stuck with me now, Angel. Whether you like it or not, girl, I am here to be a pain."

"Oh, I like that." Angel hugs Tracy again. "May I get you two some coffee?"

"I don't know about Tracy here, but I for one am going to bed. So you two women can get caught up. When I get up, I will take you to see that house, Angel."

"Did you get the one you were telling me about?"

"We can have it if you like it. Yes."

"Oh sweet. Thank you, Dr. Adams."

"Don't thank me yet, you haven't seen it." He hugs her and says, "Good morning. See you in a couple of hours."

"All right, we will be quiet."

"Trust me, you won't wake me once these eyes are closed. They are out for a while." Alex left the two women to have their coffee and do their catching up.

"Come on in, Tracy, and I will get us some coffee."

"I sure would like a good cup, all right. How are the wee ones?"

"They are just fine, thank you for asking."

"How about you, Angel? How are you doing?"

Angel gets the cups out as she starts to tell Tracy about what she had been planning.

"I am starting work next week. Or at least I had hoped to. I was waiting to see if you would come. I did not want to leave the children with anyone else."

"I am here now, and you sure can go to work if that is what you want to do."

"It is only part-time so I will still have plenty of time with the children."

"I think that is great."

"I think Dr. Adams is great. He is arranging all of this for me. I don't know where I would be now if it weren't for him."

"Well then, Miss, let's just be grateful that we know him and he knows the right people."

"Tracy, are you going to live with the children and me, or do you want your own home like you had?"

"If you don't mind and if there is room, I would like to be your live-in nanny."

"I don't mind at all. In fact, I would love it, and I know the children will get to love you and, most of all, trust you."

"One thing I would like."

"What is that, Tracy?"

"I would rather be known as the children's grandmother than their nanny." I could not read the expression on Angel's face, and at that moment I could have kicked myself for saying something so sensitive at this very moment. I knew Angel was thinking of her mother right now, and it was hurting her deeply.

"I'm sorry, Angel. I should not have said that."

Angel pours our coffee and sits down with the look of bewilderment on her face.

"What is it, Angel?"

"I don't know if Mom would be okay with that."

"Don't fret your pretty little head over it. I will be their nanny, it is fine."

"Just until we see how things go and how the children will take to you. Maybe it won't work out, then you will be very heartbroken if you have to leave us."

"Yes, Angel, you are right. Let's just take it one day at a time."

"That sounds great to me. Now tell me, did you sell your house already? And what about all you belongings?"

"I will rent it out if it doesn't sell soon. As far as my belongings, I had most of it taken to the secondhand stores."

"But why? You will be needing some of those things to make your rooms you."

"There was nothing that I had that I can't buy again. Some of the very special things I kept and had them stored just until I saw what I had for room."

"Dr. Adams says this place is huge, and we will have more room than we know what to do with. There is no one behind us, just a large park."

"Well, maybe we should look into getting a dog for the children. That way, we would have to go to that large park every day." Tracy was thinking more along the lines of a watchdog to make sure Chris couldn't come sneaking around; she just wasn't going to say that to Angel.

"Maybe a puppy would be nice for the children."

"Puppy? Yeah right, a puppy. The children would love a puppy." Tracy wanted to shout, "NO, A WATCHDOG!"

Halfway through their coffee, Elisabeth got up. She had a big smile for me, sitting on her mommy's knee. So I just waited out my time, and before ten minutes were up, she had come to sit on my knee. To hold this precious child close to my bosom was a fulfillment of pleasure like I have never known. To go through one's life and never have a child is one of life's biggest mistakes a woman could ever make. I can't begin to explain the feelings that flow through a woman's body at this time. The motherly instincts that kick in are as strong as any love you could give to anyone. So to be someone's grandma would have to be just as special as being a mother. I sit with Elisabeth on my knee, and it just felt so right to rock back and forth.

Elisabeth relaxed and just snuggled in that much closer. I knew she felt safe. I also saw Angel watching and wondered if she was thinking of the times she too used to be on her mother's and grandmother's knee being rocked. This is a comfort that is so easily shared and a joy to give.

"You know, Tracy, Elisabeth has never had a grandma to sit with. Of course, all of my own doing. But nevertheless, she has never spoken the word *grandma* or *nana* to anyone. She has no idea who those people are. When I think about this, I realize just how wrong I have been. And how unfair I've been to both Elisabeth and my mom. To think that my children will never have what I had, and it was the best time of my life. My mom and grandmother were the best. They also were my best friends, and I let them both down because of a man. A man who doesn't know what love is all about." I saw a lonely tear trickle down Angel's face. I thought now was the perfect time.

"Well, my dear, there is one thing you can do: and that is to be sure that you don't ever put yourself or your children last or in danger again. Remember that you all deserve the best life can give you, and you deserve—as your children do—the simple pleasures of life. You are strong again, Angel. Hold on to your health and your mind. These two things are very important, and everything else will fall into place. You will see how things will unfold, and it will all seem to be so natural if you just relax and let it happen."

"You think so, Tracy?"

"Trust me, Angel, it will. You and the children will be fine, and you will see that, in time, they will have a grandmother and a grandfather to spend time with."

"Oh, Tracy. Do you have a sweetheart I don't know about?" We chuckle, as I say.

"No, my dear I don't. I don't think, at my age, a man is what I need. After all, I don't need a grandpa."

"Me either."

"You have Mr. Alex, Angel, and I know he loves you and the children very much."

"Yeah, we do. And I guess I love him too. He has been in my life for as long as I can remember."

"Well, that is a start. You now have a built-in grandpa for the children."

"You know, it just doesn't feel right to call him *Grandpa* when he has been our doctor all my life."

"So if your grandma would have been a nurse, would you not have called her *Grandma*?"

"Oh yeah. She wouldn't have let me call her anything else. Grandma was very special to me."

"So why should it be any different with Mr. Alex?"

"I guess because he has always been our doctor. I have never though about him as a grandpa."

"Maybe we will have to test the waters and see if he would like to be called *Grandpa*."

"That would be very strange to do."

"Why don't we let Elisabeth here decide?" As she hugs Elisabeth tighter.

"How do we do that?"

"Well, we will teach her all about what grandpas are all about. They catch on very fast, these little people. It is never too late to give your children the love of grandparents."

Chapter Eleven

─────────●─────────

"Who is getting grandparents?"

"Oh Mr. Alex you are up already."

"Yes, I promised to take you two ladies to see that house."

"So you did. Are you needing something to eat first? I can get you a sandwich whipped up in a jiffy."

"Why, thank you Tracy that would be great."

"I will make something for this sweet child here as well."

Tracy gets up and taking Elisabeth with her into the kitchen.

"I will get Gregory ready to go as well." Angel leaves the room. Whether the women knew it or not, they had gotten around the grandparent question without a hitch.

It wasn't long before they were over in the house. It was a beautiful older home with high ceilings and old wood floors that were still like new. The rooms were all large and very well light up. The windows went from floor to ceiling in most of the rooms. It had three full bathrooms that you could park a car in easily. Everything was of the 1970s and beautifully kept. Angel couldn't see anything she would want to change. It was all so very practical yet so warm and inviting. This home seem like it just reached out and wrapped its arms around you.

"What do you think, Angel? Do you like it?"

"Dr. Adams, I think this is great. It gives me a sense of peace."

"Do you know why that is, Angel?"

"No, I don't. But from the moment we walked though the doors, it was like a weight had been taken off my shoulders. I can't really explain. I do feel like this is where I belong. Like it should be home or that I have been here before."

"The calm and warm feeling that you are getting comes from the aura that is in this home from the owners. These people never had a sad day in their lives. They were always happy and upbeat. They had six children who loved them and were so well behaved, it was hard to believe that they were children. They were not spoiled as you can see of the house. They were very down-to-earth people. They wanted a strong home that was warm and dry and that would see the six children raised, but not a home that the children could not be children."

"But everything still looks new in here. If it weren't for the colors, you wouldn't know that it was of the seventies."

"When you take care of something, the older it gets, the nicer it becomes."

"I can see that. Grandma would have loved this house."

"Yes, Angel, you are right about that. And it would have also been your grandmother. She was also a very practical lady, and her beauty shone through with age."

"Grandma was a very pretty lady, wasn't she?"

"Yes, Angel. She was probably the prettiest lady I ever saw. She did not think so. She was beautiful inside and out."

"Do you think Grandma was lonely all those years? I know now that you and her spent lots of time together. But still, you did not live like a couple, so she had a lot of time alone."

"Your grandmother lived just as she wanted to. She love her life and her family and most of all she loved just being her."

"I know she always seemed happy whenever we saw her. But I also know Mom used to worry about her and wished she would have remarried."

"I guess she just never found the man she wanted to share her home and her heart with. I know she was broken hearted when her first husband died. I think it was more because of Kate. She worried about what not having a father would do to Kate."

"You don't think she loved her husband?"

"Oh yes, Emma loved him all right. There are so many different levels of love. Plus respect, I know she had a lot of respect for him. She said he was so good to Kate and her that she couldn't have asked for better."

"He was quite a bit older than Grandma, wasn't he?"

"Yes, Angel, he was."

"Do you think that is why they only had Mom? He was too old to have more children?"

"Well, after a certain age, having children does not come easy, and he would not want to have left your mother with more than one child to take care of. He knew he was sick when he met your grandmother. He just didn't tell her until he really had to."

"What was he sick with?"

"That great old cancer—he battled it for years. It had gone into remission for many years for him. When it came back, there was no stopping it."

"Dr. Adams, do you think Grandma got her cancer from him?"

"Oh no, Angel, that does not happen. Some types of cancer can be inherited, but you don't catch cancer from anyone."

"I see. Do you think Grandma had her cancer a long time?"

"Yes, she had it for some time before she knew she had it. By then, it was too late to do anything for her. That is one bad thing about ovarian cancer. There really are no signs until it is too late."

"Angel, the baby is getting a little cranky."

"I'm sorry, Tracy. Of course, he will want to eat. I have a bottle in the diaper bag in the car."

"I will go out and get it."

"Thank you, Tracy."

"You're welcome."

"So what do you think, Angel? Would you like to have this house?"

"Do you think I can afford this house? It can't be cheap."

"If you want it, it is yours."

"Dr. Adams, I can't let you do this."

"Well, Angel, this house is mine. So if you want to live here, you may for as long as you live or want to."

"I thought it belonged to another doctor?"

"It did until yesterday, and then I bought it."

"You did?"

"After all, it is such a beautiful home. I did not want to lose it. So what do you say? There is plenty of room for you and Tracy and the children."

"What about a puppy?"

"A puppy?"

"Yes, Tracy thinks we should get the kids a puppy."

"Could be a great idea." If he knew Tracy like he thinks he does, she doesn't have a puppy in mind but a large watch dog.

"The yard is plenty big enough for a puppy and the big park right there."

"You have a point. So now we will have to watch for a puppy."

"All right, It's a deal." Angel puts her arms around his neck and kisses his cheek. "Thank you for helping us."

"Any time Angel. Now lets get this little man something to eat and then we will see about getting you some furniture."

"Furniture?"

"Yes, furniture, you know like beds, table, chairs and maybe even a sofa and chair."

"I never thought about needing all of that." I could see her bubble just popped.

"It's okay Angel, we will go back to my place. Where you will tend to the children so that they will be happy to stay with me. Then you and Tracy go shopping and you buy whatever you want for your home."

"No, I can't do that."

"Oh yes you can and you are." He pulls out his wallet and hands over a bank card."

"What is this?"

"It is your account, now you go and have fun. After you get the children settled. I can watch them after that."

"But." Putting up his hands and saying.

"No buts Angel, just go enjoy yourself for once. Don't think about anything but having a blast okay?" He puts his hands on each side of her cheeks and pulls her towards him and kisses her on top of her nose.

"I don't have any one to spoil so let me spoil you and the children."

"I don't know what to say."

"Thank you, is enough."

"Thank you, does not cover it."

"For now it does." Tracy brings the bottle in just as they were getting to the door.

"We are leaving now?"

"Yes, we can feed him in the car."

"Something happen?" She asked, a little taken back at the change.

"Yes, you two women have some shopping to do and I am staying at home with the wee ones."

"We do? You are?"

"Yes and yes." Looking at Angel, she sees she has a big smile on her face.

"What are we shopping for?" Tracy asked with a frown.

"Why, you two ladies have a house to furnish."

"Aw, sweet," was all Tracy could say on the way to the car.

It didn't take them long to get the children all settled down so Alex could handle them. Angel was a little nervous. She had no idea what he might know about children. Then she had to slap herself in the head and think: Good god, this man is a doctor. My children could not be in better hands. On the way out of the door, Alex yells at them, "Buy whatever it is you want, please don't look at the price. If you like it and want it, get it."

"Are you for real?" Tracy asked.

"Yes, now go have fun." He knew women love to shop and it must be more fun when you have the money. He could hear Angel and Tracy talking and laughing as they left the house. It was such a beautiful sound to hear Angel laughing again. Her laughter was the same as when she was just a little girl and that brought back memories of when him and Emma had taken Angel to the fair. Angel would have only been about three, What a blast they had that day. Angel laughed at everything that day. She especially like the clowns that were running around the fair grounds. Angel was an easy one to make laugh. Emma had said that Kate was like that when she was young. Alex had forgotten about Kate's laughter as he had dealt with her and all her traumas in the past few years. He hadn't heard Kate laugh for a very long time. Alex knew that Kate had died a very unhappy lady. That made his heart ache for her and Angel. To know that that SOB was the cause of Kate's unhappiness made Alex want to go out and find him and knock his lights out. Although he doubted at his age he would be able to do such a thing. After all he was now seventy-three. All it would do would give him the satisfaction of knowing that he tried for Kate.

When he pulled Elisabeth up onto his lap to read a story to her, he felt Emma's presence. He looks around and says, "That's right, love. I am babysitting your great-grandchildren. He could imagine her laughing at him as he began to read "The Three Little Pigs" to Elisabeth.

Before he knew it, it was suppertime, and the women still weren't home. Gregory had woken up again, and he had managed to feed him and change him, although he didn't know if the diaper would stay on. It seemed fairly simple and he thought he would just leave it at that. Elisabeth was so easy to please and she never gave one ounce of trouble. That made him wonder how any man could mistreat her. These thoughts made his blood boil. He had thought he had better get that anger under control before it caused him to have high blood pressure. One thing he knew and prided himself in was his good health. Stress can cause a lot of problems. How these battered women stay half assed healthy through it all was beyond anything he could comprehend. With that thought in mind he then heard the women in the garage. It sounded like they had, had a great time.

Scooping up Elisabeth and going out to see what all the commotion was about he was greeted at the door by the biggest dog he had ever seen.

"What is this?"

"Why, Mr. Alex, it's a dog."

"I can see that, but good Lord, it's almost the size of a small horse. Who does he belong to?"

"Us now."

"What?"

"We thought we would stop at the pound and see what they had for puppies."

"This is no puppy."

"No, Dr. Adams, it's not. But they were going to put her down tomorrow. They only keep them for two weeks, and if their owner doesn't claim them, well . . ."

"All right, Angel. I get the picture."

"She looked at us with those sad eyes as if she knew what the man was saying to us. I couldn't just leave her there."

"Well, I would say you have yourself a mighty fine watchdog. We had better hope she will be good with the children and not eat them for dinner."

"Oh, speaking of dinner, we brought it home with us. Sorry we are so late, Mr. Alex."

"Hey, no harm done. Elisabeth and Grandpa had a good time, didn't we?" He says as he kissed Elisabeth on the cheek. "What's for dinner?" Tracy and Angel are both looking at him with their mouths open.

"Chicken and fries," they answered together.

"Sounds great to us. Can we eat now? Lizzy and I are hungry."

"Lizzy?" Angel asked, but it went right over Alex's head or he was just ignoring them as he turned around and headed for the kitchen. So we followed him. Neither one of us knew what to say, so it was better to say nothing than to make him uncomfortable about referring to himself as Grandpa.

Dinner went by noisily and quickly. It seemed strange to have a garbage compactor on legs, but the dog enjoyed everything we had given her and then we sat and watched her. We had noticed that wherever Elisabeth went, the dog was with her. There was no denying that she had been a family pet at one time. So had she been lost or left behind on purpose? Was this meant to be, were we to go to the pound today? If we hadn't gone there today, this beautiful dog would have been put down tomorrow. To think we had left home with furniture shopping in mind. For some reason, we had just decided to swing around to the pound on the way home. This beautiful dog was the only one there. It was a blessing, for Angel needs a watchdog, not another headache. With this dog, I felt more comfortable that we would know if Chris ever showed up. I can only hope that the dog is a biter, if necessary. After my last encounter with Chris, I don't ever want to deal with him alone.

"It sure was strange that there weren't many dogs at the pound today." Angel had brought this up to Dr. Adams.

"The town has put bigger fines out for the people who don't keep their dogs confined."

"They said this one didn't have a tag."

"It could have just wandered into town. But with the bylaw, people won't claim them anymore. It costs too much. So they are left behind to be destroyed."

"Guess this one was lucky we came along."

"Yes, remember what your grandmother always said."

"I know. Everything happens for a reason."

"She was right."

"I know. Mom would tell me that as well."

Chapter Twelve

For the next week, Angel and Tracy were busy setting up their house. The furniture had all been delivered, and the women had gone out and bought all the small things that made a house a home. Tracy had had all her belongings brought down from storage. The women seem to have everything under control. Alex had missed them when they all moved out, but he also enjoyed his peace and quiet again. He liked to be able to sit alone with his memories of Emma.

Angel started her job and enjoyed the walk every day. For the moment, she worked only afternoons—which she found had worked out for them perfectly, stopping at the store on her way home to get whatever they would be short on.

She would leave early enough in the afternoon on her way to work to go into the park and drop off old bread for the birds that were all gathering there. Today was no different then any other day. She was standing there throwing bread out to the birds when all of a sudden the hair on her neck stood up and she got goose bumps all over. The birds were flying all around acting strange. They have never done this before. They were always quick at landing and eating, happy to see her. Not today they were acting as though they were afraid of her. This made her feel very uncomfortable so she thought she would head on to work. Even after she was back out in the open and going down the side walk she couldn't help feel like she was either being followed or she was being watched. She wasn't going to show whoever it was that they were making her nervous she would just make sure she was able to get help if she needed to. She pulled out her cell phone and punched in 911. Just in case. All she had to do was push SEND, and she would hold it in her hand until she arrived at work.

Of course, she was thinking of Chris. Could he be right behind her? She wasn't going to stop and turn around to find out. Then she got thinking that if it were Chris, he would have called out to her, not just followed her. As she got through the doors at the clinic, she slumped against the wall with a sigh. She had not realized that she had been holding her breath.

From the front desk, Helen calls out to her, "Angel, are you all right?"

"Yes, I am just fine. Guess I was walking a little faster than I thought. Took my breath away."

"Walking is good exercise, but it's not meant to kill you."

"No kidding. Guess I will have to slow down."

"Yea, it's not like you are late. In fact, you are pretty early today. How come?"

"No one was at home, so I left earlier."

"Oh now, Angel, did you get lonely?"

"I sure did. I missed you ladies."

"That's what we like to hear." They all laugh. Angel was still a little unnerved, so later that afternoon, she had called Tracy to see if she and the kids would meet her and to make sure they brought Lucky for a walk.

Tracy didn't ask any questions and had agreed to do as Angel had asked. There would be time to ask questions later. She did not like Angel walking to and from work without Lucky or someone else being with her. That afternoon, on the way home, the women were chatting about their day when they both got the strange feeling that they were being watched. The hair on Lucky's back was standing up, and she had this low growl happening, just to warn us or whoever may be around.

Tracy knew by the look on Angel's face that she was having the same feeling that she was.

"It's not just me, is it, Angel? Just keep walking," she says as she glances over at Angel.

"What do you mean?" Angel asked.

"We are either being watched or followed, and you can feel it the same as I can. Lucky here is telling us the same thing."

"So what do we do?"

"We don't look back or around, and we just keep a steady walk towards home. We do not stop for anything."

"We have to stop at the store."

"Well, we will be taking Lucky in with us."

"The store owner may complain."

"I will just tell them she is my medical support. They will understand. That way, we don't have to worry about anyone doing harm to her if it is someone after us."

"Do you really thing that there is?"

"Better to be safe than not." Going into the store did not take long. Both women were a little edgy and so they wanted to get home quickly and safely. They kept a steady pace as they walked and there were other people out and about so they felt a little more at ease, after all who would mess with two women out in public, with a large dog in tow?

"You know, Angel, this is not the first time this has happened to me."

"Oh really? You had this kind of thing before? What did you do?"

"I got into my car and locked the doors."

"When did that happen?"

"Just the other day when I went to the hospital to find Mr. Alex."

"Did you tell him about it?"

"No, I haven't mentioned it. I thought maybe it was my mind playing tricks on me."

"Me too."

Tracy whipped her head around and said, "This has happened to you too?"

"Yes."

"When?"

"This afternoon on the way to work. I had stopped to throw bread to the birds in the park. I got this strange feeling like someone was either watching me or following me, as I did now, and the birds were not landing to eat. They were acting like they were afraid of me."

"I knew something had happened when you called and asked if I would come and bring Lucky. What did you do when you felt this?"

"I got back out into the open and I punched 911 into my phone and carried it that way all the way to work. I just had to push the SEND button."

"Smart girl. I want you to make sure you charge your phone every night and you have it set up to get help as quickly as you can."

"I will, don't you worry. Do you think we should tell Dr. Adams about this?"

"I think it is worth mentioning as Lucky here is also bothered by something. The next time we see him, we will tell him and see what he has to say." The growling had stopped, but the hair was still standing up on Lucky's back, and she was looking all around as if she knew what or who she was looking for. Having her with us made me feel a whole lot better. I didn't think anyone was getting close to us with Lucky around.

We got home and tried to carry on as normally as possible. I had gone around and made sure all the windows and doors were locked and that Lucky was in the house with us. I personally felt that it was Chris. Angel wasn't saying one way or another. I don't think she thinks he would do this. I haven't told her about his visit to me, and I don't think I will. She will just believe that I want it to be him because I don't like him. These girls have a hard time accepting who these men really are that they have fallen for. She will feel like she is being a traitor if she thinks bad of him. It is going to take her some time to get strong enough to stand up to him. We can only hope to get more time between her and him. So when that day comes and she has to face him down, she will be able to do it with confidence. She will be able to stick to what she knows is right and to know that the decisions she has made were the right ones for herself and her children. We can only hope that, mentally, she will have healed enough to gain that strength.

Over the next few weeks, there were no more incidents with our follower. So we had gotten fairly laid back and relaxed. It was nice to know that life was so good again.

Angel had gone into therapy to be able to get all the help she needed. Learning to deal with how Chris treated her and the loss of her mother. The blame she carries for the loss of her mother is horrendous and whether or not anyone will make her believe that she was not the cause of her mother's death no one knows. Angel herself is going to have to be able to forgive herself first for the way she treated her mother. Knowing how some of it was brought on by Chris being so deceitful. Angel totally believed that her mother had quit caring for her as her mother had thought the same of Angel. Chris knew what he was doing with his manipulation. Angel has to learn the true meaning of this word and understand that she too was manipulated. It will all take time, and it could be years before Angel is free. This will all depend on how much guilt she is going to hang on to.

Elisabeth is doing great and she calls me Nana, and little Gregory is always so happy. You can't help but love these two beautiful children. They have fulfilled my life. They are so free with their love; this was something I myself did not realize I was missing. Not having children to me was like I was saving another soul from having the same life as I and Angel had had. So I always felt I was doing the world a favor by not having any children.

Now I realize that, by doing that, I have missed out on what every woman should know: the pleasure of motherhood and, of course, being a grandmother. I have found out over the last few months that your life as a woman is not fulfilled until you have had both. Of course, playing the role of grandma was easy. Playing the role of a mother was not. The best I could do here for Angel was probably more like a big sister. Being here for her no matter what was all I had to offer along with my love. That I hope one day she will know and feel.

I worry about her the same as a mother, I'm sure. I want only what is best for her and the children, and I feel I would do whatever it takes to keep them safe. The one place I would fail is if Angel ever needed another kidney transplant. I could not do as her mother and offer her one of mine.

I was up all night with the baby. He is teething again and I couldn't sleep, so I had told Angel to go back to bed. No need for the two of us losing sleep. The day was also long, and Gregory started to run a fever. By the end of the day, both he and I were exhausted, but the poor little man could not sleep. So I decided to call Angel.

"Hi, Angel. The wee ones and I are not coming for our walk. I'm beat, and Gregory is too."

"That is fine, Tracy. I will be home soon, and I will take over so you can get some well-deserved rest."

"Thank you, dear. Would you pick up some apple juice along with the milk today?"

"You bet, Tracy. Anything else you need?"

"No, that is all for me, dear. Elisabeth hasn't asked for anything else."

"All right, so I will be home as soon as I can."

"That's fine, dear. Don't have to rush, we are not going anywhere." Angel did rush around to get the work she wanted to get done out of her way so that she could get home early to give Tracy a hand. She knew Tracy had had a long night and knew she was looking tired before she left for work.

"Helen, my little guy is teething, and if there is no sleep tonight, would you mind if I didn't come in tomorrow?"

"I thought you had help?"

"I do, but Tracy is wore out, and I was hoping to give her a break."

"That bad, is it?"

"Yea, it is. Sorry."

"Not a problem. Nothing we can't handle until you get back."

"Thank you."

"Keep in touch."

"I will, Helen. Good night."

"Good night, Angel."

Grabbing her handbag and off she ran. Didn't take her long to get to the store. All she had in mind was milk and apple juice which, when she placed it on the counter, she then heard, "I will get this."

Angel froze on the spot.

"Is something wrong, Miss?" the lady behind the counter was asking.

"What can be wrong? I'm paying for our son's milk. Do you find something wrong with that, Angel?"

"No. It's fine, thank you."

"Now come and I will take you home." Chris takes Angel by the arm and walks her outside.

"What are you doing here?"

"What, Angel, aren't you glad to see me?"

"No, Chris, I'm not."

"Well, too damn bad for you. I want to see the kids."

"I'm sure you do."

"They're my kids, and I have the right to see them."

"Why now? You never wanted them, nor did you care when we were with you."

"Guess you could say I have had a change of heart."

"Really?"

"Yes. I have been for counseling, and they helped me see what I have missed."

"Really?"

"I see your job has taught you a new word." With that, Angel pushed by him and started to walk home.

"Come on, Angel. I will give you a ride."

"No thanks. I don't take rides from strangers."

"Strangers, who the hell is the stranger here?"

"You are, Chris. I don't know you and haven't for a long time, so please just leave me alone." Once again, she pushed passed him and headed for home. She had thought maybe she should just turn around and go back to the store. Her cell phone was at home. It was in need of charging and, leaving in a hurry, she forgot her phone.

Grabbing her arm hard and spinning her around to face him, he said, "Damn it all, Angel. I didn't drive all the way here just for you to turn and walk away from me."

"Just leave me alone."

"Come and have coffee with me. We can talk."

"We have nothing to talk about."

"Yes we do, Angel. We have two children together."

"Funny you didn't think that way before. They were mine, remember?"

"Like I said, I have gone to counseling. It has changed a lot of my thinking, and I miss you and the children."

"Oh please, Chris. Just go away. We haven't missed you. Nor do we need you."

"After all I have done for you, this is how you are going to treat me?"

"What all do you think you have done for me, Chris? You cost me my mother and stepdad—that is all you have done for me. I don't feel like I owe you a thank you never mind any of my time."

"What? So now I'm nothing to you?"

"Basically, now I have to go. Gregory is teething and not feeling well. I have to get this home."

"I said I will give you a ride, now get in."

"I said no thank you. I will walk."

"Have it your way, Angel." He turns and walks away. Angel is thinking. Thank God, finally. She picks up her pace and worries all the way home that at any time he would be pulling up beside her. This would not be like Chris to not have his own way. She was shaking like a leaf when she finally got inside of the house.

Chapter Thirteen

———————•———————

Tracy could see by the look on her face that something had happened, so she dropped the clothes that she was folding and went to her side. Putting a hand on Angel's arm and asking, "Angel, what is it?"

All Angel could do was shake her head.

"Was it that feeling again?"

Again, Angel only shook her head.

"I think we should report this to the police."

"And tell them what exactly? That we have this feeling? They already think women are strange."

"Angel, I don't think this is something we should just ignore."

"Maybe you're right. Maybe they would drive around this way a little more often if they thought something strange was happening."

"I haven't heard of any one being attacked so that is a good thing."

"I haven't either and no one at work talks about this. So maybe it is just you and me." Angel didn't want to tell her that she had just confronted Chris. She knew Tracy would be on the phone to Dr. Adams if no one else.

Tracy didn't want to tell her she thought it was Chris. That's why just the two of them are getting these feelings. How long do we wait to tell someone? After he has attacked Angel or maybe even myself?

Tracy had this gut feeling that it was Chris, and she wasn't wanting Angel to take any chances. Nor was she anymore. They will take Lucky with them always.

"Tracy, you can go get some sleep now. I will watch the children." She pulls Tracy into her embrace and gives her a very sincere hug. This brought tears to her. It had been a long time since she had hugged anyone as a mother figure. Tracy picked up on this right away and hugged her back just as sincerely. She knew that they had just made a bond like no other. They would complete each other's lives and be there for each other till their dying day.

"All right, my dear. I will take you up on this, and if you need my help, please come and wake me."

"I should be fine, Tracy. You get up when you are good and ready. The children and I will be quiet not to wake you."

"Thank you. Please let the children be children. I will sleep."

"Thank you, have a good rest."

Tracy goes to her room, and Angel takes Elisabeth by the hand, and they head for the kitchen. She knew Tracy would have supper all planned out and things all ready just to turn on. So she would check to see at what stage everything was now at. It was no surprise to see there was nothing for her to do. Tracy was very efficient and always thinks ahead. Very much like what Mom would do.

Angel got to thinking about her mom, remembering that meals never seemed to be a big deal to her. She always had things ready by the time breakfast mess was to be cleaned up. She said, that way, she was free to do whatever she wanted without having to worry about supper.

Her friends would say, "I better get home and start preparing supper." Mom just shook her head because some of her friends just could not get organized. You could tell by their houses as well. Mom believed that everything should have its place. And if it didn't then you don't need it, 'cause then it just becomes clutter. Mom always said it makes for an easy house to clean if everything was kept in place. Over the years, I have learned what Mom was saying is so true. Why have things all piled up? If you never get to the bottom of that pile, you didn't need what was under there. When Angel looked around her home, she knew that her mom would be proud of how she kept house. 'Cause Angel too likes things in their place, and Tracy does as well. The children have the odd toy out of their room, but a toy or two will not cause a dumpy looking house. Picking up the toys and setting them off to the side, she picks up a book and decides she was going to sit and read to Elisabeth while Gregory slept. The medication that Tracy had given him seemed to be working, so she would put her time to good use and spend it with Elisabeth. Pulling Elisabeth up beside her in the big chair made her think of the days when she used to sit like this with her grandma. Grandma never came over that she didn't sit in the big chair and read her a story before she left. As I got bigger, we then started having woman-to-woman talks is what Grandma used to call them. She would say, "It's funny, Angel, but if your mother was to be telling you this, you would think she were just nagging on you. But here we are having a woman-to-woman talk, and you are listening to me." Angel just smiles to herself as she opens the book to read to Elisabeth.

The hair on Lucky's back stood up, and she lay beside us with a low growl rumbling in her throat. She was either warning us that someone was around or she was letting whoever it was know she knew they were around. Elisabeth stiffened up as she snuggled into my side closer.

"It's okay, sweetheart, just someone walking by." I was waiting for the doorbell to ring 'cause I was pretty sure that Chris had followed me. Lucky got up and wandered around the house, still growling. When the doorbell did ring, I damn near jumped out of my skin, and Elisabeth was just as jumpy as I was. We just sat there. Then there was pounding on the door. Taking a deep breath and getting up from the chair to go to the door, I then heard a voice: "Angel, you in there?"

"Yes, coming." Pulling the door open to Dr. Adams was such a relief.

"Hi, Angel. The girls at the clinic said you came home early because Gregory isn't well. Thought I would come see if I could help."

"It's just his teeth, and thank you, I think we have it under control. Come on in, and I will put on the tea."

"Sounds great to me."

"I was just going to do some reading to Elisabeth while Gregory and Tracy had a sleep."

"Tracy feeling all right?"

"Yes. She is fine, just a little tired. Gregory has played her out."

"Looks like the garbage men were a little rough when emptying your garbage. They have put a hole in the back of your wall."

"I will check it out later. They do get rough with the cans. Glad we don't buy them."

"Did you want me to fix that hole in the wall?"

"No, thank you. Mom showed me how to do mudding."

"If you are sure. It will only take me a few minutes."

"I know it would, but it will also give me something to do. I will see if what Mom showed me works."

"All right. If it doesn't then let me know and I will come fix it for you. I don't know why they build it to go into your garage like that."

"Into my garage?"

"Yes, someone could get into your house through there. How long has that hole been there?"

"I don't know. I don't have much for garbage. So maybe a couple of days."

"Be sure to tend to it right away. Keep your garage door locked that comes into the house."

"I will. I don't use Tracy's car much. I leave it for Tracy in case she needs to take the children somewhere quickly. I like to walk as much as possible."

Sitting down for our tea, Elisabeth had come along, and before I knew it, she was up on Dr. Adams's lap. They were chatting back and forth and seemed to be really enjoying each other's company. I felt like I could leave the room and Elisabeth would be just fine. She has come a long ways. What would happen if she were to see Chris? Would she slip back into her shell? The place she finds to be safe. Since we have moved here, she has not asked about him once. It is a sad feeling to know that a child finds it better to be without their daddy. It is a known fact that children are smarter than adults when it comes to reading people. So Elisabeth knew that her daddy did not want her. With that thought in mind, it almost tore my heart out. I remember my daddy, and I loved him so much. When he died, a part of me died with him. Oh, how I missed him. I still do but have learned to live without him. There is no doubt in my mind that if Daddy were still alive at the time I met Chris, life would be a whole lot different today. I wouldn't have made such a mess of my life and of Mom's and poor Jake. It has been a blessing that Gregory is too young to know anything.

"Dr. Adams, have you seen Jake?"

"Yes, I have. And I was supposed to tell you to go over and see him."

"He wants to see me?"

"Yes, he does. Jake said anytime would be fine with him. He is closing up the estate and moving back into his little house. He said that you should go over and pick up your belongings and see if there was something of your mother's you might want." Sitting down heavily on the chair and pushing my hands though my hair, I look at Dr. Adams, shaking my head.

"I haven't been back there for a very long time. I don't feel like I deserve to take anything from there. Whatever is there of Mom's belongs to Jake. He loved her with all his heart."

"So did you, Angel."

"No. If I did, I would have had more faith in her than I did. I never would have let someone else turn me against my mother if I truly loved her the way Daddy and Jake did."

"Angel, you got caught by a man who knows how to manipulate women. He caught you blind sided. And when a person doesn't know how to play that game, it is so easy to have what happened to you happen. You were an impressionable young girl, and he knew it. You saw the steps he took to keep you and Kate apart. Unfortunately, you did not see it in time. You cannot blame yourself for the power of a man who knew how to play the game. I hope now that you would be able to pick out the signs a mile away."

"I don't want any man in my life."

"Oh dear, don't be saying such a thing, Angel. You are too young to be alone. Life can be a very lonely, long road when you have no one to share it with."

"I have Elisabeth and Gregory. I don't need any man coming into my life and destroying what I have left as a family."

"Your children will all grow up, and you will find yourself alone and lonely."

"Grandma wasn't lonely. She spent a lot of years alone."

"Oh, but she was lonely. She just would never let Kate know."

"I thought you spent all your free time with her?"

"Your grandmother had a lot of years before we met up again. Emma liked to keep herself busy, but in the end when she went home, she was still very much alone. It was of her choice many times. But nevertheless, she was lonely."

"Grandma always looked and acted happy."

"For the most part, she was very happy—just lonely."

"So why didn't you change that if you knew Grandma was so lonely?"

"I guess, Angel, there are some things I just can't explain. It was all about timing, and the time was never right."

"Didn't you love Grandma?"

"Oh, Angel"—as he shakes his head and looks up to the heavens—"I have never loved anyone as much as I loved your grandmother."

"Didn't you tell her that?"

"Not in so many words, I guess."

"Why not?"

"'Cause your grandmother's heart was taken by someone else. I could tell she was pining for someone, and I never wanted to ask."

"Why not? Then maybe you would have been able to let her know just how much you loved her."

"I didn't want to know who it was that she loved so deeply. Being second best was all right with me, so long as we could spend time together. We had our good times to remember and our respect for each other."

"Seems to me that you both wasted a lot of precious time."

"I want you to remember what you are saying, Angel."

"What do you mean?"

"You are going to meet a very nice young man who will love you as though you were his very own breath. Don't waste those precious moments worrying about whether he is another Chris. Time goes by way too fast. Before you know it, it is too late to make a difference."

"I'm afraid that he will have to be a real prince on a white horse before I let him even close to me and my children."

"Angel, please don't mark all men by Chris. Yes, there are lots of them out there. But you know the signs now. You will be a whole lot wiser the next time around."

"There won't be a second time around for a very long, long time. I am quite happy here with the kids and Tracy. We don't need anyone else in our lives."

"Mark my words. There will come a day when you will know that you need more in your life than Tracy and the children. I'm not saying you will love your children any less then you do now, but you are going to need more in your life."

"I can't see what more I would need other than my mother, and Tracy will do fine on that regard."

"I will do fine with what, Angel?"

Being started Angel whipped her head around so quickly Dr. Adams wondered what had her so jumpy. Getting up off her chair and going over to pull Tracy into an embrace she says.

"Being a mother."

"Whose mother am I being?"

"Mine," Angel replies with a grin and kisses Tracy's cheek.

"Thank you, Angel, but I don't think I can replace your mother."

"I'm not asking you to replace her. I'm taking you as a replacement. I don't think I could find anyone who would be as good to the children and myself as you are. My mom would be proud to have you stand in her place."

"Thank you, Angel." The two women hang on to each other in a very relaxed way. It was plain to see that they had become family. This warms Alex's heart to know that Angel would have someone besides himself that really cares for Angel and her children.

"I would have to agree with you, Angel. I think Kate would be pleased with your choice of an adopted grandma."

"Thank you, Mr. Alex. I found Angel and the children very easy to love. They fill my heart with so much joy. I could not stand to see something happen to any of them."

"Well, I must say you all make a mighty fine-looking family. Now I must get going, morning comes early to me these days. Don't forget to go over and see Jake, Angel. He will be expecting you soon."

"I will, and thank you for letting me know."

"You're welcome, and I will be back sooner than I have been. I promise." He kisses both the women on their cheeks. Then he picks up Elisabeth and hugs and kisses her until she giggles. It was so plain to see that she really likes Dr. Adams.

"So you are going over to see your stepfather, Angel?"

"Yes. He is closing up the estate and moving back into the little house. He wants me to go pick up what belongs to me and maybe take things of my mother's that I want."

"That will not be easy for you to do alone. I will come with you."

"Thank you, Tracy, for caring. But I think this is something I should do alone. Jake may not talk much to me alone, but probably less if you are there. I love you anyways." She pulls Tracy into a hug, saying, "I must go fix a wall."

"A wall where?"

"Guess there is a hole behind our garbage cans."

"Oh really? How did that happen?"

"The garbage men are too rough with our cans."

"To put a hole in the wall, they must have destroyed the cans."

"I will check it out."

"Do you need some help?"

"No, I can manage a hole in the wall." Angel goes out and finds that the hole is a lot bigger than she thought it would be. Finding it funny that there was no damage done to the cans. She had to look around to find something to fit. Going out back, she found a part sheet of plywood and decided that would do the trick. She brought it in and screwed in into place from the inside. Thinking to herself that this would take more than the gyprock that they had finished it with in the first place. Who builds a garbage box with gyprock? She could see that it had all been part of the building, and it wouldn't get wet, so the owner didn't see a problem. She had to admit it had all looked very nice.

When she went inside, it hit her that they had not said anything to Dr. Adams about what they had been feeling. Nor did she mention that she had seen Chris. She was glad in a way because it would have spoiled a great visit, and he would have left here worrying about them. At his age, he didn't need that anymore.

They all had a great sleep. Angel had told Tracy she would walk alone this morning, seeing how Gregory was still sleeping. Tracy did not argue when she knew Angel was taking Lucky.

Leaving the house, something red caught her eye. Turning around, Angel saw *BITCH* spray painted across the hole she had covered up the night before.

Chapter Fourteen

———◆———

Her heart starts to race, and she looks around to see if anyone was sitting on the sidelines watching her. When she got her mind to think straight she knew she was in no danger as Lucky wasn't putting up any kind of a fuss. Deep down inside she knew who had done this. There was no need in calling the police because they would just tell her it was some teens out doing the town in red. Teens my ass. Angel was starting to see that Chris was going to make her life as uncomfortable as hell. She only hoped she was going to have the strength to fight back or at least hold her ground. She knew if he really wanted to he could push to get visiting rights of the children. She could only hope that he still didn't want anything to do with the children and will leave them out of this game he is playing. She couldn't believe that after all this time he would even come around, what would be the purpose?

All day at work, she was a little jumpy and her mind was on overload. When the girls asked if everything was okay with her. She just laughed it off and blamed it on the lack of sleep. Which of course they all fell for because they knew Gregory was teething. Angel was so glad that the day ended and she was back home before Tracy had to take out the garbage.

"Tracy, I don't want you to worry about the garbage. It is something I can do when I get home."

"I don't mind, Angel."

"No, I will. That is the least I can do to help. You do a lot more around here than I do, so I'm making the garbage my responsibility."

"All right, Angel. If that's how you want it."

"I will feel better, knowing I have done something at home every day."

"Oh sweet child you do so much, you just don't realize it."

"So, I will do one more chore, Just until Gregory is old enough to do it." They both laugh about it and move on to get supper over with.

"I think I will take a run out to see Jake after supper, if you don't mind Tracy. If you have something else planned for tonight I will make it another night."

"Not at all, Are you taking the children?"

"Not this time. I would like to talk to Jake first and then I will go from there."

"All right, sounds like you have thought this through."

"Don't think I would say that. But the longer I wait the harder it will be. With Jake moving and all. I won't be able to get my things as easy. I don't want to drag him back to something he is trying to forget."

"I understand, please drive carefully."

"Don't need to worry Tracy, I won't be gone long."

"I will do up the dishes so you can be home before dark."

"Tracy, you worry to much."

"Someone has to worry about you."

"Now Tracy, You know I'm a big girl."

"Even big girls make mistakes."

"You don't have to tell me that. I have learned that all on my own."

"Sorry, You are right, of course you have. Just be careful."

"Don't worry I will be."

On Angel's way out, she looked at the painting and swore to herself. She would have to cover that up before Tracy saw it. It was funny cause she wasn't scared about it now as much as she was mad. Thinking she would give Chris a piece of her mind the next time she saw him. There was no doubt he would deny doing it. But that wasn't going to stop her. Angel had been getting mentally stronger by the day and felt she was a force you wouldn't want to fight with anymore. She only wished she had, had this strength when her mother was still around. Her mind was clear and she knew she would not get caught or blind sided again.

As she drove out to see Jake many memories came back to her. All the trips her and Jake had made up and down this road in his pick up truck. She had loved Jake and she knew he also loved her. Jake was the best stepdad a girl could have asked for. How she had let him down over the years. Would he ever forgive her? Hell, will he even talk to her? This thought gave her butterflies.

The thought of butterflies brings back the memories of the time she had them for the first time and how she thought there were real butterflies in her tummy. Not understanding how they got there was a little upsetting to her. But as always Mom was there to set her straight.

"Oh, Mom, I hope you are with me now. I will need your help. Jake will need your help." A breeze blows through her hair, taking a deep breath and saying.

"Thank you, Mom. I love you." For the rest of her trip, her childhood blew through her mind like a whirlwind. It seemed as though she went from being this happy little girl with the world at her fingertips to a mom with no future and no parents. It was like she had been put on another planet—no one around but her, Chris, and the children. Was that how it was for Adam and Eve? Now that was a scary thought; look how that turned out.

I guess there are still a lot of people who take a bite out of the forbidden fruit. If I remember it right, the fruit was the apple. There are a lot of people who eat apples. Is that why the world is in such a mess? Should the apple be disposed of and maybe then the world would be a better place? Wish Mom and Grandma were here maybe they would have an answer.

Pulling into the estate gave Angel a sick feeling. The day she left came back into play. She just sat there in the car and cried. Remembering those horrible words she had last spoken to her mom. *I'm sorry you're my mother.* With it being Mother's Day even makes it worse. There was no "happy Mother's Day" or "I love you, Mom" to remember. Now this is just ripping her heart out. Angel was sobbing so hard she didn't hear the first rap on the window. The second one got her attention and scared her as well.

"Miss, are you okay?"

She rolls the window down an inch and says, "Yes, I'm fine. I have come to see Jake."

"Oh, Mr. Jake. He is not well, Miss."

"I know. That is why I am here."

"Okay, I will take you to him."

"Thank you, sir."

"Yes, Miss." Angel did not recognize this gentleman, nor did he recognize her. After all, it has been a long time since she had been to the estate. She gets out of the car and follows the gentleman into the mansion.

Memories start to run wild as Angel starts to relive her life here with Jake and her mom. She could hear herself laughing as Jake would toss her up on his shoulders and carry her through the rooms as though she were a feather and hear her Mom saying, *"Jake, put her down. You are going to hurt your back."*

"Then I'm not much of a man," he would say.

Looking around, she could see some of her mother's things and all the pictures Mom did of me and her and Jake and then of Grandma. There were several pictures of us with my dad. Jake wouldn't let her put them away. He said we should be thankful that Dad had gotten us all together. Mom was great with the camera, and the pictures told the stories. Mom liked to take action shots and pictures of us when we didn't know she was. She had always said they made the best pictures. Picking up the one of me when I had fallen from my bike, I landed in the grass and my nose came inches from this big black-and-yellow caterpillar. It was huge and fuzzy. You would have thought that I was really checking it out. Mom got a great close-up of it. In one picture, you could see my bike, but the close-up one with the caterpillar was the best.

Walking around and touching some of Mom's things seemed to me as though I could feel her standing beside me. To her, each of her pieces had a story to tell. Recalling how Mom would tell me about what she wanted to put in that place. We would look until we found just the right thing. Mom used to sit and look at the rooms and say "I know what this room needs," or she would explain what the room would look like when she was done. Mom had a great way with colors and decor. She always made every room warm and inviting. She preferred to redo old homes. She said she liked to know she put life back into something that had given to so many, so in return, the home deserved a new lease on its life. Mom always believed that everything should have its place. Sometimes she moved things around and around until they looked like they belonged.

Picking up the glass doll out of the old carriage that Mom had found at an antique shop, I recall her telling me: "See this baby doll, Angel? So long as I have it, I will always have you as my baby. This doll looks just like you—perfect." I felt the tear that was running down my cheek just as the housekeeper came in.

"Mr. Jake will see you now, Miss."

"Thank you." It felt strange to be announced in what used to be my home.

"Come on in, Angel, and have a seat," Jake says to me as he sits with his back facing me. So I go around and sit in the big chair I used to sit in as a little girl by the fire.

"I see you didn't bring the children?"

"Not this time. But I will next time. I promise." He just nods his head.

"I'm told you're not well."

"Just age, I guess. Things are catching up to me."

"I'm sorry to hear that."

"You may go through the house and take whatever you wish. I take it that is why you have come?"

"Not at all. Dr. Adams said you wanted to see me."

"Yes, I am moving back into my small house and closing up the mansion, so please take whatever you want."

"There is nothing really that I want, Jake."

"So I see I'm not *Dad* anymore."

"I'm sorry. I didn't think you would want me to call you *Dad*."

"Guess that is up to you, Angel. Just remember: once a parent, always a parent." Angel just hangs her head for the lack of words. This wasn't going to be easy, and Jake wasn't helping.

"Saying I'm sorry doesn't seem to be enough. I know I hurt you and Mom very much, and I wish I could undo what has been done. But I can't. I wish every day that Mom was still here so I could tell her how sorry I am."

"That makes two of us. But what is done is done, and we can't change it. So we must go on for as long as we have left. I would hope that you have gotten your life on track now that Alex has gotten you out on your own. This alone would please your mother. I'm sure she is smiling down on you right now."

"I hope so."

"How are the children?"

"They are very well, thank you, and happy."

"The move wasn't hard on them?"

"On the contrary, I think it was a great move. Especially for Elisabeth."

"Yes, Elisabeth. Your mother was so happy when she saw her. It was all I could do to hold her back."

"Why didn't she try to talk to me when she lived across the street?"

"Would it have made any difference, Angel? You hurt her bad enough in the hospital."

"I said I'm sorry. You have no idea just how sorry I am."

"Oh, I think I do. I have had to live without my love, go to bed without her every night, and wake up to an empty bed and house every morning. Angel, you have no idea what your mother meant to me. I wish I could have died that day with her."

"Don't say that, Dad." Jake looked at her with surprise. She was just as surprised to have it come out so easily.

"The kids and I need you around."

"No, Angel. I'm afraid I wouldn't be much good to have around the children."

"They might do you good. You will have to spend time with us again and see."

"Maybe after I get moved again."

"What are you going to do with this place?"

"Remember, Angel, it is yours and your children's and theirs. So it is yours whenever you want to live here."

"Oh, I couldn't. But thank you."

"Well, you should because it is a home that needs children and pets."

"I did love it here. I wish I could go back to being that little girl again."

"I have wished that for a very long time, Angel. But now you have your children, and you must move on. That is what life is all about. It is a circle of life that is never ending. Now you and your children must carry on where your parents have left off. It comes to an end way too early for some of us, and others get to take the longer route around. But in the end, we will all be in the same place again."

"Do you really believe that, Dad?"

"Yes, dear, I do. I know in my heart that I am going to see your mother again. That is all that has gotten me this far since she passed away."

"I'm so sorry, Dad, that I wasn't here for you."

"No need to be sorry, it is done and over. Yes, I was very angry with you. For all the pain you caused your mother, and then I blamed you for her death. Alex has made me see that you didn't have that choice. It was Kate who took that chance and lost. I know in her heart she would feel she won because she gave you life again and a second chance to be with your children. You and your children meant everything to her."

"I know that, Dad."

Jake looks at Angel with a frown so deep, his eyes were barely open. He shakes his head and then says to her, "If you knew that, why the hell didn't you call or get in touch with her all this time?"

"I had sent my address with the phone number on it just after we moved."

"Really, we never got anything. I know your mom would have been on cloud nine. She waited every day after you left. She made that trip to the post office every day to see if anything came from you. Every day, she sunk further and further into depression. Angel, your mother almost died of a broken heart long before she did. I don't know if I can ever forgive you for that. You were her life. Yes, she loved me, but I was second on her list. I don't say that if she could have gave me part of her to survive that she wouldn't have. But I knew no one would change her mind when it came to you."

"Dad, didn't they tell Mom how dangerous it was?"

"They told her there were risks. She didn't care. After you turned her away the night before the surgery, I don't think she thought about the risks. She just thought she would show you just how much you meant to her. And if it meant that kind of risks, then so be it. I begged her not to. I wanted her to wait and see if there would be another donor. Even if she would have gave it another week, maybe you would have talked to her and she would have felt she had a reason to fight. As it was, she felt she had nothing to lose and you had it all to lose."

Now he had the tears flowing, and through them all she could say was "Damn Chris."

"Damn Chris? Why do you say that?"

"'Cause, Dad, he did all this."

"What do you mean, Angel?"

"When I made up mail to send to you and Mom, he would always say he would send it. Then when he got mad and threw things around, and Tracy was helping me clean up the mess. She found the mail stuck inside of his mechanic book. I should say it fell out when she picked up the book."

"Angel, is this for real?"

"Yes, Dad. So I took it that Mom didn't love me anymore, that was why she wouldn't answer the cards I sent to her."

"Oh my god. Kate struggled with this for so long. She could not believe that you would just walk out of her life and not return."

"I felt the same way. Whenever I asked about coming home, he would always say 'we'll see.' But it never happened. Then he started telling me that it was plain to see that you and Mom didn't want me around, otherwise she would have answered the cards or at least called."

"So why didn't you call?"

"Chris wouldn't let us get a long-distance plan, so he said I couldn't. And besides, if Mom wanted to talk to me, she had the number. I believed him because I didn't know he didn't send the mail."

Jake gets up with some trouble and paces the floor. He had become an old man in a short time.

"I hope I get to see that SOB soon."

Chapter Fifteen

"Now, Dad, you can't go getting into trouble at your age."

"My age is what gives me the strength that I need. I have nothing to lose."

"You could get hurt, Dad."

"Don't you worry about that. If I get hurt, so will he."

Getting up and going over and squatting down in front of Jake, Angel takes his hands into hers.

"Please, Dad, there has already been too much pain caused by me. I don't want anyone else to have to suffer at my hands."

"Oh, my sweet child. If what you have just told me is true, then it isn't by your hands that the pain has been caused. But by the company you kept."

"Isn't that the same thing?"

"No, not even close. Did you know you were a prisoner in your own home?"

"Dr. Adams told me that. I didn't see it until Tracy found the proof."

"All those wasted days and years. Angel, I just want to tear the heart right out of that man for both your mother and me. It is what was done to us. An eye for an eye."

"Dad, Mom always told me that two wrongs don't make it right. Doing anything to Chris is not bringing Mom back to us."

"I know that, but I'm sure it would make me feel better."

"No, it wouldn't. You're not that type of a person."

"You're right, but damn it anyway. It isn't right. Nor was it fair to your mother."

"I know. I wish I could change things."

"I live with the saying that your mother always told me."

"What is that, Dad?"

"Everything happens for a reason. I just haven't figured out what the reason for losing her was."

"I know." Angel wraps her arms around him, pulling herself into his chest. She couldn't help but notice he had lost much of his body mass. Jake was like a feeble old man, not the man who would toss her over his shoulders and carry her for blocks.

"Please promise me that you won't do anything silly if you see Chris. He is not worth it."

"He deserves to suffer as we have all had to."

"He will, Dad. God will see to that. Mom would not want you to do anything that could hurt you, and neither do I. I want my children to get to know their grandpa."

"Angel, why has it taken you all this time to come around?" Looking up at him, she could see the years had taken the sparkle that once was in his eyes away. They now were empty and hollow. How this tore at Angel's heart.

"I honestly didn't think you would want to see me."

"Oh, Angel. I was angry with you, but you have always been able to get to my heart. I never stopped loving you. I guess I should have been there for you after your mother passed away. I'm sorry. I just didn't have the strength once she was gone. Self-pity is a horrible thing. It can also kill."

"Dad, can't we just move forward now? You, me, and the children. They need a grandfather. I need my dad." The tears came easy to Jake, and he nods his head.

"Maybe we should try. But we have to go slow, Angel. I have been alone for so long, I don't know if I can take having the children around. They are full of energy, and they make noise."

"Yes, they make noise, and a lot of it. But we will start with short visits, okay? Maybe you should come see us at first. That way, you can leave whenever you find it's getting to be too much."

"That might be a wise idea."

"Would you come for supper on Saturday? I don't work, so you could come whenever you want. I can make an early supper if that is better for you."

"Let's see what happens in the next few days, okay? Maybe I will feel up to going out then."

"All right. I will call you Saturday morning and see how you feel then."

"All right, that would be fine." Not knowing how to ask but it had been sitting on the edge of her tongue now for the past half an hour, she decides just to put it out there and see what Jake might say.

"Dad, may I go and see my room?"

Jake looks at her with a frown. "Why would you ask me that? It is still your room, Angel. You may go to it anytime you wish. I know your mother didn't move anything, she stayed in her study a lot."

"Mom finished her book she was writing, didn't she?"

"Yes, she did. But without you, she wouldn't do anything with it."

"Why not?"

"She said it didn't mean the same, not being able to share it with you."

"So where is it?"

"I put it on her desk."

"Would you mind if I looked at it?"

"Your mother would love you to."

"What about you?"

"I would also love you to. I know what that would mean to your mother."

"Thank you. I won't be long."

"Take all the time you want."

Getting up and going up the long flight of stairs, I got the feeling that Mom was with me. If she hadn't talked to me about the sixth sense, this would make me jumpy. Instead, I wrapped my arms around myself as I knew Mom would do, saying, "Mom, I'm sorry it has taken me so long. Hope you can forgive me."

The door to my bedroom opened up just as I went to reach for the doorknob. So I was right. She is here with me. I wondered if she visits Jake and if he knew she was here. Does he exercise his sixth sense as Mom would tell me to do? Or is he oblivious to anything around him.

Stepping inside my room was like going back twenty some years. Nothing had changed, and my doll was still on my bed. She was what they called a Mona Lisa doll. Her eyes would follow you wherever you went. It was creepy at first. I grew to love her. She became someone to talk to, and so long as I walked around the room, it was as if I were talking to a real person. She just didn't answer, but her eyes followed.

Everything was still in its place, and the shades were drawn, so I went over to pull them up, bringing some light into the room. I got this wave of heavy feeling in my feet as if I weren't to move. I stood there and just looked around, and everything had its story to tell. Although it seemed that they were all sad stories. Yet I knew that everything I had gotten was on happy occasions.

Reaching over and picking up a medallion off the dresser that lay in front of Grandma's picture that read: *Grandma, I love you!* I rubbed it through my fingers, and I remembered the day I had bought this for Grandma. Then, turning it over, I read the script. *Grandma, when I think of you. I remember the warmth of your eyes and the beauty that blooms like a rose every time you smile.* It was Grandma's birthday, and we were at the dollar store. I was so proud because I had enough money of my own to buy this for Grandma. She had told me that the smallest gifts meant more to her than the large ones and that she would always cherish this. Mom had given it back to me after Grandma had passed away. I had always kept it with her picture. Jake was right; Mom had not moved anything. For the life of me, I couldn't remember why this wasn't something I hadn't taken when I left home.

"Oh, Grandma. It wasn't because I wanted to forget you, 'cause I didn't. Please believe me and forgive me. I'm sorry I have not talked to you for a very long time. Things are better now, and I will have more time, I promise." I kiss the medallion and laid it back beside the picture. Looking at the picture and seeing Grandma. She was still a beautiful lady at her age. I was thankful that I had not seen her while she was sick. Yes, it would have been nice to say good-bye, but this picture is how I will always remember my grandma Emma. The beautiful smile and the love that shone in her eyes. Grandma always gave from the heart. She and Mom were alike when it came to that. I guess she and Mom were alike in many ways, but I took things better coming from Grandma than I did my mom."

In behind Grandma's picture was Mom and my father Ben's wedding picture, as well as Mom and Jake's wedding picture. In both pictures, Mom was so happy and beautiful. She made a gorgeous bride. Mom should have been a model for a bride's magazine. She made any groom look just as happy as she was. She and grandma had the same smile. Looking into the mirror, I smiled at myself to see if I had their smile. I could not tell. Two beautiful women, both dead at an early age. Does this mean that I too have a short life span? That thought sent shivers down my spine.

"I love you both, but I hope not. I pray that I will be around for my children for a very long time to come." As I walk around my room, a picture on the nightstand caught my eye. Minnie. Oh my god, all this time I had forgotten about her. Picking up the picture brought back memories of my dog and me and the fun we had had. I must remember to ask Jake about her. Leaving my room, I went to Mom's study to see her book.

Pushing open the door, I just stood there. I have never been in her study because when she was writing, she never wanted to be disturbed. Now I was standing on the threshold of the make-believe room. Mom always said it was her dream room where she made make-believe come alive. I stood there looking as if I would see all the characters in Mom's book sitting around talking. But her room didn't look any different than my bedroom. This was disappointing as I had thought it would be exciting; instead, I found I was nervous, to say the least. I could picture Mom sitting at her desk in front of her computer.

When Mom first started to write, she would do it all in handwriting. Then she bought an electric typewriter from the church garage sale. Jake had surprised her for Christmas our first year with him and bought her the computer. Mom left it in the box for a whole year before she got brave enough to attempt to use it. She had thanked Jake so many times. She said once she got the hang of it, it had made things so much easier for her, and it made her want to write all the time. We always knew where Mom would be. Mom was a stay-at-home mom, and she always said she loved that job. She never wanted for anything. She was a simple person when it came to the house. It was clean in order with furniture she would pick up from garage sales or secondhand stores. Mom always said she was rescuing the furniture that still had many years of life left in it. Even her desk was old but beautiful. When she was doing her study, Jake wanted to buy her all-new office furniture. She wouldn't hear of it.

Her book lay on top of her desk in pride. I had thought it would be covered in dust, but it was plain to see that the housekeeper kept Mom's room very clean. It didn't even smell closed up.

Picking up her book brought tears to me as I knew she would have been so happy to have had it published. She had told me that once it had a cover, her story would have a face. The cover had a very young pregnant girl on it standing on a bed of blue roses. The title was called *You Made Your Bed*. I pass my hand over the book cover, and it was if I could feel Mom's hand on top of mine.

So I ask. "May I read this, Mom?"

There was a breeze go though her room. So all I could say was, "Thank you. I love you." I put the book to my chest and hold it tight. Looking around Mom's tidy study, I noticed the closet door wasn't quite shut, so I went over to close it properly. I knew Mom would not have left it like this. I push it closed and turn around, and it popped open again. So once again, I close it. Once again, it opens. Hum, something must be in the way. Putting Mom's book back on her desk, I go over so I can open the closet door right up so I could see what might be jamming it. What in the world? All I could see were shoe boxes, and on them was written: To My Darling Daughter Angel. Standing with my hand over my mouth and holding back the tears, I could see that they were all dated by month and year. The first one was the month of May, which was the month that I had left. So I pull it out of the pile and opened it. On top was a folded white paper, so I took it out to see what Mom had done. I found that it was a letter written to me.

My Darling Angel:

My sweet child. I want you to know how much I miss you. My heart breaks more each day that you don't call or come and see me. To me, life is nothing without you. You were always my purpose and the reason to go on, especially after your father died. I do not understand what I have done to make you forget me. Please believe me when I say I'm sorry for whatever I have said or done. I have tried to be nothing more than the best Mom I could be. I want nothing more for you than happiness and good health. I miss our shopping and all our girl time together.

I do love Jake, but he is not my daughter. There are certain things only a mother and daughter can do. Jake has tried to make me go on, but to me, life has come to an end without you. These shoe boxes are a gift box for you. For every month you have been gone. You may not have been in my sight, but you have always been on my mind and in my heart. So anytime I saw something that would express how I was feeling and I knew you would like, I bought it for you so that you would know when you came back that your mother never quit loving you. Nor did I forget you.

I will never understand what happened, and I only pray that you will find your way back to me one day. I hope it is while I still have my mind, although I feel it slipping as the depression is taking over. I had set a goal that whatever I bought must be compact to fit in a shoe box because I wanted you to understand that there is a whole lot of love in something as small as my heart, and it is mainly for you. So, my darling, I hope that each shoe box will bring you pleasure and that you will feel the love that has been stored inside each and every one. Please remember that there is no greater love than the love of your mother.

So, my precious Angel, I trust now that you are reading this letter, that you have found your way back home. I hope that in time all will heal, and you and you alone will understand the meaning of unconditional love.

Loving you and missing you with all my heart.

MOM

Chapter Sixteen

———————•———————

Choking on the tears that were now flowing freely, I could feel the pain that my mom had been feeling. I lift out the cards that were stacked all neatly inside. Each envelope had the month written on the outside that it was for. It looked like Mom had bought one for every week of the month. She had wanted me to find the shoe boxes—that was why the door would not stay shut.

Picking up the tan-colored envelope, I found inside a thanksgiving card. In it was a charm bracelet that had a turkey on it. It was a simple verse that read:

Although we are miles apart. I still give thanks for a loving
Daughter like you.
Missing you and love you always, MOM

Then there was Halloween. Inside the card was another charm of a pumpkin. The card read:

Wishing you were here for a Spooktacular time.
Missing you and love you always, MOM

October was a fun month for Mom; she would decorate the house for both Thanksgiving and Halloween. It was something she had a blast at doing. We had the largest pumpkin in town. Mom made it out of papier-mâché and then put a coating on top to make it stand up to the weather. The pumpkin was something she could use for both occasions, so she made it huge. It was made to be split down the middle so she could easily store it. Sometimes I think she enjoyed Halloween more than the children that came to the house. The house was so scary to some of the children, their parents had a hard time getting them to come up to the door. Mom always dressed up to hand out candy, and she always dressed up and would come to my school's Halloween party. I would never know what she was until I got home. Mom wandered through all the classes, and the teachers all thought they knew who it was but were wrong each time. Mom always got the last laugh and never wanted to embarrass me with my friends or teachers, which she never did. I was always proud that my mom would take the time to have fun with us.

Taking the box out that was dated for December.

Christmas was the next huge celebration that Mom went all out for. The inside of the house as well as the outside. It looked like a fairy tale come to life. She always started right after Halloween. With all the work she put into it, she didn't want to wait one week before Christmas just to take it all down in two weeks' time. Mom had won the decorating prize many years in a row. It was always a nice gift certificate for grocery shopping. She would always pass it on to someone less fortunate than us. She said she hoped that she had helped them to have a better Christmas. Mom had the biggest heart and always said Christmas was for giving, and she always went all out. You could be a total stranger, but to Mom at Christmastime, there were no strangers. We loved it, and so did all my friends. This breaks my heart to know that my children will never see this.

Opening a red envelope, I pulled out a card that has a beautiful white Christmas stocking with red ribbons. On the front it read:

For my Special Daughter with love at Christmastime.

I almost couldn't open it. I knew the inside would tear my heart apart. I opened it to find a silver chain with two hearts intertwined, and in the center of the two hearts was a diamond. Taking the chain into my hand and holding it while I read through the tears.

The best gift of all can't be wrapped up in ribbons and bows, and it won't be found under no Christmas tree.

The best gift of all can't be bought, nor sold. It is more precious than gold or silver, and it is free for the taking.

The best gift of all may rarely be mentioned but is treasured each day all through the year.

The best gift of all at Christmastime and always, my dear, is having a daughter like you.

This was so like Mom. She would find a card that would say just as she meant. Holding it close, all I could say as I cried was, "Oh, Mom, what have I done?" The rapping on the door got my attention.

"Ms. Angel, Mr. Jake wants to know if you are all right."

"Yes, Bella. Tell him I will be right down."

"Yes, Miss."

Putting the cards back into the box. Going through these boxes was something that was going to be very hard to do. Angel knew that each one would be full of love and yet would bring her such pain. She knew that she was going to go through all the pain her mother had done over all that time. Whether she would have what it would take to go through the boxes, only time would tell. Putting the boxes back up on the shelf and stopping at the bathroom to wash her face before seeing Jake. She did not want to upset him any more.

She had found him dozing in his chair and wasn't sure whether she should wake him. As she turned around to leave, she was startled by him saying, "Did you find everything in order?"

Jumping while he spoke and turning to face him again. "Yes, Dad, I did. Mom never changed anything in my room."

"No, she said no one was to touch anything. It was to be left just as you had left it."

"Why?"

"She had hoped that when you came back, you and her would pick up where you had left off. So she wanted everything to be the same."

"Dad, Mom was very sad all this time?"

"Yes, Angel. She lost the lust for life after you left. I was not enough for her."

"I'm sorry." I just hung my head. I didn't know what to say. How could one person cause someone so much grief and not know it?

"Did you find your mother's book?"

"Yes, I did."

"Where is it? Are you not going to take it and read it?"

"Yes, I was. Then I put it down and forgot about it. I will get it before I leave or another day."

"All right, whichever you prefer."

"Dad, did you know about the shoe boxes in Mom's study?"

"No, I didn't. Why would she keep her shoes in her study in stead of her closet? I never cared if she bought shoes. I never understood why women needed so many shoes. But your mom loved her shoes. I didn't know where she would put them if she bought many more pairs. Maybe that's why she started to put them in there?"

"No, Dad. Each box has been dated, and my name is on them."

"Why would she buy you shoes?"

"They don't have shoes in them. Mom bought cards and different little things that she thought I would like. She put them in the shoe boxes and has them all in her closet."

"I knew she bought things for you. I never knew what she did with it, seeing how she didn't have an address. Like you, I never went into her study. That was her private space, and I never violated her trust even after she had died."

"That was very kind of you, Dad. I should not have gone in there either."

"You would not have found the shoe boxes that she made up for you."

"No, but it was Mom's space as you said, and we never went in there."

"It's okay, Angel. Your mother would have wanted you to. Otherwise, she would not have left those boxes in there."

"Do you think I was supposed to find them?"

"Yes, Angel, they were meant to be found." That made me feel a little bit better about betraying Mom's trust.

"Are you wanting to take the boxes home with you?"

"NO! I mean no, Dad. I will go through them here. It will take some time, and I want to be able to do it when I have time of my own. I think it will be too upsetting to do it in front of the children."

"All right, whatever you think is best."

"It's also hard to read of so much love when I don't deserve it."

"Your mother would disagree with you."

"I know she would. I don't really feel that I have the right to accept anything that Mom has left for me. I had caused her so much heartache."

"You will have to find a way to forgive yourself and move on."

"I guess so."

"You know that's what your mother would want you to do."

"That is so sad, Dad. I know that it's not really my fault because Chris hid the mail. But I know I should have tried harder to get in touch with Mom. I knew Mom, but I let Chris mess with my head."

"That's how these guys operate. He knew when you left here that you were ticked at your mom and she was ticked at you, so he played on that."

"How stupid I was."

"I will have to agree with you on that. Because if anyone should have known your mother from the inside out, it was you."

"This makes me sick inside. I just want to throw up."

"Let this be a lesson, Angel, although it has cost you big."

"A lesson? What do you mean, Dad?"

"If something like this happens between you and your daughter, make sure you do whatever it takes to let her know how much you love her. Don't let anyone else do any message sending. Do it yourself by hand delivering it."

"You are so right." Thinking of Chris and my mail.

"Dad, I must get going now. I didn't realize it was getting so late. I would like to spend some time with the children before they go to bed, if I'm not too late already."

"I understand. Thank you for coming."

"Thank you for asking me." I get up and go over and hug this feeble man that once was a man of strength and energy. Now he's not either. He reminds me of the old men that are in those nursing homes. Wondering if that was where Jake would end up as I climbed into Tracy's car.

It was cloudy, and this made it even darker out than it should be. I surely hoped that Tracy would give the children a late snack so I could see them.

The big trees that overhung the driveway made it that much darker and eerie. This lane should have been in movies for both beautiful in the winter and eerie when dark out. I realized that I had not driven this driveway in the dark before. It was nice to get out onto the lit-up pavement. I didn't know why the drive was bothering me so.

I felt uptight, and yet the visit with Jake went very well. Now if the vehicle behind me would just dim their lights, it would be much appreciated. They seemed to me a little too close, and it was hard for me to see. So I pulled over and slowed down so they could go by, as I had no way of letting them know their lights were on bright and killing my eyes. As I did that, so did the vehicle that was behind me.

Don't stop, don't stop, a voice in my head was saying. So I pulled back out and decided to speed up a little. I didn't have far to go, and I didn't plan on stopping until I was in our garage. Those small hairs on the back of my neck stood up. Funny how we don't know we have them until now. Now I had a reason to be uptight, or to be downright scared. The vehicle behind me would surely run into me if I had to stop fast. All of a sudden, the car jumps ahead. I grip the steering wheel for all I was worth.

"What the hell was that?" I try to look in the mirror. I couldn't even tell what it was or the color. The lights were so damn bright and blinding. Again, the car jumps ahead. The idiot was running into me and pushing me. Now my heart is in my throat, and I was scared to death. I have seen this happen on TV shows. They never turn out for the best. Where was my phone? Glancing over at my purse and pulling it towards me, my stomach falls as I could not see my phone in the side pouch. Then I remembered I left it at home charging, not thinking I would need it. I was just going out to Jake's. Now what? Then *wham!* My head jerked, and I damn near lost control of the car.

"Please, God, help me here." All of a sudden, the vehicle pulls out beside me and comes in so close then speeds away. I was too scared to take my eyes off the road, so I never did get a look at what kind of vehicle it was. If this was some kind of joke, I wasn't finding it amusing. Who does that to another person while they're driving? A drunk. With that thought in mind, my house came into view.

"Thank you, God, for seeing me home safe. Or should I say 'thank you, Mom?'" Whichever one it was, thank you for riding along. Parking the car, I could not get into the house quick enough. I wanted to try and keep cool so I wouldn't scare Tracy. She has had enough on her plate since she met me. But I was going to tell Dr. Adams in the morning about this and see what he thinks. There was no use in spoiling Tracy's sleep along with mine. One zombie in a household was enough.

Tracy was just tucking the children into bed.

"Hi, Tracy, I will do that. Sorry I'm so late. I didn't watch the clock."

"There is no need to apologize, Angel. It has been a long time since you visited your stepfather, so it was well overdue. I have not minded one minute. The children were good as always."

"Thank you, Tracy. You are so kind and thoughtful."

"No, dear. That is what families do for each other." I go over and wrap my arms around her. It was something that felt so good. I made a mental note that I needed to do it more often. I felt safe and secure in Tracy's embrace. It was how I felt when my mother would hug me. I hope that my children feel the same way when I take them into my arms and hold them to my heart. I only hope that they know that with every beat they feel, it is packed so full of love for them as my mother's was for me.

"Well, it sure is great to have family like this then. I love you for that."

"I love you and the wee ones here very much. You have become the most important part of my life."

"That is so sweet of you to say, Tracy. But you have to have a life of your own, not just us."

"Who says I do? Besides I'm very happy with my life. Happier than I have ever been. Now I will let you finish tucking the wee ones in, and I will go make us a cup of tea." Kissing Elisabeth's forehead before getting up off the bed, she then kisses my cheek and leaves me to tend to the children. Of course, Gregory will already be sound asleep.

Elisabeth was almost there to, so I kissed her.

"Goodnight sweetheart, Mommy loves you as big as the sky." Getting up and leaving I hear Elisabeth say in her sleepy voice.

"Me to Mommy." Stopping and turning around to blow her another kiss brought back memories of my mom and I. Some things are passed on down from generation to generation without people even realizing they're doing it. I wondered that if Mom were still alive, would this jump out at me as it has, or would it be something else I just took for granted as so many other things? Like thinking I would have my mother at my side for many years to come. Never once did I think of my mom dying at such a young age. The saying "Here today, and gone tomorrow" is so true. Taking things for granted is so easy, and we all do it.

Chapter Seventeen

———————⧫———————

I had fallen asleep fast, but it didn't last long as visions of me being jerked as the vehicle behind me kept ramming into me. At one point, it had me going off the road down a long bank, and there was water at the bottom. I woke up in a cold sweat and could not go back to sleep. I was puttsing around in the living room when Tracy came staggering in.

"Why are you not sleeping, Angel?"

"One of those nights, I guess."

"What's on your mind that would keep you up? Have I done something to upset you?"

"No, Tracy, you have not done anything. I'm so lucky to have you in my life. Just bad dreams and I will be fine. Once I was awake, there was no going back to sleep. Now why are you up?"

"I thought there was a mouse in the house, but it turned out to be you."

"I'm sure glad of that, because a mouse would have to be damn large if it woke you up."

We both laugh.

"I will make us some chamomile tea. Maybe then we can both get back to sleep."

"Sounds great to me."

We drank our tea and chatted about many things, and before we knew it, it was time for me to be getting ready for work, and Gregory had woken up for a change and a feeding. Tracy took care of him while I took care of myself. I left a little earlier than usual, seeing as I was up and ready to go. Maybe I would get off early 'cause there was no doubt I would be tired by the end of this day. So if I started early, I could leave early.

Getting to the office, I saw that Dr. Adams was already there. Thinking that was great because I really wanted to tell him about last night. When I went into the coffee room I saw he was not alone. There was a young man with him that looked like he was built for the football team, and good looking as well.

"Well, good morning Angel. You are in early today. Couldn't sleep or the kids have you up all night?"

"Couldn't sleep."

"Same old story, hey? Angel, I would like you to meet our new med student. This is Trevor Anderson." He steps over with his hand out. So I stick mine out to shake hands with him, and he takes hold of mine ever so gently.

"I have heard a lot about you, Angel, and it is nice to put a face to the name." I know I turned many shades of red. I could feel the heat on my face. He pretended not to notice that I was blushing.

"Sorry, I can't say the same about you." He still had a hold of my hand, and all I could do was look into those huge brown eyes. His hair was wavy and a mixture of colors. Not sure if it was natural or if he had had it streaked. He wasn't a redhead, but he wasn't really brown either.

"Well, I've never been put on the table for discussion either." Pulling my hand away now as that remark made me feel uncomfortable. Yet I couldn't help but look at his eyes.

"That means what exactly?" I asked.

"It was my father who did your kidney transplant."

"Oh," was all that would come out.

"Yes, and I got to stand in and watch the procedure."

The first thought that ran through my head was, Oh god, he saw me naked. I know I was as red as anyone could get. This made me turn away from him, saying, "I hope you learned something by it."

"My father is a great teacher. Best in his field."

"I'm glad to hear it. I guess I'm living proof of that."

"How have you been doing, since your surgery?"

"Great, thank you. I'm very grateful to your father."

"Thank you. I will let him know I have finally met you, and that you are doing so well."

"Thank you."

"I hate to be the one to say, it's time to go to the hospital Trevor."

"All right, I'm ready. Angel, I hope to see you again soon." I didn't have time to say anything before Dr. Adams spoke up.

"Oh you will. She works here every day."

Nodding his head, he says, "All right, then. I look forward to meeting you again, Angel. Bye for now."

"Yes, bye." They were off to the hospital, and it wasn't until I got my coffee that I remembered I wanted to tell Dr. Adams about last night. Damn, I will have to try and catch him later.

The day went by uneventfully, and as I was getting ready to leave, in walks Trevor. I couldn't help but look at him. He was a very good-looking man. He walks over and bends down so he could look me eye to eye and says.

"May I take you for coffee before you go home?" I'm still staring into those beautiful eyes as I answer him.

"Sorry, but I have two children waiting for me at home."

"I know. Dr. Adams told me about them and how sweet they are. He was going over to give Tracy a hand until you got home."

"He is? Well then, I best get going. Thank you all the same."

"He was going, so you could have time to come for coffee, or whatever it is you like to drink."

"So Dr. Adams arranged this with you?"

"Yes, he did, I guess."

"I must remember to talk to him about this when I get home."

"So I take that as a yes?"

"All right. But it has to be quick one."

"A quick one it is then." He opens the door with a smile like none other I have ever seen. I was starting to think I must not be in touch with reality anymore. This guy has my head spinning. I'm sure I should be running in the opposite direction. He didn't really seem too full of himself. I think he was just taking a chance because Dr. Adams set us up. Surely he wouldn't send someone over if I would be in any danger. That thought made me feel a whole lot better.

We go for our coffee at the little cafe on Main Street. Before we knew it, two hours had gone by and I don't think there was anything we didn't know about each other. I made it very plain to him that my children came first in my life. He just smiled and said that was great to hear. In his time working at the city hospital, he had seen many sad situations where the mother didn't really want the children. But they were her meal tickets. He said he often thought he should open up a drop-off center where these women could just drop and just walk away, no questions asked. He was sure the children would have had a better life.

Trevor had told her about a little boy who was brought in three times with broken bones. They were always told he fell off of something. The fourth time in, he didn't make it, and the mother was charged with murder.

"He was the cutest little boy, how anyone could hurt him was more than I could understand. I don't understand why she wasn't investigated before it went so far. Someone should have known the signs. I was sick for weeks after. I felt I should have done something. But now it was too late."

"Did you think he was being abused?"

"I have watched enough TV to make me think that way. When no one else took it seriously then I just put it off as I watch too much TV. The mother was very convincing, and she acted like she really loved him. She also was very good-looking and well dressed, so I think that threw people off."

"How old was the little boy?"

"He was just turning two."

"Oh my."

"Too young to tell anyone what really happened."

"Did they even ask him?"

"They tried to talk to him about him climbing on things all the time, and what can happen. He never said a word."

"That is so sad."

"Yes, it is. So I am glad that you put your children first."

"Thank you. Speaking of which, I think I should be getting home now."

"May I walk you home?"

"You don't have to. Then you have to walk back to get your wheels."

"The walk won't kill me."

"All right then. Thank you."

We headed on out, and we still found plenty to talk about. When we got to the path that went into the little park that I usually feed the ducks at, I got that feeling of being watched again. For some reason, we both got quiet.

"Are you okay, Angel?"

"Yes, I'm fine."

"You sure? You don't look fine." Trevor felt it too, and he didn't want to say anything to scare Angel. He had never felt anything like this before in his life, and it was a little unnerving. He could also tell in her reactions that she was feeling it too. He just stepped in closer to her and took her hand. She looked up at him and smiled. Although it was a weak smile, he knew she was sincere. They walked the rest of the way home in silence.

When they reached the house, Angel said, "Maybe you can get a ride back with Dr. Adams?"

"I might just do that."

Angel didn't want to say she didn't want him walking back by the park alone. He would think she was crazy. When they go inside, she finds that Tracy had invited Dr. Adams for supper. She was sure that Tracy had an eye on him. It was kind of cute, even if he was a few years older than her. Everyone needs someone at one time or another.

"Thank you, Angel, for the company. I must be going now. I will see you tomorrow."

"You could stay for supper as well. I have cooked enough for an army."

"That is so kind of you to ask. But I really have to go. But I would love to have a rain check if that is possible?"

"I think I could arrange that."

"Thank you."

"See you tomorrow then, boy," Alex says as he puts a hand on his shoulder and shakes with the other.

"You bet." Trevor left without a big farewell, and we all sat down to eat. Things were pretty busy around the table and with everyday chat. Dr. Adams never brought up the subject of Trevor, and I was thankful for that. Maybe I would find a friend in him. It would be great to have someone my own age to relate to now and again.

It seemed like all had quieted down around the table as we all got to eating when the sirens started to wail.

"Oh, they seem close tonight?" Dr. Adams said as he picked up the potato bowl to take another helping.

"That happens now and again. Guess that's what we get for living so close to work."

"You're right, Angel. My area is pretty quiet most of the time. You would think with more seniors living over there, we would have more action."

"Count your blessings that you are all healthy," Tracy added in.

"I do, Tracy. At our age, it doesn't take much."

"I try to be careful and eat all the right things and get my rest."

"You don't get much rest with these two." Angel points to her two little ones.

"I get all the sleep I need to keep up with them."

"I hope you will let me know if that changes. I will take less days at work or find someone to help you part-time."

"That will never be necessary. I love these wee ones. They keep me young at heart."

"Please, Tracy, promise me that you will let me know."

"Don't sweat it, dear. I will."

Angel just raises an eyebrow at her.

"I will. I promise."

"Okay then."

Just then, the doorbell rang. They all look at each other, and Tracy and Angel exchange a second look at each other. As Alex watches this, he is wondering what was up. The doorbell rang again.

"So should I get this, ladies?" Alex says as he gets up and heads for the door. Angel and Tracy are both glued to their seats. They each knew what the other was thinking. Had he finally decided to show his face here? They were both glad that Alex was also there this time.

"Well, come on in, you're just in time to eat."

Both women jumped up and went to see who had just come in.

"Dad?"

"Dad?"

"Yes, Tracy, it's my dad."

"Well, I will be."

She hurried to get another chair as Angel went on over to greet her father.

"I'm glad you decided to come over, Dad."

"Yes, Jake. I'm glad to see you out and about too."

"Was in the neighborhood so thought I would drop in."

"That is great. Come in, Dad, and sit. Have something to eat with us."

"Don't mind if I do."

"I will put on a pot for tea."

"Thank you, Tracy."

"Tracy, this is my dad, Jake."

"It is so nice to finally meet you, Mr. Jake."

"Likewise, Tracy."

"Are you getting moved out, Jake?"

"Not yet, Alex. I'm waiting for Angel to get her belongings out that she wants first."

"I'm sorry, Dad. I haven't been back."

"That's fine. I know it won't be easy for you."

"This can't be easy on you either. How about on the weekend I come over and start to get things out of your way?"

"All right. You don't have to rush for me. I'm in no hurry."

"Maybe not, but it would be good for you to be all settled down again in your small house."

"Yes, and no."

"Are you sure you really want to move out?"

"Why are you moving back home? If you are, then I would stay. That is if you would want me to?"

"Dad, you know that wouldn't be a problem. The kids and I would love to have you around."

"You're young, Angel, and you don't need the worry of an old man."

"You're not an old man, Dad."

"Then you need glasses, girl—'cause if I get any older, I will be a mummy."

"Oh please. You have a lot of years to go."

"I hope not."

"Please don't say that, Dad."

"Do you think the weather is going to change soon, Jake?" Alex thought he best change the subject.

"My bones tell me it is going to."

"That is one thing we have to count on, hey, Jake. Our body barometers."

"Mine hasn't let me down in years."

"Mine either. Good old dependable joints. I think we would be lost without them."

"Most times, I wished I didn't have them."

"I hear you there, old-timer."

"Dr. Adams, Dad is not old. Neither are you."

"Oh thank you, dear girl, but your father is right. You do need glasses."

"Well, you are only as old as you feel," Tracy says.

"Yes, we are, and now we will go to the sitting room. You young ladies can bring our tea in to us when it is ready. Come on, Jake, we will go get the soft chairs. We have some catching up to do."

"Sounds good to me."

As they were walking, Jake commented on the action down the street as he came.

Chapter Eighteen

———————•———————

When Tracy and Angel were done in the kitchen doing cleanup, they then got the tea and cookies ready to take to the men. As Angel approached the sitting room, she saw both men in the recliners, and they were both sleeping.

Turning to Tracy, she said, "Well, maybe Dr. Adams was right and they are old."

"Or they found each other boring?"

Angel went on in and put the tea down just in case they would only be having a short nap. She stopped and put her throws that were on the sofa over each of the men. Standing back and looking at each one of them, she knew then that Dr. Adams was right—they were both old men. Where had all the time gone? She remembered them both as strong young men. But they were both old and getting feeble. She had wondered how much longer Dr. Adams was going to be able to practice. When he was done with that, where would he be going? Into an old folks' home with Jake? Would they even last that long? She had her doubts about Jake as he seemed to be willing himself to die. She knew he still missed her mother very deeply. She also understood that feeling.

Standing there watching them with her arms crossed, a thought came to her. Just maybe I should be planning on setting up one of our places to be able to take care of both of these men. As their health fails, they will be needing someone to take care of them. After all, they both have had a big part to play in her life and in her health. Wasn't that only fair that she gave back some of what she has gotten from both of these men? After all, she believed in what goes around comes around.

Looking up, she said, "What do you think, Mom? Think I could do it?" Just then Tracy came in. She heard Angel talking and was thinking that the men were now awake. But, entering the room, she saw Angel looking up and talking. So she looked up and around before saying anything.

"Think you could do what?" Tracy asked her in a whisper.

Angel nods her head towards the door, and they leave the room. Once they were back in the kitchen, she told Tracy what she was thinking.

"I'm thinking of making sure one of our places is set up to take care of Dr. Adams and Jake, once they are both too old to take care of themselves. I just don't know if I have what it would take."

"I think that is a fine idea. And yes, you could do it, especially with my help."

"Your help? I couldn't ask you to do that."

"Yes, you could. But you don't have to because I'm offering."

"Are you sure you would want to do such a thing? It could be hard work."

"*Could be* is not even close. It will be. Taking care of seniors is a very hard job, but rewarding. It would be great for them to have the care they will be needing come from someone who loves them and not from someone who is doing it just for the money."

"I would have to pick which place would work for all of us."

"That shouldn't be too hard for you to do. You do know all the places."

"That is true. I will have to think on this."

As the evening came to a close, the men still had not woken up, so Tracy and Angel just went to bed as well. Angel had lain awake for some time, putting plans in order of how she would get a place ready to take care of both Jake and Dr. Adams. Satisfied with some of her decisions, she finally fell asleep.

Waking in the morning, she found both chairs empty. This was not a surprise to her. In fact, she would have been surprised to see them both still there.

The morning went as smooth as every other morning, and before she knew it, she was at work. Now that was a different story. There was so much happening there, and she could tell by the way Dr. Adams was talking on the phone that he was in a very upset state, and she wasn't able to make heads or tails out of what was wrong. She knew something had happened but wasn't able to get a straight answer out of anyone. She would wait until Dr. Adams was off the phone. She knew he would tell her; in the meantime, she would go get herself a coffee. Taking it and sitting at the table and waiting made her a little edgy. What could have happened that would have Dr. Adams so upset? Perhaps he had another patient die. That always hits him hard. Dr. Adams thinks he should be able to save everyone. With that thought in mind, he came through the door. He looked like he had just lost his best friend. So I get up and go over to him.

"Dr. Adams, what's wrong?"

He swallows hard and says, "It's Trevor."

I look at him with a frown and say, "Like in Trevor Anderson?"

"Yes, I'm afraid so."

"What happened, where is he?"

"After he dropped you off, he was caught by some thugs by the park. They have beaten him badly. He is in serious condition. His head is spilt in the back. He has three broken ribs, one has punctured his lung. He is in a coma, which I'm hoping is just his body protecting itself while in shock. He should come out of it in a few days."

"Oh my god. Is he going to be okay?"

"At this point, all we can do is pray for him and hope that the head trauma hasn't been too much."

"Who would do this to Trevor?"

"Thugs don't really need a reason, but usually for money. They need a hit, so they need money. A park at night is a good place to wait."

"So those sirens that we heard were all about Trevor."

"Looks like it."

"Can I go see him?"

"I'm going over to the hospital now if you want to come with me? They have called his parents, so they should be here in about four hours. Then we will leave him to them."

"Okay, I will let the girls know that I'm going with you for a while."

"I will wait for you outside."

With that he was gone, and Angel's stomach was churning. She thought back to the feeling she had when she and Trevor walked past the park on her way home. She should have said something then. He would not have walked back and would not be in this condition now. It was her fault that this happened to Trevor. Now she didn't know if she should say anything or just deal with the days ahead as they come.

When she and Dr. Adams got to the hospital, it seemed like everything was in an upset state here as well. Dr. Adams was able to get the chart that he needed on Trevor and we then went to his room. He was in ICU. As we entered his room, the machine that they had pumping air into him made a *shush-shush* sound, and he had tubes coming out all over. There was a clear one that had reddish-colored liquid flowing into a jug, and his head was wrapped. You could see the blood seeping through the wrap. His face was swollen and black and blue. I would not have known it was Trevor if Dr. Adams had not told me it was him.

I felt like I really had to throw up, and the floor kept wanting to come up and meet my face. So I finally pulled a chair over beside him, and I took his hand in mine. I just sat rubbing my fingers up and down on the back of his hand. The guilt ran through me rapidly. I knew if his eyes were open, I would not be able to look him in the eye. How could I have not said something to him as we walked by? Things would be so different now. If he doesn't pull through, do I tell someone about it then? Or would it be best to keep it a secret?

"Angel, is something wrong?" I just shake my head, but what I really want to do is cry.

"No," I answered, but I kept looking down.

Dr. Adams comes over and lifts my face up, holding my chin in his hand as he says, "Why do you look like you have the weight of the world on your shoulders?"

He didn't let go of my chin, and I felt the tears start to flow as I mumbled, "This is my fault."

"What? Why would you say such a thing, Angel?" He pulled a chair over and sat down, waiting until I got control of myself so I could tell him about the walk home.

"There was someone there when we came home."

"Someone where, Angel?"

"In the bushes by the park. I could feel them watching us. I never said anything to Trevor. He knew something was wrong with me 'cause he just moved in closer and took my hand. He never asked, and I didn't say. But if I had said something, he would not have walked back there. He would not be lying here now like this."

"That may be all true, Angel, but you have no idea if what you were feeling then was from the same people or not. Maybe someone else was in the park when you went by and you picked up on that. It would just be your sixth sense kicking in, that's all. Your mother and grandmother both had a high sixth sense. I believe it has been passed on down to you, that is all. So please don't blame yourself for what happened to Trevor. It could have been anyone passing by at that time. It is what you call being in the wrong place at the wrong time. Thugs come out more later at night, so chances are they weren't even there yet when Trevor walked you home."

Some of what Dr. Adams was saying made sense, but I really wasn't feeling better.

"Now listen. I want to go talk to his doctor. I want you to talk to Trevor and see if maybe you can bring him around. Do you think you can do that?"

Once again, I just nod my head. Dr. Adams turns and leaves me there with a stranger that I was to talk to. What would I talk to him about? I didn't really know him. I sat there and I looked Trevor over. He didn't look anything like the man that walked me home the night before. He has now become a real stranger. I drop my eyes and let the tears flow silently down my cheeks. Some was from guilt, and some was for Trevor. Although I didn't know him well, no one deserved this. Trevor didn't seem like a person who would have any enemies.

She felt a slight tightening of his hand, and that made her look around as though there should have been someone else in the room with them.

This time, he squeezes her hand a little harder.

"Trevor. Oh my god, Trevor." She jumps up so she could look into his eyes, although she didn't think he would be seeing too much.

"Do you need a nurse or a doctor?"

He shakes his head weakly from side to side. She could tell that hurt him, to move that little bit.

"Don't move, Trevor. I can get you some help."

She goes to leave, and he just squeezed her hand tighter.

"I'm not going anywhere, Trevor. Just rest. You need to rest, Trevor, to get strong. I can't believe someone would do this to another human being. I'm so sorry."

He frowns at her.

She knew he didn't know what she meant, so she takes a deep breath and holds it while she said, "Trevor, I knew someone was in the bushes when you walked me home. I should have said something. This would not have happened to you."

He closes his eyes, and she took this to mean he was disgusted with her. She goes to pull her hand away once more, but he held tight. Opening his swollen eyes and looking through just small slits, he tried to relay the message, that it wasn't her fault. She wasn't sure what he said with his eyes. And he could tell by the look on her face that she didn't understand. He was getting frustrated because he didn't know how to tell her.

"Why did you walk back alone? Why didn't you ask Dr. Adams for a ride? Oh, Trevor."

He just shakes his head from side to side and squeezes her hand.

"Don't shake your head, Trevor. I can tell it hurts. How about if you want to answer yes, you blink once. If no, blink twice."

He blinked once.

"See? That doesn't hurt so much, right?"

He blinked once again. That made her smile.

"Okay, I think you best rest now. You will be too tired to talk to your doctor when he gets here."

He blinked once.

"Good. I will just sit here and keep you company until then. But no more talking."

He closed his eyes, and before she knew it, he was sleeping again. She must have dozed off too because a hand being placed upon her shoulder startled her awake.

"Sorry, Angel, I did not mean to startle you."

"I'm sorry, Dr. Adams. I did not mean to doze off." She still had a hold of Trevor's hand.

"I take it that our sleeping beauty here hasn't come to yet?"

"Oh yes, he did!"

"He did?"

"Yes, and he squeezed my hand and was blinking in answer."

"Thank God. They said he may not wake up for days. I hate it when that happens. Perhaps this is a good sign that the blow to the head wasn't as bad as they thought."

"Could there be brain damage?"

"Did he know what you were saying to him?"

"Yes, he did."

"Then I doubt it, but only time will tell. When he is able to talk, we will get more answers. For right now, we will be thankful for whatever he is able to do."

"Don't you think he will be able to carry on with his medical training?"

"I pray that he can. This will take some time to heal from. He has taken quite a beating."

"I know. Who does this to another person?"

"Someone that has brain damage already."

"This is a horrible thing to happen to anyone."

"You are right, Angel. No one deserves to be beaten no matter how severe the beating is or isn't. To use your hands on another person in this way is just not human."

"I know."

"I know you do. I'm sorry. I didn't mean to bring back bad memories for you."

"That is okay, Dr. Adams. It has made me understand what Trevor may be going through."

"I suppose you are right about that. I could only imagine where you know firsthand. You know, Angel, you could put your experience to good use."

"I could? How would I do that? It is a horrible thing to remember."

"You could do talks at schools and other community functions. Starting about grade-seven level and up. Sometimes a person young like yourself can get through to students better than, say, myself. They always think us old people don't know what we are talking about. You get the pictures that the hospital have on file of you and blow them up so they can really see the impact of a beating and what being in a control relationship can do. You could save some girls from going through what you did. Even if you only save one. You will have made a difference, and what happened to you would not have been in vain."

"You really think I could help someone?"

"Yes, Angel, you could help many."

They sat in silence for a while. Then Angel says, "Dr. Adams, did you know Tracy was from an abusive relationship?"

"I sort of gathered that but never asked. After all my years of doctoring, you get pretty good at picking them out of a crowd. There are scars that they wear on the surface and don't realize it. Some are more profound than others."

"Do I show that too?'

"Yes, Angel, you do."

"How so?"

"Your reluctance to be around men. You have this wall up, and it will take someone very special to get through it. That is if he will have the patience it is going to take to gain your trust. Most men will just quit and move on. They don't want to deal with damaged luggage as they call it."

"I get all tense when men are around."

"That is to be expected. But you will have to learn to relax and trust again, or you will have a very lonely life."

"I have the kids and Tracy. I will be just fine."

"Your children will be all grown up soon, and Tracy will be a lot older and probably be moving on when the kids don't need her anymore. Then you will find yourself alone. It is not good to be alone."

"Grandma lived alone for many years."

"Yes, she did. But she also had me as a friend. She was not afraid of men. It will make a difference to you, you will see. I hope you don't wait that long to find out you need a man in your life as a friend. Some best talks you will have will be talking to a man when he is a good friend."

Angel raises her eyebrows in the meaning of "yea right."

"It is true, mark my words. Your grandmother and I could talk about everything. Sometimes I just listened 'cause that was all she needed."

"Grandma could talk to Mom whenever she wanted."

"Yes, she could. There were times when Kate was the topic and Emma just had to talk to someone to get things straight in her head. Especially when your dad died, she had a hard time getting through to Kate, and she needed a helping hand."

"I remember Mom not being Mom then."

"That tore Emma apart inside to see her daughter, her girls, in such a state. And there was nothing she could do to fix it for you two."

"Grandma sat with me a lot then. She would wrap her arms around me and make me feel safe. I thought Mom was going to die too."

"She had a rough road to go down, that's for sure."

Chapter Nineteen

---•---

The nurses came in and out, checking on Trevor. They didn't believe me that he had woken up. I had begun to think maybe he hadn't as he has not moved since he went back to sleep. I was still holding his hand when his mom and dad came in.

I barely remembered Dr. Anderson's face. He looked at me as if he should know me, but all I said was hi. Trevor's mom was a beautiful woman. They made a great-looking couple. No wonder Trevor was a looker. She had gone right over and picked up Trevor's other hand and started to talk to him.

"Oh my poor baby. Who would do this to you? You never hurt anyone in your life to deserve this. But don't you worry, son. I will take you home, and you will get well."

"Now, Alice, you don't know if he will want to come home. He is in pretty good hands here." He wraps his arm around her shoulders and pulls her in for a hug.

"Of course he will want to come home."

"The nurse said that you had said he had woken up?"

"Yes. Him and Angel had communicated before he fell back to sleep." Once again, he looks over at me. This time he asked, "Are you the *Angel* I done the kidney transplant on?"

"Yes, I am."

"Well," he said as he leaves his wife's side and comes around to our side of the bed. He reaches out his hand to me and says, "You are looking great, Angel."

I place my hand in his, and it was as if life had just been ignited into me again. It was a strange feeling, but warm, and it made me feel great. It was the same feeling I had gotten from Trevor the night he walked me home and took my hand. Trevor too made me feel safe and warm inside. Perhaps it's because of the father-and-son relationship.

"Thank you, Dr. Anderson."

"So life is good for you?"

"Yes, sir, it is. Thank you."

"Trevor had told me that he had met you and that you were looking great and doing great."

Taking my hand back, I nod my head as Trevor had started to stir. His mother was on it like a loving mother would be.

"Trevor, it's Mom. What can I do for you? Should I call a nurse?"

"Just give him a moment, dear, and let him wake up more. Maybe then we can see what he really wants."

"But he does want something."

"Give him a few minutes, Alice. We will figure it out."

She fussed with his blankets and dumped his water jug and refilled it. Not sure why 'cause he had a tube in his mouth that was taped on both sides, so he wasn't going to be drinking water. She could not find enough to do.

Trevor squeezed my hand twice, so I got up so he could see me through what were to be his eyes. They seemed like they had swollen even more.

"Are you okay?"

He blinked once.

"Good. Did you need a nurse for anything, Trevor?"

He blinked twice.

"Good. So what's up?"

He smiled with his eyes, and I knew he just wanted to see me.

"You are so funny. I was just sitting here watching you sleep. But I will have to leave soon."

He squeezed my hand hard, and I could see the fear in his eyes.

"You will be okay, Trevor. I have to go to work."

He blinks once. That made her feel better. He was still agitated about something, but she could not read it.

"I will come back after work. I must call Tracy and let her know, okay?"

He blinked once again.

"I will go now so you can visit with your parents. I will see you later."

"Oh dear, that won't be necessary. We will have him transferred home."

Trevor started to squeeze my hand and was blinking so fast, I couldn't keep up.

"Slow down, Trevor. I can't read you when you go so fast."

"You're going home, so maybe I can come there to see you on my days off."

He blinks twice.

"You don't want me to come see you?"

He blinks once.

"So what don't you want, Trevor?"

He moves his eyes slowly towards his mother and back to me. How was I going to say this without her getting upset?

"You don't want to go home with your mom?"

He blinks once.

"Oh hogwash. How do you know what Trevor wants and doesn't want?"

"He talks to me with his eyes, Mrs. Anderson."

"Hogwash. I will get a pen and paper. He can write what he wants."

"Mrs. Anderson, he blinks once for yes and twice for no."

"Like I said, I will get him a pen and paper. I'm his mother, and I do know what's best for my son."

"Now, Alice, Angel and Trevor seemed to have this all under control."

"We are taking our son home. I will take care of him."

Trevor starts to toss his head back and forth saying no, and I knew this was hurting him. So I put my hands on each side of his face and look into his eyes, saying to him, "Please, Trevor, don't do that. You cause yourself more pain. Please just blink." I could tell by the tension in his face that he did not want to go home. "Please, Trevor, promise me that you will just blink." It took him a couple of minutes, but he finally blinked yes.

"Okay, now I'm going to go to work and I will let you discuss this with your parents. I will check to see if you have gone. If not, I will be back. I promise you."

He blinked once and no one else said anything, so I turned around and left. I just got out of the door when a hand grabbed my arm firmly and turned me around. I came face to face with his mother. I know my eyes were wide open, and I was about to speak when she started in on me.

"I know that Trevor is in this condition because of you. So I think you have done all the damage you can do. I would appreciate it if you would just stay away from my son."

"I didn't have anything to do with what happened to Trevor."

"This happened after he walked you home, didn't it?"

"Yes, it did. Like I said, I didn't have anything to do with it."

"Why don't you drive to work like everyone else? My son would be just fine if you had your own car."

"Excuse me, Mrs. Anderson. I do have my own car. I choose to walk to work and anywhere else I can. Have you not heard that walking is good for you? No, let me guess. You have someone drive you to wherever you go. Why is that? Don't you have a driver's license?"

She went all red in the face. I knew I had hit the nail on the head.

"Now if you will excuse me, I have to go to work. I'm not as lucky as some women. I have to do this to survive."

She stood there with her mouth open, and if she said any more I don't know. I didn't stick around to find out. I was fuming inside. These women that have everything handed to them make me sick. What makes her think she is better than me—money? My mom and Jake had money, and they never treated anyone like this. Grandma had money and was still a kind soul. Bet Trevor doesn't take many girlfriends home to meet his mother. Probably not guy friends either.

I got back to work, and the day was long, and I was down all day. I had been asked so many times: what was wrong? I would just say nothing. I decided to go home and see the kids and Tracy before calling to see if Trevor lost his battle. I'm pretty sure he would lose. There was no doubt that she loved her son and would give him the best of care. But poor Trevor didn't want that. If he gets depressed, it will take him longer to heal.

Tracy could tell when I got home things were not right. I had told her everything. She could not believe that all the commotion that we heard that night was all over Trevor. She was sick to think that as we sat and ate Trevor was lying just down from our home almost dead.

"Oh, Angel. That could have been you. I think you should take the car. You are taking too many chances. Did they catch who did this to Trevor?"

"I don't think so. Thugs are hard to catch."

"That's who did this?"

"So they are saying."

"Well, they will kill people for five bucks. I knew a man that they jumped on his chest so hard, they exploded his heart all for five bucks."

"Are you kidding me?"

"No, I'm not. You have to be more careful, Angel. That park is dangerous."

"I know what you're saying. I never go there in the evening."

"I don't think any time is safe. That park rings out trouble."

"I will be sure to be more alert while going by there."

"I wish you would drive. I know you like to walk and all, but you have us waiting for you." Tracy comes over and, giving me a hug, says, "I don't know what I would do if something ever happened to you."

"Now don't worry so much. We will all be just fine. What happened to Trevor was just horrible timing. After all, we have been here how long now? This is the first time we have heard of anything like this happening."

"You are right about that. Please be extra careful just the same."

"I will, promise. Now I will call the hospital and see if Trevor is still here. I doubt it, but no harm in trying."

"You think his mother would have that much power over him?"

"He can't say or do much on his own."

"Poor man. Maybe he should go home until he is healed."

Angel dialed the hospital, and to her surprise, she found out that Trevor was still there.

"That is good news, thank you."

"Well?"

"He is still here, so mommy dearest didn't win."

"Not yet, anyway. Maybe they want him to stay put for a bit before moving him."

"I never thought of that, it is a good possibility." Angel did not know why but she felt better now than she did when she came home. She had supper with Tracy and the kids and helped Tracy clean up the mess before going to the hospital.

"I will only be an hour or so."

"That is fine. He probably will enjoy your company. Lying there like that must be boring."

"He looked tired more than bored."

"Give him a couple more days and he will be bored."

"He has a long stay ahead of him, so I hope he is easily entertained."

"Say hi to him and wish him well for me, dear."

"I sure will, Tracy. Thank you for watching the kids again."

"No need to thank me. Now go along before it gets late."

Driving over to the hospital, I felt giddy inside. I didn't know why because I should be scared of running into Mrs. Anderson again. If she talked to Trevor, he may not want to see me. I should have asked the nurse to check with him to see if he was up to company. The giddy feeling took over, and I continued on my way. Nothing or no one would stop me from going to see Trevor—well, maybe Mrs. Anderson.

NO, not even her. Mother or no mother, Trevor can have friends visiting. Besides, he has learned to talk to me with his eyes. This I found romantic. I have never talked to a man before with just him using eye contact. Trevor's eyes were beautiful. I hope they will look the same when the swelling goes down.

I stopped at the nurses' station just to make sure I could go in.

"Sure you can, Angel. He will be glad you came. His parents have turned in for the night. They were exhausted."

All I could do was think, yes!

"Thank you." I hurried down to his room. He was sleeping so I thought, but he must have sensed me in the room. He started to wave his hand around. I go over and take his hand, and once again, I get that warm feeling.

"Hey, how are you?"

He smiles with his eyes.

"Are you good?"

He blinks once.

"You're getting good if you could tell I was in the room."

He tries to take a deep breath through his nose. I knew right away what he was saying.

"You could smell me?"

He blinks once.

"I'm glad I had a shower."

He blinks once and smiles again.

"So when do you go home?"

He blinks twice.

"You're not going home?"

He blinks twice again. This made me happy, and I knew he could tell. Squeezing my hand as I sat down on the high stool someone had brought into the room.

"This was a great idea. Let me guess. Mom."

He blinks once.

"You know, they say mothers know best."

He blinks twice but has a smile to go with it.

"You're lucky, Trevor, to still have your mother. She loves you a lot."

He blinks once.

"Bet she wasn't too happy to leave you here."

He blinks twice.

"Do you like to read, Trevor?"

He blinks once, so I started to name some authors to see who he liked to read. When I got to James Patterson, he squeezed my hand.

"All right, I love to read his books. So now let's find one that you haven't read, and I will bring it up and read to you."

He blinks once and squeezes my hand again. I knew he liked that idea a lot.

When I mentioned the Women's Murder Club, I found out he had not read them.

"I have the full series at home, so starting tomorrow, I will ask Tracy if she would mind if I came and read to you each night for a couple of hours."

Squeezing my hand, I could see a very large smile. I knew this would give him something to look forward to each evening.

"I'm going to put a pen and paper on that table and ask the nurse to keep it close so you can right down things that you would like or need. You make me a shopping list, okay? And each day I can bring you whatever you want."

He blinks once.

"You know, you are easy to get along with like this. I also know that you will be here for four to eight weeks, so you best be prepared to listen."

Squeezing my hand, I knew he was happy.

"I heard they're taking your respirator off in a couple of days. Your lung should be healing some by then and able to do the work on its own. Then you have to do deep breathing exercises to make them work properly. It was a small hole, so you are very lucky that way. Good thing you didn't get all three ribs jabbed into you."

He squeezes my hand, and I knew he was so glad that it wasn't worse.

"My grandma used to tell me that things could always be worse, so count your blessings. Sometimes I couldn't see where she felt things could be any worse. So she would point them out, and she would be right."

Trevor just held my hand while I talked. I didn't know I would find so much to talk about, especially when it was a one-sided conversation. He fell asleep holding my hand, so I just set it up on the side of the bed and left. The medication must still be making him drowsy. The doctors still wanted him to stay calm for a couple more days, then they would make him work. I slipped out and let the nurse know that I was leaving so they would have to keep an eye on him.

I was looking forward to tomorrow. Tonight I would get the book that I planned on reading to Trevor and start it tomorrow night. Once again, I felt giddy—which made me feel strange at the same time. I was alive again. Looking up, all I could do was say, "Thank you. I love you all."

Chapter Twenty

———————◆———————

Tracy had the children in bed, so I went right up and had my bath, thinking about Trevor the whole time. It had been a long time since any man had kept my attention. Perhaps it was just because I felt sorry for what had happened to him. I did feel somewhat responsible. If I had driven to work, he would not have been in that area. His mother was right to be put out with me to a point. That's how I feel, anyway. Making sure I put the book in my bag tonight so I don't forget tomorrow, I go downstairs to get a cup of hot chocolate.

"Oh dear," Tracy said as she jumped back. "I did not hear you come home."

"I'm sorry, Tracy. I should have looked in on you so you would have known. I sure didn't want to scare you."

"Yes, dear, you should have. I might have mistaken you for a burglar and hit you over the head with my broom."

"Please remind me next time. I'm making hot chocolate, would you like one?"

"I have one already but you may join me."

"You bet. I would love to."

We had our hot chocolate and talked about everything that had been going on. Somehow we got on to the topic of Trevor, and it was exciting to me to have such a pleasant man to talk about. I told Tracy

I would like to read to him in the evenings if she was okay with taking care of the children that much longer.

Tracy had said that so long as she had her Tuesday and Thursday evenings free for her bowling group, she didn't mind at all. I didn't see any problems with that either. So we were all set. Drinking our hot chocolate then going to bed was a waste of time for me. I could not sleep no matter what I did. I ended up reading until it was time to have my shower and head for work. I couldn't believe I was the first to get there, so I just hung around outside until the linen was delivered, and I went in at the same time as he did. I showed him my name plate, and he was fine with it. He had a simple name to remember, so I called out to him when he was leaving.

"Thank you, Bill."

He just waved and kept on going. The other girls would be along soon, so I decided to put on a pot of coffee. I felt like I could sure use one. I was just pouring myself a cup when a hand was put on my shoulder, and I knew who it was before I turned around. His touch made my blood run cold.

I didn't turn around right away. I finished getting my coffee ready, saying to him, "What are you doing in here, Chris? This is for staff only."

"No one will be around for another half an hour."

"You better leave now."

"I came to see you and find out how our children are, so is that any way to talk to me?" As he slid his hand down my arm and grabbed my wrist and yanked me around to face him.

I was not going to show him he scared me, so I pulled my hand back firmly, saying, "Do you mind?" Moving away from him with my coffee in hand gave me something to keep my hands busy so he couldn't tell he was making me nervous. I prayed that someone else would show up early as I had. Right now, it wasn't early enough.

"So you think you're some kind of big shot now working here with the great doctor?"

"I'm no different than I was before. Just doing my job and taking care of the children."

"And your boyfriend?"

"Sorry, I don't have a boyfriend."

"Oh really. Who was that idiot you walked home with?"

"What?"

"Oh don't play games with me. You know who I mean."

"Trevor walked me home, but he's no boyfriend."

"So you just hold anyone's hand?"

"How do you know this anyways?"

"Don't matter how I know. You just remember you are mine and will be until you die."

That made the hair on my neck stand up, and I wanted to vomit.

"I don't belong to you or anyone else. Do you understand, Chris? I am Angel Sanders and no one else. I am my own person, and I don't need you trying to make me think otherwise. It won't work. You don't have that hold on me anymore and never will again, so you best leave or I will call the cops."

"They won't do anything. After all, I'm here to see a doctor. I have the same rights as anyone else."

"Everyone else is not allowed back here. They will take you out until the doctor comes."

"Don't you worry your stupid pretty little head about me. I know when to get out. Not like your boyfriend."

"Get over it, Chris."

I turned around to get out and he grabbed at me, and my hot coffee went all over him.

"I'm sorry. Here, let me get a cloth."

Then things went black. Chris hit me so hard, I thought he snapped my neck.

A patting to the face and a cold cloth was on my forehead.

"Angel, are you okay? What the hell did you do, black out?"

Looking around, I could see that Chris had left.

"Boy, do I have a headache."

"You didn't eat this morning, did you?"

"No, Dr. Adams, I didn't."

"You get up and sit over here. I will make you some toast and jam with orange juice, and that will give you the pickup you need right now."

I wasn't going to say anything different, so I did as he said. I had no idea how I would explain the black eye. With that kind of hit, I was sure to have one.

"When you feel up to it, you come out to work. Take your time, there is no hurry. The filing is not going anywhere."

"Thank you. I shouldn't be long."

I was glad it was Dr. Adams that came in first. This would be embarrassing to explain to the girls. I finished up the toast, and I have to say it tasted damn good. I will have to see what kind of jam that was. I could hear the other girls talking to Dr. Adams, so I thought I better get out there so he didn't think he had to explain anything.

"What happened to you?" was the first thing I heard.

"She didn't eat and blacked out is what happened to her."

"Oh my, your eye took the blunt of your fall."

Putting my hand up to it and saying, "Ouch, it feels like it." I could see Dr. Adams looking at me funny, but he never said a word. I knew what he was thinking 'cause he found me in the middle of the floor. There was nothing for me to hit my eye on. So what happened? I knew he would be asking questions soon. I would have to tell him the truth if he hadn't already figured it out.

"I think you should take a couple of days and rest that eye. If you use ice, it will heal faster."

"Thanks, Gloria."

I go to the bathroom to take a look.

"Oh my god. This is bad. I will be lucky to see out of it tomorrow. Damn you, Chris. Damn me, how could I be so careless?"

Gloria was right. I will take the day off and see what happens. So I pack up my things and head for home.

I found Tracy in the laundry room; saying she was surprised is an understatement.

"Angel, why are you home? What happened to your face?"

Not knowing if I wanted to tell her, I could read what—or should I say who—was on her mind.

"It was Chris, wasn't it? Did he catch you on the way to work this morning?"

"Yes. And no, he caught me at work. No one was there yet, and he got in with the guy that delivers the linen."

"Why did he hit you?"

"I spilled my hot coffee on him."

"On purpose? Good girl."

"Thanks, but no. I was walking away from him, and he grabbed me and spun me around, causing him to wear my coffee. He was wild right now."

"I guess he would be, and of course, it was your fault and deserved to be hit like this. Let me get you some ice. Come sit down."

"That's not all."

"Oh really? What else? Tell me while I get your ice."

"He hit me so hard, I thought he had snapped my neck. I had blacked out and came to when Dr. Adams was patting my face and using a cold cloth on my face and forehead."

"Did Mr. Alex have him charged?"

"No, Chris was gone by the time Dr. Adams came in. Dr. Adams thinks I passed out from not eating. At least, he did until he saw my eye swelling and changing color."

"What do you mean?"

"Well, when he found me, I was lying in the middle of the floor. There was nothing to hit my face on to give me this." I put my hand up over my eye. My cheek was damn sore as well. "Chris had hit me with all the anger that he had been holding inside since I left."

"You are going to charge him, are you not?"

"No. I hope he will think I am and will disappear because he will be scared."

"That is a big mistake you are making by not charging him."

"Maybe, I will have to wait and see. If it happens again, I will charge him."

"He will think you are running scared and he will be back, mark my words. You should go to the police and let them know and have a restraining order put on him."

"Next time."

"Damn it, Angel. I wish you would listen to me, just once."

"I listen to you all the time, Tracy. Please, we will see if he comes around in the next couple days."

"The police won't do anything if you haven't at least made a complaint. Remember, I have lived this life. I do know how it works."

"I know you have, Tracy, and thank you for caring. I promise I will do something if he comes back around. I will also be more careful and have an eye open. Literally one eye for sure."

"Just so you know. If he comes around here, I will call the police and ask questions later. One encounter with him in a lifetime was good enough for me."

"When was that?"

"After you had moved here. He came to my house looking for you. He had me so damn scared, and I have no idea what would have happened if the movers had not come when they did. He was going to find out what he wanted to know, no matter what he had to do. The movers knew something was not right, and they watched over me all the time they packed up my house."

"What about later, didn't he come back?"

"I don't know. I didn't stay at the house. I got myself a room in the busy part of town. I think he thought I had left town once the house was packed up."

"Oh, Tracy. I'm sorry that happened to you because of me."

"Now don't be silly. Guys like that are mean and are bullies all the time. It wasn't you. So don't you ever take the blame for something he does."

Tracy got up and got me a cold cloth to take the place of the ice for five minutes.

"I think I will go up to the hospital early to see Trevor. Then I can be back in time to put the children to bed."

"All right, do whatever works for you."

"Elisabeth is going to ask you about your eye when she sees you. This might frighten her. It could bring back memories of when you were still with Chris."

"Oh god, I hope not."

"What are you going to tell her when she asks?"

"I will tell her that I fell and hit the coffee table at work. She won't know there is no table there."

"Okay. I will make sure to use the same excuse when she talks to me about it."

"I'm sorry. I know you don't want me to lie about it, but I don't want her to know her dad is here. She will be too worried about him coming here."

"I know, and I understand. I will try to keep the worry from her."

"Thank you, I appreciate that. I think I will go see Trevor now."

"All right. Please take the car. There is no doubt that Chris will know you have come home. Bet he is watching for you."

"He has been watching me. He knew about Trevor. He thinks he is my boyfriend."

"Why does he think that?"

"'Cause he saw Trevor holding my hand on the way home that night."

"You mean he was—"

Tracy never got a chance to finish.

"OH MY GOD! Chris did that to Trevor because he saw him holding my hand. When he was talking about it, I didn't put two and two together. How dumb could I be?"

"Do you think Trevor saw who did this?"

"I don't know, but I'm going to find out."

"If he did, I hope he can charge him."

"If Trevor can describe Chris, then I will push him to lay charges."

"I wonder why he didn't gloat over what he did to Trevor?"

"He never asked how he was doing?"

"No, he didn't."

"Maybe he thinks Trevor is dead."

"I didn't get that feeling, but then I never caught on to any of this until now. All he kept asking was if Trevor was my boyfriend and said I was still his and would be until I died."

"Oh, Angel. I don't like the sounds of that. He is a very dangerous man. Please go to the police."

"I think I will, on my way to see Trevor. If he did this to Trevor because of me, Trevor could still be in danger."

"ANGEL, YOU ARE STILL IN DANGER. OF THIS GUY."

"You are right, Tracy. I will go to the police."

"Thank God. Call and let me know when you get to the hospital."

"I will. Please don't worry so much."

"We are blind to the danger that we are in because we lived with them. We walk around thinking we know them and they're not all that bad. But deep down in here"—Tracy puts a hand over her stomach—"we know better."

Stopping at the police office like I said and asking about if they had any leads on what happened to Trevor Anderson. Of course, the answer was no, and they asked me if I knew anything. I told them I wasn't positive, but maybe I could shed some light on it.

That's when they asked me what happened to my face. Going into detail, I had told them the whole story about Chris and myself. I told them they could check it out with Dr. Adams. This made them take notes and start to believe what I was telling them.

"Why have you not come sooner to tell us this?"

"I did not know any of this until this morning, and it wasn't until I got home that I put two and two together. Until now, Chris has not bothered me. He has talked to me, but he had not hit me again until this morning. In fact, I thought he had left town."

"These guys know how to hide until it suits them."

"Looks that way."

"Thank you for coming in, and we will talk to Mr. Anderson as soon as he is able to talk to us and see what he has to say."

"If I hear anything else, I will let you know."

"Thank you again, and have a safer afternoon than you had this morning. Have you been checked out by a doctor?"

"Yes, Dr. Adams."

"That's right, you said he found you. We will go talk to him as well."

"Thank you, good-bye." I was going to the hospital.

Chapter Twenty-One

G etting to the hospital was something I had been looking forward to. So I hurried on inside, and there was no one at the nurses station. I found that strange with Trevor in ICU. I carried on to his room. The drapes were closed, and all was quiet. Pushing the door open slowly so I wouldn't wake him. What I saw took me back a bit, and my heart was in my throat. The bed was stripped clean, and nothing of Trevor's was on the shelves. Okay, think. One of two things happened. Either he took a turn for the worse and passed away, or he went home with his parents. Neither idea sat well with me. I knew I would miss him either way. I couldn't figure out why Dr. Adams had not said anything about him this morning. I felt like I had lost my best friend. Now what? Turning around, I bumped into a cleaning lady.

"Sorry."

"That's okay," she said to me as she continued into the room to clean it.

"Did you forget something in here? Perhaps I can check to see if it was moved as well."

"MOVED?"

"Yes, Miss. This young man was moved to a ward."

I slumped against the wall in disbelief. Trevor was still here with us.

"Are you okay, Miss?"

"Yes, you have no idea how okay I am. What room is Trevor in?"

"He is in room 212, Miss. Second floor."

"Thank you. I took off, almost running. I knew people were looking at me, but I didn't care. I also knew I was earlier than I should be as visiting hours don't start yet for another hour. Riding the elevator gave me time to think. Why would they move him? What happened? Did his mother get him put in a private ward so I couldn't see him? Would she do that to him, treat him like he couldn't choose his own friends? Friends—yes, Trevor and I are friends. With that bubbly thought, the elevator door opened. I came face to face with Trevor's mother.

"Good morning, Mrs. Anderson."

"It is a good morning, Angel. Take care, and we will be seeing you." She steps onto the elevator as I step off. The door closes as I stand there and stare at Mrs. Anderson. All she could do was smile, so I smiled back.

Pushing Trevor's door open, I found him sitting up in a chair in front of the window. All he had was one drain tube in his side for his lung, which would be in for a few more days.

"Hi, Angel." His voice was just a whisper but, nevertheless, he was talking.

"Hi, Trevor. What a surprise this is. You must be a very happy man not to have that respirator taped to your mouth anymore."

"That I am. Come, sit down."

So I pull up a chair very close to Trevor so I would be sure to hear what he had to say. It may not be much yet as he will find it tiring to talk.

"Your eyes look better today too."

"Do they?"

"Have you not looked at yourself?"

"No, I'm scared to. The way my mother explains it, I would scare even a ghost away."

So I dug out my compact and flipped up the mirror. "Here, look for yourself."

He hesitated for a brief moment then took my mirror. "Wow, those are some colors, hey?"

"Oh yea, you have very nice colors, especially on this side."

He turns his face to take a better look.

"I'm not as bad as Mom made me out to be."

"Now you know moms think that every hurt is a horrible one when it comes to their children."

"I forgot, you are a mom."

Trevor and I sat and talked for about half an hour, then he wanted to lie down.

"I think I've been up long enough. I feel like I have worked all day."

"Okay, let me help you into bed."

"Thank you." Now I could hardly hear him.

"It is a real strain for you to talk, Trevor, so maybe you shouldn't do so much. Your throat will be sore from that tube."

He nods his head in answer.

"See, doesn't that feel better than talking?" He blinks twice. All I could do was laugh.

"If you feel like you have to sleep, you go right ahead. I won't mind. I will pull up this chair and just sit awhile." When I turned to get the chair, my bad eye was facing him. The feel of his hand on my arm made me tighten up, just for a moment, until I remembered it was Trevor and not Chris.

"What happened?" I could see the concern in his eyes. Now do I tell him the truth or make something up? I choose to go with the truth.

"My ex-common law decided to pay me a visit."

"Are you kidding me?"

"Afraid not."

"Did the police do anything?"

"Not yet, they are going to be watching for him." I could tell Trevor was very agitated by this. So I decided to change the subject.

"When do you start your breathing therapy?"

"Tomorrow afternoon." I could see there were thoughts going through his mind, and I knew he was full of questions. Which I will gladly answer when it doesn't hurt his throat anymore. Trying to keep the conversation going now was almost impossible. His train of thought was somewhere else. This made me uneasy. Was it because of what Chris did to me, or was it because he thinks I still care for the guy? Even after this. If I had said I laid charges, would it have made a difference in how he is acting now? So I tried another approach.

"Do you think maybe you should have gone home with your parents?"

Shaking his head and reaching his hand out to me, he says in a very tired whisper, "No, I don't need their help. I have you." Then he showed his beautiful breathtaking smile. That smile and his eyes were enough to catch any girl. With this thought in mind, I wondered why Trevor wasn't married. He squeezes my hand as I had gone into deep thought.

"Where are you?"

"I'm here. Was just wondering how I can help you."

"By reading the books you promised me that you would read to me."

"I can sure do that. In fact, I brought book number one."

"Then let's hear it."

"All right." Digging it out of my bag and showing him the cover. He raises his eyebrows and nods his head.

"Okay, how about you just lay back and relax while I read." Again, he smiles and nods. So I started to read to Trevor and realized how much I really enjoyed this guy's writing. It didn't take me long before I was right into the story. When a nurse came in to see if Trevor needed anything was when I realized he had fallen asleep.

"Guess I'm not an interesting reader."

"I would say the drugs still are working on him. You will be surprised of how much he heard. Those are a good read." The nurse points to my book.

"Yes, I love his writing. I collect his books. I think I have every one he wrote. There was only one that I could not get into."

"He would have to be pleased with knowing that he only wrote one bad story."

"Oh, I'm not saying it was a bad story. There was just something about it that didn't hook me. Usually, I can read his book in one evening."

"So you are a fast reader?"

"If I have no distractions, I do pretty good."

"That's me too. It has to be in the evening after everything and everyone has been done for the day."

"I hear you there. I have never been able to take a book to work and read on break time. I like to get into the story."

"If I have too many interruptions, I forget what I have read."

"Me too."

"Seeing how sleeping beauty here doesn't need anything, I will check back later."

"Okay, thank you."

The next four weeks went by fast for me. I don't know if they did for Trevor, but for me it was like there wasn't enough time in the day for all I wanted to do.

I did manage to finish the Women's Murder Club for Trevor, and he really enjoyed them. He said he would have to start buying that author's books.

Our visits became more lively as he had asked me to bring the children up to see him. I think this was part of his own therapy. He and the children got along great, and every time I took them up, he had another storybook to read to them. He had told them if their mommy could read to him, then he could read to them. He always made the children laugh.

Trevor's therapy went well, and on the day they took his drain tube out, he felt so much better. He said he felt like he had a lump in his side and it bothered him. He could feel it when he moved. It turned out to be the drain tube. It didn't take long for that hole to heal over. There was a little seepage when they took the tube out, but every day it got less and less. The doctor was happy with how he healed, and so was Dr. Adams. Before we knew it, it was time for Trevor to go home. He was excited, and I was too. But I was also sad. This meant that he wouldn't need my company anymore, and it also meant that I wouldn't be seeing him on a daily basis. This had me sad inside. Over the four weeks we had gotten to know each other, he had told me about his lonely childhood due to the wealth that he was raised in. He had said people think that having money is the answer, but to him, it just bought loneliness. We had also talked about why he had not married. He said that his parents were always trying to marry him off to someone's wealthy daughter. They didn't care whether we hit it off or not. It was always about money with them. So he stayed away as far as possible from those girls. He knew that the girls were all looking for money too. Happiness to them meant money, and to him, he wanted more. Although being a doctor would bring him money, he still would get to do what he loved, and that was to help children. Sick children didn't care if you had money or not. He had said if he couldn't make it as a doctor, then he wanted to be a teacher of the slum areas so he could do some good for the young children that had nothing or very little and no one to be there for them. He had said he would like to build a place big enough to get all of them out of the slum, but he knew he could not do it alone.

I had told him about my childhood and how we had money, but I didn't think it was quite like what he was raised with, and I knew Mom and Dad were helping out whoever they could from time to time. My mom had a big heart. She had her standards, but she would not stand by and watch anyone suffer if she could help.

I told him how Chris and I got together and what my life had become since then. What my life is now without my mom. It too was a lonely life. Although I have Tracy now and she is a great stand-in mom, it's just not the same.

Trevor understood, He loved his parents even with their faults. Or with the fact that they let money rule their lives, But he said it will be a sad day when he loses either one. They mean well, just in a different way and you can't hold that against someone because they don't see things the same as you do.

"Hey, Angel, why you so sad?" He asked me while we walked out to the car the day he was discharged. I didn't know how to tell him that I would miss him. My children would miss going up to see him.

They thought that had to be the best thing they ever did. We had laughed about an outing to the hospital being the highlight of everyone's day. I think for Tracy it was harder for her to let go for that little bit of freedom, as it gave her every late afternoon off. She said she was lost at first then said she couldn't believe all the things she had been neglecting to do for herself. She to was a woman with a big heart and helped everyone around her and forgot about herself.

In the end it had worked out for all of us in one way or another. Now we would all have to go back to our old ways. I just dodged around Trevor's question.

When we got to the car he slid up on the hood and pulled me into his side. Holding me close he said.

"Angel, can we carry on the way we have been?"

"Meaning what, Trevor?"

"You and I and the children doing things together in the afternoon and weekends."

"Have you not seen enough of us? Don't you have friends you want to get back to?"

"No, I don't. There is no one I would sooner be around than you and the children."

"I thought you would be tired of my children."

"Are you for real? Your children are so much fun to be around, they bring life into one's life. They are easy to like. In fact, they would be easy to love. Something like their mother." With that said, he bends down and kisses me so gently. I must have had a startled look on my face as he started to apologize for doing so. Putting my hand on his chest and saying, "It's fine. It was great."

I lay my head on his chest. I can't say I didn't have mixed feelings of pleasure and fear, but I do think the pleasure overrode the fear. I had hoped so anyways.

"I do want to live again, and I do want to love again."

"Hey," he takes my face in his hands and says, "we can take it as slow as you want. But I'm telling you now, Angel, I do want you and the children in my life. I enjoy the feeling that you all bring to me."

"You make us feel great too. I know the children really like you."

"I'm a likeable guy, what can I say."

"Me for one says you best get your butt in the car, and we should make a mile."

"Where you taking me? To your house?"

"My house? I thought you wanted to go home?"

"Are you kidding? I would like to see the children at your house on their own ground."

"What, is this some kind of test, to see if you are sane?"

"Maybe."

"Well, I think your crazy."

"Your not the first to say that." We both chuckle as we drive to my house. I was sorry it wasn't a longer drive. I wasn't ready to share him with everyone. I really enjoyed his company. Pulling up to the house I was surprised to see Dr. Adams car parked out side.

"Looks like they already have company."

"Does Dr. Adams come to your house often?"

"I wouldn't say often, but I think more lately that he and Tracy have become good friends."

"That sly old fox hey."

"Yes, he sure is. I must remember to ask Tracy if something more has become of their friendship."

"Guess you are never to old to need some loving."

"Guess not, But if it ever came to that I would be surprised."

"Why is that?"

"Dr. Adams has loved my Grandmother for years and I don't think he would ever let anyone into that part of his heart."

"I thought you said your grandmother had passed away."

"Yes, She did many years ago but he still holds her very close to his heart."

"Can you imagine loving someone like that? Truly loving to where you are the one and only."

"It is a dream that is for sure, and some people have been lucky to live it.

Chapter Twenty-Two

W e found Tracy and Dr. Adams on the floor playing a card game with the children. They looked totally surprised to see us come though the door. Parents would ask "what have you done?" as they both had the guilty look of "oh god, we've been busted."

Trevor and I let it pass and just went and watched them finish their game. The children were more excited about getting to spend time with Trevor than they were in finishing their game.

"You sure know how to spoil the fun," Dr. Adams said to Trevor.

"Sorry. What can I say?"

"I have to be going now anyways. I'm glad to see you out, Trevor. When do you plan on coming back to work?"

"Tomorrow."

"Tomorrow? Are you sure?"

"Yes, I am. Been lying around too much."

"Good to hear you feel so strong."

"Hell, I feel like new and ready for whatever comes my way."

"That's a boy," Dr. Adams says as he slaps him on the shoulder on his way out. "See you tomorrow then."

"You bet, bright and early."

Trevor spent time with the children until it was bath time. We had made arrangements to take the children bowling on the weekend after Trevor found out I loved to bowl and had done it from an early age. My children would also know how to bowl at an early age. Trevor himself had not spent much time in a bowling lane, and this could be cute. He and Gregory should make a good team—not team leaders, but a team. This brought back good and bad memories of my childhood and, of course, my dad's death. When I told Trevor about that, he wanted to cancel. I said "no way." It had been so many years; it was fine. But I had not been in a bowling lane since then, so I didn't know how it would be when I first walked into the last place my dad and I had been the night he died. My mom had kept us clear of the bowling lanes. I never did know whether it was for me or for her. I never asked to go bowling again. I thought it would be too hard on Mom. I think she was thinking of me. That would be just like Mom.

So the Saturday came, and off to the bowling lanes we went. Yes, my stomach was doing flip-flops, but I felt like I had it under control.

Trevor opens the door up and that night came back in a flash so quickly I could feel the floor coming up to meet me. I could hear the voices of all my little teammates, and it was as if I were back in time. The room looked the same. It was still the same people running it, and even the floor still had the same covering on it. I felt a hand wrap around my waist, and I heard a voice say, "Let's sit down for ten minutes or so. I'm sorry, maybe this was not such a good idea."

I shook my head and looked at Trevor, but his face was that of my dad's. I was sure he was saying, "It's okay, Angel, you can do it. Come on, now. You're my little trooper." Then I was being shook.

"Angel, are you going to be okay? You look like you have seen a ghost. Are you going to be sick? Do you want to go to the washroom?"

"Mommy, you okay?" I could hear myself as a little girl.

"MOMMY, YOU OKAY? WHAT'S WRONG, MOMMY?" Elisabeth started to cry. It only took a couple of minutes of hearing her cry, and I was back in today's world.

"I'm sorry, sweetheart. Mommy is just fine." Although I didn't really believe it. The look on Trevor's face was telling me he didn't either. My voice was barely a whisper.

"Come, let's go get our shoes."

"Are you sure, Angel? We could do this another time."

"No. It's now or never. I will be just fine." How could I make them believe that when I didn't. We all went and got our shoes and got into the bowling. It took some time, but with the children needing my help before I knew it, it was myself, Trevor, and my children at the bowling lane. My dad had gone back to rest.

The event went by quickly and enjoyable for all of us.

Once we were back home and the children were settled down for the night. Trevor and I sat out on the deck and enjoyed a cup of hot chocolate. We had talked about what had happened at the bowling lanes. This was something I had not told Trevor about all the time he was in the hospital. Sure I had told him my dad had passed away when I was very young, but I had not gone into details. I had never thought about how it would effect me when I went back to the lanes. Now I should be able to go back and nothing would change. I have faced that demon and won.

Trevor apologized over and over again. I could not stress to him enough, that I was glad we had gone and I was especially glad that he was the one I had gone with. This was just another mile stone that I had to walk and it is now over and done. I may move on now to the next.

Trevor and I had started dating after that, alone. Yes, I was nervous and I sure didn't want to spoil anything by having hang ups over the past. It was a hard road to travel alone. Many times I had asked my mom if I were doing the right thing.

It was so easy to be with Trevor, he was not a pushy type of man and he didn't seem to want to rush into anything serious which showed me he was not a controlling man.

A TIME TO RUN

Dr. Adams seemed to be so happy that we were dating and Tracy couldn't say enough good things about Trevor. It was as if she thought if she didn't talk fast I would let him slip right through my fingers.

Mom and Grandma always said that if it was meant to be it would happen. I believed in that as well. Nether one of us had a reason to rush anything and Trevor knew how badly I had been hurt so he was more than willing to go slow.

It went so slow that I thought just maybe we would never really be a couple. I had talked to Tracy about it and had asked her if maybe he could be gay, as he never approached me in a sexual way. I thought she was going to choke on her hot chocolate.

"Gay! Are you kidding me? Trevor loves you so much, I think he is scared too."

"Scared of what? I don't bite."

"It's not the biting he is scared of. It's the possibility that perhaps he too could hurt you."

"Trevor wouldn't hurt anyone."

"There are ways of hurting people without being physical, Angel."

Hanging my head, I knew she was right. I had never laid a hand on my mom, but I had hurt her so deeply.

"I know. But even that way, Trevor is not the kind."

"Maybe you should talk to him, if you think you are ready for more."

"Tracy, it has been six months now since we started dating."

"So? Six months is not that long."

"In today's world, it is."

"It is?"

"Yes, Tracy. It is." I could see her frowning, and I knew the wheels were turning inside that kind head of hers, and it was all over Dr. Adams. I didn't know for sure and I wanted to ask, but my respect for both of them stopped me. I also felt that if she were waiting for Dr. Adams to be intimate with her, she was barking up

Darleen Turner   203

the wrong tree. He would never let go of Grandma. He had already told me that she was and would be his only love. He had made a mistake once and had paid for it for the rest of his life. Although he and Grandma got back together, they never married—something he regretted totally, and because of that, he would never take another woman to his bed. His loyalty was very strong and true. This put me in a hard spot because I cared so much for both of them, and the fact that I knew this, I wondered if I should be the one telling her what I knew. Is that what a good daughter would do? Or was there a line that I shouldn't be crossing?

It was August 17, and a hot day it was. Elisabeth would be four today. We had planned on a big outside party for her at Jakes as he had the swimming pool. Jake was happy that there was going to be a happy celebration on his grounds. I could not help but worry about him. Jake had become a very old man in a short time. He kept saying there was nothing wrong with him. Maybe he was right physically but mentally he was dying. Jake was dying of a broken heart. Love that deep is dangerous although it is great to have there is also a disadvantage to it. I couldn't help but feel guilty each time I saw him. I felt he still blamed me. Even though he said he'd come to terms with the fact that no one could have talked Mom out of the choice she had made. I have wondered many times if I had known she was my donor, could I have changed her mind if I would have been talking to her at the time. In some ways, I blame Dr. Adams. He knew Mom was my donor, and he came to talk to me the night before surgery. He knew I was scared. What about Mom, was she scared too? Was Jake with her until they took her into the surgery room, or did she lie there in fear waiting to help me? I was on my own; the nurses were there, but I had no one to talk to about it. Chris stayed as far away as possible. The only one that came to see me was Dr. Adams. I had wondered what happened to Mom. He had said a team of wild horses wouldn't keep her away. I waited and waited. I thought she would come through my door at any moment. I prayed for that because, at that moment, I needed my mom to hold me. I was more than ready to have her take me in her arms and tell me everything was going to be okay. She was there now and all would be just fine. Not knowing she was in the room just down from me waiting for the same life-threatening surgery that, in the end, would save me and take her.

Now it's Jake who is paying for my mistakes the most. Yes, I love my mom. And yes, I miss her with every beat of my heart. But I still have a good life. My two beautiful babies and a man that I hope will love me as Jake loved Mom and Dr. Adams loved grandma. The only thing is I'm afraid of the pain such love can bring. It seems to be the less of two evils.

You can have deep fulfilling love and appreciation or an empty heart with no love. I wonder if the good lord intended for this choice to be so difficult, or are we all too much in a hurry to tie the knot with someone? The world is such a large place, and so many of us do not venture farther than home to try and find our mate. Our true love for life. When you think about it, it makes sense to travel.

Our day with Elisabeth was fun, and Jake had such a good time with the children. When Dr. Adams finally arrived, the children didn't know which one they wanted to be with the most. They were taking in all the grandpa time they could soak up in one day.

Trevor had come and brought a couple of children from a halfway house, a boy and a girl. They were Elisabeth's age, and the sadness in their eyes was heart ripping. Trevor was in his glory playing with these children. To put a smile on their faces was all he wanted to do.

They ate their fill of ice cream and cake and had fun playing in the pool.

I found out later that they were twins and that their parents had been killed in a plane crash, and there were no relatives to take them or wanted them. They had been at the halfway house since they were very young. I found it strange that no one adopted them. Even now, they weren't too old to get to love and mold them the way you would want them to be.

As the day dwindled down, the children all got tired fast, and we knew it was time to get them to bed.

Trevor had left early to take the children he brought back to their house of doom, and I had packed up my children and said good-bye to Jake.

"Dad, I will be back soon with the children. I promise. Thank you for letting us have the birthday party here."

"You don't have to thank me. This is your home—remember, Angel?"

"I know, Dad. I would like you to come to see us more often. It would do you good to get away more."

"I like to sit over there." He points to where the bench was sitting in front of the angel that Mom's ashes were put into.

"I know, Dad. It is a beautiful spot. You keep it looking great."

"That is my piece of heaven over there."

I didn't know what to say about that. I just nodded my head and in answer to the children, "All right you two, say good-bye to Grandpa. We have to go now."

The children hugged and kissed their Grandpa and we were off for home.

It didn't take long when they were dozing in the backseat. I had looked at them in my mirror, and when I looked back to the road, I had time to slam on the brakes and say, "What the hell? Now what does he want? Why is he out here?" Chris stepped right out in front of me, and I was a fool for stopping, but then running over someone wasn't my forte either.

I wound my window down.

"Chris, what are you doing out here?"

"It's our daughter's birthday, and I had hoped to see her today."

"So why are you out here instead of coming to the house? Where is your truck?"

"Oh, I had to pee, so I pulled over. Then I heard you coming, so I wanted to stop you before you got too far. I see you had them at Jake's."

"How did you know we were out here?"

"I had checked at your place and even drove around town looking to see if you had taken them somewhere special in town. Seeing how I couldn't find you, I figured I would try out here. So you did have them at Jake's?"

"Yes, Chris."

"Did they have fun?"

"They had a blast and wore themselves out, as you can see. So I really would like to get them home and into bed, before they sleep too long and think they should be up half the night."

"Well, I bought her a birthday present."

"You bought her a gift?"

"Yes, why do you sound so surprised?"

I just shook my head.

"Actually, I got her a few things. Guess you could say I'm trying to make up for what I missed."

"Oh really."

"You know what, maybe you could just take them for her. I see they are sleeping, and she can open it later or tomorrow. Would you help me put them into your car?"

"Sure, just give me a minute."

He had turned and headed to his truck. I checked on the children, and I undid my seat belt and got out and followed him. He had disappeared into the bush and, fool that I was, I followed. It had been a long, busy, hot day for the children. I just wanted to help him so I could get the children home to bed.

Chapter Twenty-Three

———•———

As I came down the hill and around the corner of the bush that he had disappeared from, Chris grabbed me and threw me to the ground. I scrambled to get to my feet with the words of Dr. Adams going though my mind: *I HOPE YOU KNOW WHEN IT'S TIME TO RUN, ANGEL."* With that thought in mind, I tried to do just that. I took off, which I thought was fast, back towards the car. But Chris had me by the arm and, this time, threw me so hard it knocked the wind out of me for a short moment. That was all the time he needed to get on top of me and hold me down.

"Please! Chris, don't do this. The children."

"To hell with the kids." He was groping me and trying to kiss me, and I knew I was fighting a losing battle. I tried to push him off. There was no way. I didn't think he was that strong, but I was sadly mistaken.

"I told you, you were mine till the day you die. And damn it, Angel, I'm going to prove it to you." This statement had my heart racing with fear. Was Chris going to kill me when he was done raping me? Don't most women die after they have been raped?

Oh god, please help me. Mom, please help me. I went numb after that, and he got rough, and he took and took. I have no idea what kept him going for so long.

I thought maybe if I didn't fight him, he wouldn't hurt me. He would just take what he wanted to prove his point and then leave me alone. He did just as he said he would; he took until I was hurting and he was laughing. Being raped was not the highlight of this day that I wanted to remember, but it was happening and there was nothing I could do about it.

The thought of my children in the car kept me calm. I could only hope that he would take what he wanted and then let me go. Then, all of a sudden, he lay still for a moment; and I figured he would just get up and leave me. That thought ended with a hard slap to the face, and then the beating began. The kicking and kicking went on forever. He had taken what he wanted just to show me he still had power over me. Be it right or wrong, he didn't care.

The pain in my side got so bad, I was going in and out of consciousness. I could feel the blood running down my face from when he hit me. I knew he had split my lip. At this moment, my face wasn't getting any more of the beating, but my back and sides were having the shit kicked out of them, and the pain was unreal.

Hearing something about "teaching you, bitch" was all I got to hear before I passed out.

When I came to, it was starting to get dark. I saw that my car had been moved off the road and was down in the bushes where he had his truck parked. Remembering the children, I tried to get up and get to the car. Things were numb until then, and the pain hit again. I moaned and just lay there. If Trevor came looking for me, he would not have seen me down here. Will anyone find me in time? Has anyone even missed us yet? My children, were they still in the car? Or had he taken them with him. Not likely, but who knew what he was thinking now? The black wave came over me once again, and it was Elisabeth calling me that woke me up.

"MOMMY, MOMMY! WHAT'S WRONG, MOMMY?" She had somehow managed to get her seat belt undone. I was trying to get my mind wrapped around as to where we were and why were we outside. When it came back to me, I remembered. "Where is Gregory, Elisabeth?"

"He is still in the car, Mommy." She starts to cry.

"NO, Elisabeth. Please don't cry. Mommy needs your help. I want you to give Gregory his bottle. Bring Mommy her purse. PLEASE! Now hurry. PLEASE! Then come back to Mommy." I needed my cell phone badly. If I could stay awake—but within minutes the pain got so bad, and the blackness took over.

Jake was sitting in front of the fireplace going over the day in his head. Even though it had been hot outside he always lit the fire place at night. He and Kate would always end their evening sitting in front of the low fire with a glass of wine. He had great thoughts of today and had hoped that maybe they would have more of them. He had really enjoyed having the children around and having Angel back home.

His doorbell started to ring, and he waited for the housekeeper to get it. Who would be calling her this late at night? Jake himself never had anyone in after supper. Then all hell broke loose. He heard crying and screaming, and his housekeeper yelling, "Master Jake, come quickly. COME QUICKLY!"

"What the hell?" was all Jake could say, and he moved as quickly as he was able. Getting out to the foyer, he could not believe his eyes. Rose was down on her knees trying to quiet the little girl. Elisabeth was talking so fast between her crying, no one could understand a word she was saying.

Jake took her and gave her a shake just to snap her out of her hysteria. He noticed the blood all over her shirt and pants.

"Where is your mom?"

"In the bush."

"In the bush? Why, did Mommy have an accident?"

"I don't know." And she started to cry again.

"Okay, okay. Take me to where Mommy is. Rose, I will get the truck. Grab some blankets and a cell phone. She can't be that far away if Elisabeth walked here."

"Okay, I will hurry."

Jake took Elisabeth with him to the truck and had her all buckled in when Rose came. It seemed like they drove for a long time. Every time he would ask if they were close, Elisabeth would say no.

"Are you kidding me? We must have missed them." So he pulled over to turn around and Elisabeth started to scream.

"NO, NO! Mommy is there." And she points down the road.

Jake looks at Rose and says, "Do you really think this little girl walked this far?"

"She seems to know we're not in the right place."

"So you think we should keep going? We have been driving for about ten minutes now."

"Mommy! Mommy!" And she points down the road.

Jake speeds up, and he did go by where Angel was. And again, Elisabeth called out, "MOMMY! MOMMY!" Now she is pointing behind them.

Jake does a fast donut in the middle of the road and slows down. He had missed them by maybe fifty feet. Elisabeth was a bright little girl, and he was thankful for that because she let him know right where Angel was. We could not see the car, but somehow this little girl knew where her mother was.

Stopping, Jake put on his four-way flashers in hope that someone else may stop and help them. Jake got Elisabeth out and grabbed his flashlight while Rose brought the blankets. They headed towards the bushes.

"Elisabeth, are you sure this is where Mommy is?"

"Yes, down there." Pointing to the clump of trees that Chris had taken the car to. He scoops Elisabeth up and starts to walk faster.

"I don't like this, Rose. Call 911."

"You sure?"

"Yes, something is horribly wrong with this picture."

Rose starts to dial just as Jake saw the reflection of the taillights with his flashlight.

"Stay here," he said to Elisabeth as he put her down and takes off on a run. Shining the flashlight in the car, he saw the baby sleeping but no Angel. He opens the door slowly not to scare the baby and looks inside. There was no blood, so where did all that blood come from that was all over Elisabeth? Rose comes up beside him.

"Did you find her?"

"Not yet. I don't understand."

Then he heard a groan, or he thought he did.

"Did you hear that, Rose?"

"Yes, sir. It sounded like a wounded animal."

Then it came again, and this time Jake was able to follow it. There, lying in a heap, was his daughter—his beloved Kate's daughter. Scrambling to get in close to her so he could lift her head out of the dirt.

"Angel, honey, it's Dad. Can you hear me?"

"God, Rose. I hope help is close by."

Now they could hear Elisabeth crying.

"Rose, I want you to get the baby and Elisabeth and go wait in the truck, please."

"Yes, sir. I sure will do that."

Rose went and got Elisabeth first. She knew the poor little girl was scared out of her mind. Standing in the dark with no one close by, knowing something was wrong with her mother. By the time Rose had both the children in the truck, the police and ambulance had arrived. They loaded up Angel as quickly as they could. They knew she was in dire straits and needed help immediately.

"Do you know what happened to her?" the one police officer asked.

"We have no idea."

"How did you know she was out here?"

"Her daughter came to the house to tell us."

"We will have to speak to her daughter then."

"Her daughter just turned four today."

"Don't you live like ten or fifteen minutes down the road?"

"Yes, sir. I do."

"And you say the little girl came to your house?"

"Yes."

"Did she get a ride with someone?"

"Not that we know of."

"I'll be damned," was all the officer could say. He had no idea that we felt the same way.

"Maybe in the morning I can come and see what she might be able to tell me. If that will be okay with you?"

"I am taking them back with me. I am their grandfather, and I will let their housekeeper know where they are."

"All right. I will come see you in the morning. I'm going to go to the hospital now and see if she has come around enough to give us a start."

"As soon as the children are settled, I will be there. I have a couple of calls I will have to make first."

"I will see you there then." He tips his hat and leaves.

"Oh sir, they were there for a long time. The children will have nightmares for a very long time."

"How do you know that, Rose?"

"'Cause the baby is soaked from head to toe."

"Please bathe them, make sure they eat."

"For clothes?"

"Did you not get the diaper bag?"

"No sir. I was not thinking."

"Okay, do the best you can I will call Tracy, and she will bring some over."

"Yes, sir."

Jake called Dr. Adams first, and he could tell how shook up the good doctor was by the call. Alex said that he had gotten a call from Tracy wanting to know where Angel was. He had told her they were probably with Trevor, not to worry about them, they would be home soon. Alex said he would call Trevor.

Jake then called Tracy, and she went off the deep end. It took Jake a little while to get her calmed down enough to tell her that they needed her help as far as the children went. Tracy finally calmed down enough to agree to take some clothes over to Rose before coming to the hospital. She said she would have to take a cab because Angel had the only car. Which was being held until everything was checked out to why it was in the bush, so they were hoping to get fingerprints.

Trevor and Alex were at the hospital at the same time. Trevor was on a run, and Alex walked a very fast pace. They met at the door.

"What the hell happened?" Trevor asked Alex.

"I have no idea, son. It's too early to know any details. I think she had an accident on the way home."

"This late? Where had she been all this time?"

"I can't answer that either. I thought she was with you when Tracy called me, looking for her."

"Oh my god. She was lying hurt somewhere all this time."

"Now don't get all worked up. We don't know what all is wrong or what happened." They continued walking in the hospital while talking and found Angel in ICU.

"Gee, I was just here."

"Maybe Angel liked what she saw in here and decided to visit."

Trevor gave Alex a strange look.

"Hey, son, just kidding. I'm just as scared as you are. I'm just trying to keep it together. She is all I have left of her grandmother and so that makes her very special to me."

"I'm sorry."

"Don't be sorry. We have a lot to be worried about, it is not a time for jokes. Forgive me."

Trevor could hear how choked up Alex had gotten and could see the tears in his eyes. He knew men cut jokes to try to make things okay. He walks over and puts an arm around Alex. "WE will see her through this. Right?"

Alex nods his head as he waited for the nurse to be finished with Angel so that he could go over and talk to her. He hoped she could hear them. He hoped that she wasn't in a coma. Alex could tell that

Trevor was very worried as well, so he tried to return the comfort. Trevor did not say much at first.

"Why the hell didn't I pick her and the children up and take them home? There was no need for her to be traveling alone with the children. I have no idea what I was thinking of."

"Now, Trevor, don't go blaming yourself. Angel probably would have wanted it this way because it would make too much driving for you with those other children."

"She and the children come first. She knows that."

"Yes, she does."

The nurses finished up with Angel. Trevor and Alex went right to her bedside, both taking a hand. Trevor let Alex talk first out of respect.

"Angel, it's Dr. Adams. If you can hear me, please squeeze my hand." He waited, but there was no response.

"Angel, you are going to be okay. You just have to fight, that's all. We are all here for you, so please try hard to open your eyes."

Angel could hear Dr. Adams, and she could see his face in her mind, but her eyes were not ready to open. At a distance, she could see Kate and Emma. Why they weren't coming for her, she couldn't understand. She started to call out to them.

"Mom, Grandma, wait for me."

"No! Angel you don't want to go with Mom and Grandma yet. Elisabeth and Gregory are waiting for you."

Trevor looks up at Alex with fear in his eyes.

"Don't worry, Trevor, we can talk her out of this. She is talking loud to us, it's not something that is happening just in her mind. So we can help control this. We just have to talk lots and loud."

"May I talk to her?"

"By all means, go ahead."

"Angel, sweetheart, it's Trevor. I would like you to open your eyes. I got something for you today, and I wanted to surprise you. But looks like the joke was on me and you are surprising me. But I think you would really like my surprise. Would you like to see it, Angel? How about it, will you open your eyes for me PLEASE?"

Angel moved her head, and Dr. Adams took this as a sign that she heard him.

"Keep talking, Trevor. She is coming around."

Trevor reaches into his pocket and pulls out a small ring box. Dr. Adams raises his eyebrow and says nothing.

"Angel, I love you very much. I would like you to be my wife." He slips the ring onto her finger. "Here, feel this," he says as he takes her other hand and rubs it across her ring. Dr. Adams had noticed he had not spared any money on the ring.

"Please, Angel, tell me what you think. Did I pick the right one? If you don't like it, they told me we could exchange it. The only thing is we don't have much time, so you have to let me know right away."

Angel starts to thrash back and forth and then starts to call out for Gregory and Elisabeth.

"Angel, the children are fine. They are with Tracy and Rose. They are safe and warm, and they just want their mommy to come home."

"Don't hurt the children. Please."

"The children are fine, Angel. Come on now, talk to us."

"She is talking to whoever did this to her," Trevor said.

"I think you are right."

"You do?"

"Yes, and I'm pretty sure I know who is responsible for this."

"You think you know?"

"I'm pretty sure this was the work of the children's father."

"You think he would do something like this in front of their own children?"

"He has done it before."

"Oh my god. She never said anything."

"She was waiting to hear from the police 'cause she is sure that he was your attacker to. We are all sure of that."

"I never saw anything. They got me from behind."

"It wasn't *they*, it was him."

"I can't believe such a dangerous man is still on the streets."

"That makes two of us."

"Angel talked about him a little but never told me how dangerous he was or is."

The doctor on call came in and said they would like to take Angel for tests; they would be back in a couple of hours.

"Okay, can we go and talk somewhere?"

"Sure, Trevor. Let's go for coffee around the corner."

Chapter Twenty-Four

A lex knew that Trevor had a lot of questions he wanted answers to. They would have a couple of hours, so they could get many things cleared up about Angel. Alex knew it would come to this eventually, but he did not feel it was his place to say anything. He had thought Angel would have told him more than she obviously did. Seeing now there was no way to hide her past from him, he might as well tell all he knows. He would deal with Angel later. It also looked like Trevor was being brought into her past without knowing it—if she were right in thinking that it was Chris who had attacked Trevor. Angel knew him better than anyone, as far as what he would be capable of.

They were well into their second hour when Dr. Adams got paged to come back to the hospital. The look he had on his face told Trevor he was worried, and Trevor got the gut feeling that he should be worried too.

When they got back, they were asked to go straight to the doctors' lounge. Opening the door, they found four more doctors. All had a gloomy look to them.

"So what's up?" Dr. Adams asked. He wasn't waiting for no run around the bush.

"My name is Dr. Dick Collins, and these are my associates. We have checked Angel Sanders out from head to toe and we have found she has one torn kidney that, of course, is bleeding. So we will go in as soon as she is prepped and repair that one and one that is not functioning to full capacity. She may need a transplant. We will give it a few days to heal and see if it will start to work more on its own. She will be on dialysis until we see what happens. Whoever did this was really concentrating on her kidney area. She is black and blue right up to her armpits and halfway down her hips."

Trevor turned white, and Dr. Adams grabs a chair and slips onto it, saying, "That bastard."

"You know who did this to this young lady?"

Dr. Adams nods his head and answers, "I'm pretty sure I know who is responsible for this. Proving it is another thing."

"Do the police know?"

"Yes, I have talked to them."

"This girl is in serious condition. I suggest her family be notified and start screening for donors."

"She has only a stepfather left besides her two infant children, and she has already had one transplant."

"Yes, I saw that. She doesn't have many options open to her then."

"I will go see Jake."

Trevor had heard all he wanted to hear. He slipped out of the meeting and found his way to Angel. He knew where they would be holding her while getting her ready for surgery.

Slipping in and taking her hand, he said, "Angel, I love you. Please, love, be strong and come back to me." Angel moans and turns her head towards him.

"Trevor?" she says in a whisper.

"Yes, dear, I'm right here with you. I'm glad you are awake."

"Where are my babies?"

"They are with Tracy and Rose. Don't you worry about us, just get better soon. Be strong, okay? We need you. I want you to be my wife, Angel." Angel has a faint smile come to her lips and goes back to sleep. The tears roll down Trevor's face as the nurses come in.

"I'm sorry, Trevor, but we must take her now."

"Yes, I understand." Trevor bends over and kisses Angel on her lips, whispers in her ear. "I love you, Angel. Please come back to me." He holds her hand while they wheel her away for as long as he could, then she was gone.

He left the hospital with a heavy heart and a mission in mind. He knew he would have about six hours before he could see Angel, and he was going to make the best of it. First stop, he was going to see Angel's babies for her just to hug them for their mother. He was hoping to be able to pass her love on to them, to make sure that they were okay. He figured that Elisabeth had seen more than she should have and would have trouble sleeping. After he saw them, he had some pals to go see. He had not seen them in a while but felt the need to go and look them up. He would pray later.

Alex in the meantime headed to find Jake. He knew he had been at the hospital. When he asked the nurses if they had seen him, they said he had gone home. They too had heavy hearts.

It seems like Angel just can't get on with her life, and he knew deep in his heart it was Chris standing in her way. If only they could pin something on him, but he is one smart crazy man. This time he can only pray that Chris didn't go too far. Angel has no one else left to help her out, and she is running on borrowed time. Alex wondered if he would outlive Angel as well as her mom and grandmother. This was not right. Angel has had a rough go of it with a little bit of happiness in between.

Could the good Lord just this once see to it that she gets what she deserves and Chris gets what he deserves? Just this one time. Was there no justice out there anymore?

As he rings Jake's doorbell this late at night, it came to him that perhaps this poor man came home and went to bed. To his surprise, Rose answered the door, and everyone was still up sitting around the fire. This was going to make it easier than having to tell the story three times.

So he got right down to the details. And in the end, he had the two women weeping, and he saw the tears drop off Jake's cheeks.

"Is there any hope of a donor this time?" Jake asked.

"She is on the list, and they can only wait. They don't come by kidney donors often. Because of her age, she may be bumped to the top of the list. I have no idea how many are waiting, or their ages."

"Can we be tested somehow to see if we could be a match for Angel?"

"Yes, Tracy. You can if you wish to be a live donor."

"Oh god, Mr. Alex. If I could do that for Angel, I sure would. Where do I go?"

"Thank you, Tracy. Just go to the hospital and tell them what you want to do, and they will set it up for you."

"I will do that first thing in the morning. If Rose will watch the children?"

"Oh yes, then I will go when you get back."

"Ladies, thank you so much for even doing that. People don't want to be live donors, for many reasons."

"I know it is risky."

"It is."

"That is okay. Angel would do it for someone else."

"Could they not use Elisabeth?" Jake asked Alex.

"She is too young, and we can't just make that choice."

Jake nods his head in answer.

"Trevor came by to see the children. Poor lad doesn't know what to think, he doesn't know what to do. He said he had some pals he was going to go meet."

"I know, Tracy. Guess he has to deal with this his own way. He did put an engagement ring on Angel's finger, hoping it will give her the strength to pull through."

"Oh, Mr. Alex, that was so kind of him. He does love her, and he would be good for her and the children."

"Now we have to pray that it all works out for the best."

"The children were so excited when he came. He was good about explaining that Mommy was sick and would be home soon. They seem to be okay with it."

"Let's hope he is right, and she will be coming home soon," Alex says.

"I wish I were younger."

"Why is that, Jake?" Alex asked.

"I would go find that SOB, and he would never be hurting Angel again."

"Well, my dear friend, that makes two of us. Do you think the two of us together could do enough damage before he got us?"

"It sure the hell would be worth a try."

They all sat in silence with their own thoughts for about an hour and then Alex left. No one knew just how much Alex wanted to take Chris out. But he didn't even know where to start. After all, he was all about helping to keep people alive, not taking them out. Then maybe he wouldn't have to take him right out, but he could make it so he would never be able to walk on his own. And in that shape, he would not be able to hurt Angel again. This played on Alex's mind all night, so there was no sleeping.

He had also thought about Emma, and she would not agree with his thoughts. He could hear her saying. *"Alex, two wrongs don't make it right."* Saying sorry under his breath for the woman he still holds in his heart with so much love it hurt. Emma also believed in what goes around comes around, and she would say, *"Chris will meet his match, and he will have to pay for what he has done. Give it time, and you will see."*

As far as Alex was concerned, this had not happened soon enough, and he wished he could make it happen. He had never in his life wished bad on anyone. But he felt, at his age, what did he have to lose? Emma always told him: *Watch what you wish for, it could come back on you.* To think of it, she had so many sayings. Her mother must have been some kind of witch. As he thinks that, he looks around his room. Like he was expecting Emma's mother to show her face or maybe throw something at him. He had seen pictures of her, and she and Emma could have passed as twins, so they probably had the same personality. He did not consider Emma a witch, but she was a very wise woman with her words and a very generous woman with her heart.

Before he knew it, the heat from the sun had awakened him. The sun was shining in his bedroom window, and this was a first for him. He had always been gone to work before the sun came up, so this told him he was finally getting old. It might have only been for a couple of hours, but he had gotten some sleep. Guess his old body was starting to let him down. He goes and has his shower and heads for the hospital. He had not gotten a call, so he figured Angel must be holding her own.

Arriving at the hospital, Alex found nothing but chaos. When he asked what was going on, he was told that there had been another gang-related beating, and it didn't look like this guy had a very good chance of surviving. At this time, Angel's doctor came around the corner.

"Good morning. How is Angel this morning?"

"She is holding her own, but I don't know for how much longer. A donor is not looking too positive right now. It is something that girl needs in the worst way."

"Maybe the guy that got beaten should be checked. Would be great if he would be a match. If he is as bad off as they tell me, it could be for the good instead of a waste."

"We already set that up. His drivers said he wanted to be an organ donor."

"I guess prayers are answered in many ways, hey, Dick."

"Yes, they are. But to lose a life to save a life doesn't seem right to me."

"I think it's because of the oath that we took."

"You are quite right, Alex, although it seems that so many things have changed since we took our schooling."

"There was no such thing as donors then."

"Man, doesn't that make us sound old?"

"Let's not think old. Let's think that, with time, we have advanced way beyond our imagination. I know I did not think about putting other people's parts into someone else, and having it work."

"Guess we can say we have seen the day."

"CODE BLUE, ROOM 4. CODE BLUE, ROOM 4."

Both Alex and Dick make a run for room 4. The crash cart was already on standby because they had expected this.

Alex and Dick got right in on the action and in no time had the man's heart beating again. As they get him settled and stand back, Dick looked at Alex with a worried look on his face.

"What is it, Alex? Are you all right, old-timer?"

"This the guy that was brought in beaten?"

"Yea, it is. Why? What's wrong? Do you know him?"

"Yea, I do. His name is Chris. He is Angel's ex, and probably the guy responsible for the shape she is in."

"Are you sure, Alex?"

"Oh I'm sure, all right. We should have let the SOB die."

"Now, Alex, you know we can't do that. I understand how you feel, but this is what we do."

"She had better not die because of his hands and he lives by ours. There would be no justice in that."

"You are right, but unfortunately, we don't have control over it all."

"We are not God. I know that. I have learned that the hard way over the years."

"It sounds to me like it might be time for you to retire. You are letting things get to you."

"Just assholes like this one." Alex turns and walks away before he says anymore. He was going to see Angel then going to get a coffee.

The drapes were open to the ICU room and Alex could see Trevor sitting there holding Angel's hand and watching a lone tear fall to the floor as he rolled the ring he had placed on her finger back and forth. Angel was still in a deep sleep and came around once in while but never stayed awake really long enough so we could ask her anything. The fact that she came around was a blessing. We could only hope that she would hang on instead of going the other way. How much time she was going to give us, we didn't know. But the hunt was on, and every hospital had the word on the need of a kidney.

Leaving Trevor to Angel, Alex went for his coffee. Sitting and listening to the staff all talk about the poor man in room 4 and what a horrible beating the gang had given him was turning Alex's stomach. He wanted to scream at them. *He is the cause of that young girl's beating and the loss of her kidney!* But he knew it wasn't the time or place, so he took his coffee and headed to a quiet place. Sitting in the chapel, he said a prayer for Angel.

"Dear Lord, I know I have been out of line today, and I know you are so very disappointed in me. I am not happy with myself or my behavior. Please find it in your heart to forgive me. I am sorry."

With that said, he sat in silence for a few minutes before looking up and talking to Emma.

"My darling Emma, I wish you were here with me now. Sometimes I feel as though you are right beside me, but today is not one of them. Although I could use your strength and wisdom at this time, I also know you will guide me in the right direction. I feel like I have failed you and Kate so many times since you both left us. I have tried to be there for your granddaughter, but I'm always too late. This time, my hands are tied, and she is in the hands of God—and, hopefully, another great doctor.

"I am also praying that the love that Trevor is showing for her will make her hang on long enough for a donor to be found. Please, Emma. You and Kate also have to push her from your end. I can't do this alone. I'm so sorry, my love. I guess old age is taking over."

With that said, he hung his head and shed a few tears of his own before returning to Angel's room.

Trevor was standing outside her room talking to his dad when Alex came back.

Reaching out his hand to Alex and saying, "I'm so sorry, Alex. I came as soon as I could. I will help with Angel as much as I can, but you know there is only so much we can do without a donor."

"Of course I do, and thank you for coming." Alex felt the life that everyone else feels when they shake this man's hand. He could only bow his head and say, "I'm going home now, I will be back later." He had thought perhaps he would go see Jake. They had told him he had sat with Angel all night. He had thought Trevor would have been the one to be at her side all night, but then it doesn't really matter as long as she is not left alone. He did not like anyone to die alone. Alex was also sure that if Angel dies, Jake won't be far behind her. He was more attached to that girl than anyone understood. Right now, he also is feeling like he is letting Kate down.

Alex thought maybe Jake would be in bed, but the groundskeeper said no, Jake hasn't been to bed yet. The crazy old fool was going to kill himself, one way or another. Jake was pleased to see Alex.

"Do you think Angel has a chance this time?" Jake asked as he showed Alex to the big chair he always sits in when he goes to see him.

"She always has a chance, Jake, and you know that."

"Not much of one without a donor."

"You're right. We can only pray, Jake, that happens soon."

Alex's phone starts to ring as Rose comes in saying, "Mr. Jake, the hospital is calling." Alex looks at his phone and see's that it is also the hospital. He and Jake exchange glances as Alex answers his phone and Jake reaches for his.

Chapter Twenty-Five

———————•———————

Within minutes, both men were scrambling for their coats and headed to the hospital. They had been told that Angel had gone into cardiac arrest and was going downhill fast and to get there as soon as they could.

Jake jumped in with Alex, and neither one said a word all the way to the hospital. Both men were too busy praying. Emma always said that prayers were stronger done in groups. Alex wondered if he and Jake would be considered a large enough group. There was no doubt in his mind that Jake was doing the same thing as he was. Alex also felt sick at this time and wondered if his friend felt the same way but was afraid to ask. Jake looked too fragile, and Alex really worried about him.

They sat at Angel's bedside for two straight days and nights. She had no changes in her condition, and she was what they considered stable for the shape she was in.

Trevor was silent and never left Angel's room. He sat with his head down, and when asked if he was okay, he would just nod his head. His eyes were red and puffy from the tears he had shed, and he looked like hell. It was a good thing he had taken some sick time from work. It wasn't like everyone didn't know where he was, but there has to be a paper trail.

Alex and Jake finally got up the nerve to go for a walk and get themselves a coffee. It seemed like coffee had been their only nourishment for so long they had forgotten what real food tasted like. Both men were like Trevor and were afraid to leave Angel's side. At this moment, they felt it was safe enough to go and stretch their legs and get some fresh air. Leaving Trevor alone with Angel can also be a good thing. He doesn't say much to her when we are in the room. Giving him his time, we felt, was necessary.

We actually had something to eat, and Jake said he would like to go home and have a shower and change his clothes. Alex felt the same way, but he was stopping by Angel's room to let Trevor know to call the minute anything changed. As he slipped into the room, he heard Trevor talking to Angel, and it stopped him in his tracks.

"I'm sorry, sweetheart, that I let it get to me the way it did. I really didn't mean to lose control and have it go this far. I would do anything to change it if I could. I can only hope you will find it in your heart to forgive me."

What the hell was Trevor talking about? Did he beat Angel? That's what it was sounding like. But why? We all thought he was at home while Angel was being beaten. How could we have been so wrong? And Chris—what about him? Was it a gang that saw he got what he deserved?

Trevor choked back his tears as he continued, *"I took an oath to help our human race not to beat someone until they were damn near dead. Oh god, Angel. I'm so sorry."*

Alex swallowed hard and was just about to grab Trevor by the throat when Trevor spoke up again, *"Seeing you in here and knowing that he was the cause of this and all your pain and maybe making two little children orphans was more than I could stand. I just meant to break a leg or maybe two so he would know never to get close to you and the children again. But when I started to swing the bat, I couldn't quit. It was like the devil himself had taken over. I was so full of anger and rage at the time, and now I'm full of regret.*

If I lose you, it has all been for nothing. If he dies, I don't just have your death to deal with, but a murder charge as well."

Alex had to slump against the wall to steady himself with what he had heard and, in doing so, knocked over a tray—which made Trevor jump to his feet. Alex felt very sick at this point. He had heard more than he wanted to. Now he would have to figure out whether he was to tell the police everything he knew if Trevor didn't. With tears running down his cheeks Trevor walks towards Alex. "I'm so sorry for what I have done." And he falls into Alex's arms, weeping like a child.

Alex held him for what seemed like forever before saying, "It's all right, son. There's a couple of us that wanted to do that ourselves, but our ages stood in our way." He could not tell if Trevor heard him or not, but he didn't want this to fall on anyone else's ears. He gave him a strong hug then pushed him back so he could look into his eyes. He could see the fear that the boy was now carrying and shadowed with regret.

"Listen to me, Trevor. You don't say a word of this to anyone. Not even Angel, do you understand? We will talk later in private in my home."

Trevor nods his head.

"Have you told your father anything?"

"No sir. I couldn't bring myself to do so."

"Good. Don't say anything now either. This is between you and I, and this is where it will stay. You don't want to throw your future away, so forget it even happened."

"Oh sir, I can't do that. There is a man almost dead."

"Quiet, not another word. We will have a chance to talk about this. Just look at her and know what you did was for her and her children. I, for one, thank you." Alex takes Trevor's hand and shakes it. "Now please stay with Angel. I want to go home and shower and change my clothes. I won't be long. Then, if you wish, you can do the same."

"I brought a change here so I could shower here."

"Good thinking. I won't be long. If Angel wakes up, tell her I love her."

"Yes, sir. I will."

Alex leaves, and Trevor sits back down feeling better than he had all night. Not that what Alex said excused the way he had behaved towards another fellow man, it was just a good feeling to get it off his chest. It wasn't like they had a long conversation about it, but Trevor was feeling like he was ready to explode inside, and perhaps it would have been to the wrong person. He had always talked with his dad, but this was different, and he just could not bring himself to say a word. What would his father have said when Trevor told him he had beat a man and left him lying and possibly dying on a street in the middle of the night?

Trevor was the one to put in the call to 911 right after he had left Chris lying in his own blood. He also said a silent prayer for Chris, and he really did hope he got better. He, for one, knows how Chris is feeling right about now.

Trevor worried about what Angel was going to think of him once she knew what he had done to the man who fathered her children. Trevor was feeling like he had lost his mind. All he knew was he had feelings for Angel that he has never had for another girl, and perhaps that is what pushed him over the edge. Seeing the girl that he hopes to marry lying close to death herself, and it was all caused by the hands of someone who supposedly loved her, brought the rage to him like he had never known in his life. This was a frightening thing to learn about oneself. So to say "I would never do that" is something everyone should keep under their hats. 'Cause we never know what reaction one can have to someone's behavior. Trevor, for one, would have never guessed that he would have been capable of such an action.

If you had a great lawyer, he would call it temporary insanity due to the circumstances and probably get him off with a small fine or a short stay in jail if Chris were to die.

Trevor knows that if charges are going to be laid, he will have no future and all his dreams will die that day. He felt it will only be a matter of time before the police come for him. Sitting with his hands on his knees and holding his head, he felt that his life as he knew it was over. If Angel dies, he didn't care; she and the children had become his world. He was sorry that he hadn't told her earlier. He was wanting to tell her when he gave her the ring. Now there is a good possibility that she will never know just how much he loves her.

He looks up at her and she reminded him of snow white. She was so pale and yet so beautiful. If only he could be the prince to wake her up and make her world whole again. With that thought he got up and kissed her so gently as if she were made of china. Whispering in her ear.

"I love you, Angel, now and always. Please be strong for us." He lays his head down on her chest and lets his tears that he had been holding back flow freely. He thought he had dozed off for a bit but then was woken by a soft hand rubbing his face and hair. It startled him, and he jerked his head up just to see the eyes of his Angel.

"Well, hello there, sleeping beauty," he whispers and kisses her again. This brought a slight smile to her weak lips. "Boy I've waited a long time to see those beautiful eyes of yours and that smile." Angel was to weak to say much she just blinked once and Trevor caught on right away. "We have had a lot of communicating like this, guess we just changed places. Lets see if I'm as good at it as you were." Angel blinked once. Her blinking was far apart, as if she were too tired to open her eyes while blinking. She did go back to sleep, but Trevor felt better that she had at least opened her eyes and communicated with him. This time he sat back and laid his head on the edge of the bed and, holding her hand, slept as Angel did. He didn't know how long it had been when he had been awakened by the nurse and asked if he could move so they could attend to Angel. Angel did not seem to know they were even there. They bathed her and brushed her hair and changed her gown. It reminded Trevor of something maybe a mother would do with her child. Although he figured the child would have woken up at some point.

Watching the nurse change her bedding was something. They did it without really moving her. They were very skilled at their job. He was glad of this because he didn't want any more pain brought to Angel.

Trevor decided to go and have a shower and change his clothes while they were finishing up with Angel. They said they still had a bit to do with her, so he could feel safe about leaving her alone. He wanted to tell them that wasn't the problem. What he was worrying about was if Angel were to pass away, he wanted to be there to hold her while she went on her journey. He knew no one would understand, and in the hospital, they see many die alone. This is so common that even the nurses don't seem to feel it. It becomes just a natural happening in their day's work. Over time, they get hardened to these facts of life; otherwise, it would drive them crazy. Trevor, for one, didn't know if he would ever be able to harden himself enough to be able to carry on as long as his father or Dr. Adams had done. He had met a few young doctors that had called it quits after dealing with someone they loved coming in from an accident and losing them in the end. They have to learn that they are not God, and they can only do so much, and the rest is in the hands of our Lord. Trevor has become a great believer in God and felt that with him by his side he should be able to handle anything. Angel had been a test, and he failed God, and he knows he has a lot of repairing to do. So he will put in extra time at no charge, and he will also help out more at the children's center. Trevor will also check on Chris and make sure he gets all the right help he needs. Just maybe he was someone who has been swept under the carpet along the way, and it has turned him into the monster he is today. He didn't want to make excuses for the guy, but God knows we are not born this way. Trevor could only hope that his help wasn't too late coming for Chris. He also hoped that if Angel pulls through, she will forgive him for the horrible thing he has done. Trevor did not know how men back in the days when they believed that it was an eye for an eye, tooth for a tooth, could sleep at night. He hasn't been able to really sleep. Yes, he has dozed. But to fall into a deep sleep wasn't possible as the scene keeps coming back to him. He wakes up shaking and sweating and scared.

Knowing he could possibly have a man's death on his hands played a big part in him not being able to sleep. He was going to go check on Chris before returning to Angel's room.

In the meantime, Jake was getting ready to go back to the hospital. He had some sleep and some toast and his shower and thought he should be good to sit with Angel for another few hours. Walking past Kate's study, he stopped and pushed the door open slowly as if he might see her sitting at her computer. This was something he had often done when she was alive. He would stand and bask in her beauty, and he enjoyed watching her work. Most of the time, she would be so into her story, she never knew he was even there. Noticing the novel that she had had published sitting on her desk, Jake goes on in and picks it up. There was a white envelope sticking out of the top of it, so he opened the book to that page. He read: To My Darling Kate. Wondering what it was, he pulls the pages out from inside and opened them up. He looks at the back page and sees that it was a letter to Kate from Emma. Going back to the first page, he started to read. It made him a little uncomfortable, reading Kate's mail, but something was pulling him to do so, so he carried on.

My Darling Kate:

It is with a heavy heart I write to you as I know I don't have many days left on this earth. There are a few things I want you to know, and I hope that you will understand them. First off, please know that I loved you more than life, and whatever I chose to do was always in the best interest for you. Some things may be clearer to you once you have finished reading. I hope that in the end it will all make sense to you and maybe even make a difference in your life.

As Jake read on, he had to find a chair and sit down.

"Oh my god, Kate. It can't be. If it is, how long have you known this? Why did you not tell someone? Why had you not told me?"

Jake's mind was racing, and he didn't know what to do first. Should he call Alex? Or should he go straight to the hospital like he was going to and see Angel? YES. He would go to the hospital. Folding up the letter and putting it inside his coat pocket, he headed for the door. Then remembering the book, he turned around and grabbed it off the desk. He would take it for Angel to read while she was laid up. There would be no better time than now to read what her mother had written. Both her novel and the letter from her grandmother. Jake was sure that they would both prove to be very interesting reading and maybe help Angel in the long run.

Alex had had his shower and was putting on his coat; when he went to put his handkerchief in his pocket, he found the letter that was from Emma so many years ago. Thinking, gosh has it been that long since he had that coat cleaned, taking it off and setting it aside for the cleaners. He reaches in and pulls out a dark blue one that was still in the wrap from the dry cleaners, so he knew it was clean. Laying it on the bed, he said, "Yea, I have time for you today, dear," feeling a little guilty for not remembering to read her letter so long ago. I could really use you right now, and so could your granddaughter."

Sitting on the edge of the bed, he opens his letter and a warm feeling came over him as soon as he saw Emma's handwriting.

My Darling Alex,

I hope that somewhere you will find it in your heart to forgive me for what I am about to tell you. Remember, dear, I have always held the highest regards and respect for you, both as a doctor and as a man. I waited for the right moment, but it never seemed to arrive. So now I can only hope that you too will understand why I did what I did and be able to forgive me and move on with brighter hopes of the future. Please remember one thing. I loved you always.

As he read on, it got painful and hard to believe of Emma.

Alex could not believe what he was reading. Had Emma lost her mind? How could she have let so many years go by—wasted years? Oh, Emma. Why? Better yet, how could you have done this? Why had I not known? I thought I knew you so well. Alex was beside himself. He didn't know what to do. He wanted to crumple up the letter and throw it in the garbage. For the first time in his life, he wanted to scream at the only woman he had ever loved and never had a moment of unhappiness with. The fact that it was the last letter he got from Emma he chose to keep it. Perhaps he will reread it later and be able to understand what Emma was trying to say. Now he must go back to the hospital and see Angel; maybe something will make sense of all this. Guess today was not the day to be spending time with Emma. Now he has a very unsettled feeling, and he has no one to talk to about it. Grabbing the coat he had laid on the bed, he stuck the letter into his pocket and left for the hospital.

Chapter Twenty-Six

---•---

A lex got to the hospital the same time as Jake. "I'm glad to see you, Alex. I have to talk to you." As he reaches in his pocket to pull out his letter to Kate.

"Yea, me too. But I have something I have to do first. We can meet for coffee"—looking at his watch as he kept walking—"say, in a half hour." Alex was walking a pace that Jake wouldn't be able to keep up with.

"But I think we should talk now."

"Sorry, old chum, can't do right now. In a half hour in the cafeteria, okay?" Alex waves at Jake as he heads for the elevator.

Jake stands in a dumbfounded way; he couldn't believe that Alex just brushed him off that way. This was important and could help Angel. He would make sure he was in the cafeteria in a half hour, and Alex was going to hear about his actions. Jake stood thinking about what he knew and what he should do with the information that he had in his hand. He decided to go up and see Angel before going for coffee. He never made it back last night like he had planned.

He found Angel still sleeping, so he pulled up a chair and just sat. Taking her hand in his, he says a prayer for her:

"Dear father in heaven, I know I have not talked to you much since I lost Kate. But if you could find it in your heart to forgive me

and give our daughter here another chance, I would be forever in your debt. Amen."

Alex was headed to see Angel as well but decided to stop off and see Chris first. He was worried about his outcome because of Trevor. Personally, he didn't give a damn about how he was. He was concerned, however, about how this was going to affect Trevor. So he thought he should find out firsthand what his chances were. Chris wasn't in the ICU room, and Alex's stomach dropped.

"Oh, good heavens, no." His heart was racing as he went behind the desk to pull his file. Standing there reading it as the nurse came back to her station.

"Good morning, Dr. Adams. May I help you with someone?"

"The guy from ICU, what happened to him?"

"Nothing, but he stabilized very well and has been put in room 320."

"Right on. I will go up and see him."

"Do you know him?"

"Why do you ask?"

"'Cause he isn't your patient."

"Yes, I know who he is. Told a friend I would check on him."

"He hasn't had anyone come to see him." Alex wanted to say something like "do you think?" but kept his mouth closed and just walked away. He was taking the time to check him out, even knowing that he was out of danger. Until you see it with your own eyes, it is sometimes hard to believe, and this was one of them. Alex himself didn't think he would make it through the night. Trevor had really laid a beating on him, and Alex really wanted to shake his hand and say "Well done, son." He knew it wouldn't be appropriate, so he kept his feelings to himself. The nurse was with him as Alex came to the door.

"Good morning, Dr. Adams. Are you here to check Chris out?"

"Guess you could say that."

"Then I will leave you to it. If you need anything, please just ring your bell and a nurse will be right in," she says to Chris.

"Thank you." He sounded like a wounded mouse. Once the door closed, Alex went closer. He looked Chris over and saw that besides the broken legs and one arm, he had a swollen face. No doubt took a hit to the face as well.

"What do you want? Chris asked.

"Nothing, really. Just wanted to see how you were and to ask you if it felt good to have someone do this to you."

"Get out."

"Do you think you know how Angel feels right now? To think that it wasn't a woman that she tangled with. Not like you who met up with someone who plays as dirty as you do. But what does it feel like to be on the losing end this time? Do you feel like a big man, a real hero? Like the other times, or do you feel like the weasel that you really are?"

"Get out, I said."

"Or what? You going to call the cops on me, you loser? I didn't think so. You must have lots to tell them though. Did it make you feel good to beat Angel in front of the children?"

"They didn't see anything." Turning red in the face as he caught himself saying too much.

"You SOB," was all Alex could say as he reached over and grabbed him by the throat.

"Now look who's the tough guy, picking on a man while totally out of commission. Do you feel like a big man now?"

"Shut up, you good-for-nothing waste of skin. Whoever done this to you should not have stopped until you stopped breathing. The world would be better off."

"Angel needs me."

"Angel doesn't need you, nor does she want you. Can't you get that through your thick skull?"

"She has nobody else. All she has is me, and I am the only one who will ever love her."

"LOVE. You don't know the meaning of that word, and she has got people who love her."

"You mean that young punk doctor?"

"She also has family that loves her."

"Her family are all dead. All she has is me and those brats."

"That's where you're wrong, sucker." Alex slaps the white envelope down hard onto one of Chris's legs, making him cry out in pain.

"That one is from Angel."

"What's this?" Chris says as he picks up the envelope.

"Read it and weep," Alex says as he turns and walks away.

It took Chris a few minutes but it finally got to him, so he opened the letter. He read it over a couple of times as he couldn't believe what he was reading. Laying back on his pillow all he could say was "I don't believe it."

Alex got to Angel's room and saw no one around, so he kissed Angel and whispered in her ear. "Your grandmother sends her love, and so does your grandfather. I love you, Angel. Please be strong. The children and I need you." Angel moans but doesn't open her eyes.

Her eyes felt so heavy; all she wanted to do was sleep. She could see a bright place beyond where she was lying and she seemed to want to drift that way. She had gone there a couple of times but her mom and grandma would always send her away. Telling her to go back to the children, they needed her. It was so bright and peaceful there she didn't want to go back, not that she didn't love her children but seeing her mom and grandma again made her realize how much she truly missed them and wanted so much to be with them. She knew the children were in good hands so she didn't need to fight. Why can't they see that she needed them. Was her mom still angry with her because Angel never talked to her before she died? Would Angel never get to heaven because of what she did to her mother? Surely God would understand that it wasn't her fault. He would know Chris was behind everything. He stopped her from seeing her mother. Then it hit her. Chris would get the children if she didn't go back.

"NO, NO, I won't let him," she was saying and tossing her head back and forth.

"It's going to be okay, Angel. Just hang in there a little longer." Alex bends over and kisses her on her forehead.

"I will be back. I promise." He leaves to go to the cafeteria to find Jake. He was a little over his half hour, but he knew Jake would wait for him.

Jake was no where to be found and Alex found that strange. Did he go home or maybe to the washroom? He got himself a coffee and thought he would check in at the doctors' lounge then go back to the cafeteria. Jake should be back there by then.

When he got to the lounge and opened the door he found it was full of doctors. Dr. Anderson was there as well. They all turned and looked at him as if he had two heads.

"Sorry, did I interrupt a meeting of some kind that I wasn't told about?"

"Not at all," Dr. Collins said as he came over to shake Alex's hand.

"Then what is up? Why did everyone look at me that way?"

"I'm sorry, Alex. Just that we know how close you were to Angel and her family all these years. So I guess this is all very hard on you, and the stress must be wearing you down."

Alex's first thought was that Chris had laid a complaint against him, and now he was going to be asked to go on stress leave and asked to stay away from the hospital willingly or they would have to get a court order if he didn't agree on his own.

Putting his hands up in the air and saying, "Hey, I'm sorry, but a man can only—"

He was cut off by Dr. Anderson as he steps up and shakes Alex's hand.

"No. We are the sorry ones, Alex. Even with all the best doctors standing by, we can't do a thing about Angel. It is killing her, and every day she gets weaker. We are running out of time, our hands are tied and we have no other resources. Angel won't hang on much longer, there are too many on the waiting list ahead of her. You know what we are doing for her now only works for a short time. It is meant to give us time to get a donor and that is not happening anytime soon."

"Excuse me," Alex says as he goes and sits down. He was pale and tired and getting somewhat weaker with age. He pushes his hands through his hair a couple of times and then rests his head in his hands. He was thinking, can I or can't I? Just then, Jake came barging though the door.

"Alex, there you are. I have been looking all over for you." Then he stops and takes a good look at Alex, Gosh when had Alex gotten so old? He had not noticed how the years had crept up on him, On both of them. But Jake always felt that Alex would out live him but now he wasn't so sure. He was now snow white and had lines on his face that Jake never noticed before. His hands were shaking like the hands of an old man. Maybe because he is a doctor, people look at them differently. Like they're never going to get old, how crazy that is. They are only human, after all.

"Alex, are you all right?"

Alex nods his head and looks up at Jake with tears in his eyes. Jake squats down in front of Alex and asks, "Did something happen to Angel that I'm not aware of?"

"Oh no!" Dr. Anderson said as he steps up and puts a hand on Alex's shoulder. "We were just telling Alex that we are running out of time. Angel is not going to hold on much longer, and there is no donor in sight. What we are doing for her now was just to buy us time and, unfortunately, that is almost up. We know how hard this is on Alex here as she has been like family to him."

"Family. Yes, that's what I wanted to talk to you about, Alex old friend." Jake reaches in his pocket and pulls out the last letter Kate had received from her mother. Waving it in front of Alex.

"Do you know what this says, Alex?"

"No, Jake, I don't."

"It says that Angel still has living family Alex."

"Are you sure?" asks Dr. Anderson.

"Yes, I'm sure."

"Does it tell you who they are?"

"Yes, it does."

"May I see the letter? If you don't mind sharing it with us."

"Of course, here."

Jake hands it over and waits for him to read it. Dr. Anderson read it once then looked up at Jake with a frown and reread it. Then he turns and hands it to Dr. Collins who, by now, has gotten very curious by the look on Dr. Anderson's face. He also read it twice then looking at Jake he says, "Does anyone else know about this?"

"I'm not sure. We would have to ask the party in the letter."

They look around the room then at each other.

Chapter Twenty-Seven

After reading the letter twice he still couldn't believe what he was reading and had turned a bit on the pale side. Dr. Collins turns to the other associates that were in the room and says.

"Would you all please go for coffee and meet back here in an hour." There were a lot of heads nodding and no one was saying anything.

"Thank you." Dr. Collins says as they wait for them all to leave.

Dr. Anderson and Dr. Collins look at Jake then at Alex. Jake pulls a chair up beside Alex, saying.

"Alex do you know what is in Kate's letter?" And goes to put a hand on his shoulder and Alex looks up and the tears were falling silently as he explodes. He jumps up and kicks his chair and heads for the door. He didn't stop for anyone. He got many strange looks as no one had ever seen this side of Alex.

"Just give him a day, I will go and see him in a while. This has come as a real blow to him and at his age and the stress he has been under, he may not be able to think straight. We have been friends for many years and he will talk to me. If not today then tomorrow." Dr. Collins hands him back Kate's letter, saying.

"I understand fully, Good luck."

"So you think in a day or two Alex will talk to us?"

"I think so. I should be able to let you know more tomorrow, just give me some time."

"We don't have much time, or I should say Angel doesn't have much time."

"I know. I will do my best." With that said they all left the lounge and Jake went to find Alex. No one could know how he was feeling right now, and you don't want to say you do. Because until you are in their shoes you have no idea how it hits you when you get information that changes your life and the way you felt about someone that you held so high on a pedestal. Was Alex going to be able to accept what Emma had told him, or was he going to burry it as he has Emma so many years ago.

Alex's truck was parked outside or it looked like it had been abandoned. Alex had walked away from it in a hurry. This bothers Jake. What kind of condition will he find Alex in? This was a worry.

The door was left ajar so Jake just slowly pushed it further open and walked on in. Calling out to Alex.

"Hey, Alex are you in here?" Not a sound came back. This made Jake uneasy but he kept on walking. Where had Alex gone? He could not find him down stairs so he went up the stairs, which Jake had never been further than Alex's sitting room. He just never had any reason to go any further. As he walked the hall he could here sounds of distress. Stopping and waiting to see what was going to become of it, but all went quiet again. So Jake went to where the sound had come from and he pushed the door open gently and he found Alex sitting in a large overly stuffed chair and he held a picture in his hands and tears were streaming down his face. Jake walks on over and sits on the edge of the bed. Taking a deep breath then saying.

"I'm so sorry Alex for your loss, It seems you and I have more in common than we thought." Alex nods his head.

"Alex when did you find out?" Alex was silent for such a long time Jake figured he wasn't going to answer him.

"Just this morning when I found the letter Emma had left for me so many years ago. I never read it at first then I just couldn't bring myself to read it. Guess I thought that so long as I had something I had not read, she would still be with me. Now I had all these wasted years and I can't just blame Emma. My selfishness of wanting to hang on to her cost me more than I would have ever known."

"Don't be so hard on yourself, how were you to know."

"Well, I would have known a lot sooner had I read the damn letter she left for me way back."

"So what are you wanting to do now?"

"I have no idea. I didn't know there were two letters out there. At least, I hope there are only two."

"At this time, old friend, I don't think that is the main concern, do you?" Alex looked at Jake so confused, and Jake could tell he was. So he knew he had to approach this in a different way.

"Alex, Angel needs help, and she needs it fast. You, my friend, are the only one who can help her. Are you willing to do that?"

"What do you mean?"

"Angel needs a kidney transplant and you can help with that, or at least get tested to see if you would be a close enough match to do so."

"I'm sorry Jake I can't." Jake stands up fast and is a little annoyed with Alex now.

"You can't or you won't?" He says in a high voice almost yelling at him.

"I can't, I am to old to be a donor. The best I can do is be put on the list so that if I die before Angel they can take my kidneys then."

"Is that true, Alex?"

"YES, damn it. You don't think I would help that girl that I have loved all these years as if she were my blood kin if I could? Please don't insult me."

"I'm sorry, Alex. Of course you would, guess I want whatever chance I can get to save Angel. Her children need her."

"I understand that only too well." Jake sits back down and looks at Alex for a few minutes before bringing up the subject that he knew was hurting Alex deeply.

"Alex, do you know why Emma didn't tell you?"

"She has tried to explain it in my letter, but I can't believe that she did this. She had to have known, no matter what, I would have stood beside her. We would have been okay. I could have kept up with my practice and taken care of her. She could have still done her modeling after. She threw us away just because of my internship. How could she?"

"If it makes you feel any better. What I knew of Emma, she was not a selfish person at all. She never put herself first. She always thought of how something would perhaps cause distress to others and did things according to that. Her choices were always with others in mind. Just like when she was sick with cancer. I knew or I thought I knew, and when I approached her about it and said she should tell Kate, she told me to leave it alone. Kate never knew her mother was ill. Emma hid it very well. I would not have picked up on it if my wife had not died the same way."

"Yes. Emma had a big heart, but that doesn't excuse this. This involves many people. She has played with many lives and caused so many wasted years and uncertainty, for Kate and myself. I always felt a special draw towards Kate and Angel." Then he slaps the arm of the chair with such force, he made Jake jump.

"Damn it, man! I'm eighty-three years old and just found out now. My life is over, and how the hell do you try to build a new one now? I am just an old man, and I will die an old man."

"Come now, Alex. You know Angel and the kids will be so happy. You can have a great life for the time you have left. You are healthy, unless you are pulling an Emma and not telling all. So you could really enjoy your time with the children."

"To Angel, I will always be Dr. Adams, not Grandpa."

"Grandpa Alex. I think that sounds great, don't you? How about great grandpa."

"Man I got old fast."

"Friend we have been old for a while now."

"I want to go back to the hospital to see Angel, will you take me?"

"Alex, you don't have to go now. There is always tomorrow."

"This has been left for too many tomorrows already."

"You are right, Grandpa. Of course, I will take you." They both chuckle as they get ready to leave. Jake knew Alex was lightening up a little, but he knew the demons he were battling were going to cause him a lot of grief, especially knowing now that he was a relative of Angel's but still couldn't do anything for her. Sitting by and watching his granddaughter die could kill him. All the way to the hospital, Alex was quiet and Jake didn't want to butt into his thoughts. He figured when his friend wanted to talk, he would. Jake himself would be more than willing to listen. Alex was there for him while Kate was gone looking for Angel, so Jake knew that in time he would talk. Jake hurt for the man; he knew what it was like to have the one and only person in the world that you would trust with your life cause a tailspin.

When the two men entered the hospital, it seemed like it was on a buzz. And as Jake and Alex approached the desk, they noticed how, all of a sudden, you could hear a pin drop.

"Do you think we, or one of us, were the topic of their conversation?" Jake asked Alex.

"Seems that way. Should we carry on so they can carry on?" Nodding their heads to the woman working the desk, they back away.

"After you, my friend." Jake stands back and lets Alex go first. After all, Angel was his granddaughter. Now that had a very strange sound to it. It was also very sad for something that should be everyone's highlight of the year. How can one feel about being a grandparent so late in one's life? Jake figured it would take Alex a long time to wrap his mind around it. He had to succumb to Kate's deceit first before he was going to be able to move on. Can a man do that at his age? Maybe the best Alex could ask for would be to get early Alzheimer's disease. It wouldn't be so painful.

"You know, Jake, I'm going to see if they will use me as a donor."

"What, are you out of your mind?"

"You change your mind. Wasn't it twelve hours ago you were wanting me to be one?"

"I wasn't thinking straight. I'm sorry for that. There has already been one life lost to Angel's surgery. I don't want to see another."

"Thank you. But I have lived my life, and she does have two children to look after. What will become of them without a mother? If they end up in the hands of that sperm donor."

"Good point. But surely there will be another donor without you having to jeopardize your life."

"Huh, what life? The life I thought I had wasn't mine. I lived a lie for years."

"Now, Alex, that wasn't your fault. You had no control over what Kate did."

"I thought I knew her better than that."

"The saying is 'You don't know anyone as well as you think you do.'"

"So I'm finding out. I wish Emma could answer me. My head is spinning with so many whys and what-ifs. It's hard to think straight."

"Take time, Alex. Answers will come to you. Remember, all comes to those who wait."

"I think I waited enough years, don't you?"

"Yes, my friend, I believe you have. Emma didn't know her life would end so soon."

"Maybe not. When she knew the end was coming fast, she should have talked to me then, not write it in a letter. She had to know I would be full of questions."

"Perhaps she wouldn't have been able to stand to see the pain that we all see in your eyes, Alex. Emma would have been too weak to handle that. She died knowing you were happy with your life, except for losing her."

"You're right about that. It would have killed me to see her die in more pain than she was already in."

"Unfortunately, cancer is very painful. I felt helpless while watching my first wife die from it."

Entering Angel's room, they found there was standing room only. This made both the men's hearts quicken.

"What has happened?" Alex asked as he pushed his way into Angel's side. Jake just slid in beside him. Angel still lay in a deep sleep, oblivious to what was going on around her.

"Nothing. We were just talking about Angel's surgery," Dr. Collins said.

"I want to talk to you about that."

"You do?" Dr. Collins raises an eyebrow and then looks at the others.

"Yes, I want to donate one of my kidneys to Angel. I have always been healthy, so I should have no problems."

"That would be great, except your age is totally against you."

"I know it is, but it should be my choice. I have lived my life. Angel has two little children, and she needs to live."

"The risks are too high with you, and as doctors, we have the right to refuse."

"As a doctor, I have rights as well."

"Yes, you do. And with all due respect, we appreciate what you want to do for your granddaughter. I would like you to meet someone." Dr. Collins turns to the younger man standing beside him and says, "Alex, I want you to meet Kevin."

Alex felt the floor coming up. Looking at Kevin was like a mirror image of himself when he was much younger. Kevin puts out his hand to shake, and all he could do was hold Kevin's hand and look at him.

"Are you all right, sir?" Kevin asked.

Alex nods his head and says, "Yes. I'm fine, thank you."

"Kevin is a perfect match for Angel, and he is going to be her live donor."

"But how? I don't understand."

"Can the three of us go to the lounge?"

"Sure we can." Alex lets go of Kevin's hand, and the three of them excuse themselves from the room. Alex knew Trevor and Jake would still be there when he came back.

The three men entered the lounge without a word being spoken. Alex had his own thoughts, and he was sure the other two did as well. He was trying to remember what all Emma had said in her letter, and at this moment, nothing was making sense.

Pulling up their chairs and sitting facing each other, Dr. Collins decides he would start first.

"I stopped in to see how Chris was doing the other day."

"Chris?" Alex said with a frown. "What does he have to do with this?"

Dr. Collins pulls out the letter Alex had slapped down hard on Chris's leg.

"He thought you should have this back, or that maybe I should see it. Whatever his intentions were, it may work out for the best."

"I see. So how did you find Kevin for a donor? And how is it that he is a perfect match?"

"Kevin is our grandson. He is just a year older than Angel."

"Go on." All this time, Alex sits and watches Kevin.

"Kevin's father, Kelly, was our son. By *ours*, I mean yours and mine."

Alex whips his head around to look at Dr. Collins saying, "I beg your pardon?"

"Emma was young when my wife and I met her. She was also pregnant. My wife was her doctor. Then they found out she was having twins."

Alex went white.

"Where is your son—our son—now?"

"He died ten years ago in a boating accident."

Alex drops his head into his hands and just slowly shakes his head back and forth.

"When Emma found out she was having a boy and a girl, she was very upset. She said she could take care of one baby, but not two, and she would put the boy up for adoption. She felt he needed a man in his life. A daughter she could do on her own."

"But why? Why didn't she call me? I was just as responsible for them as she was. We got carried away on our last day together and didn't take any precautions. All the times I talked to her while she was away at her modeling school, she never breathed a word."

"Emma told us she had not told you. She said that she didn't want anything to get in the way of your dreams, and she said two babies sure would do that. My wife and I couldn't have any more children. We had a daughter, so we told Emma we would keep her son until she felt she could tell you or be able to raise him herself. After two years, we talked to her again, and she said she still had not told you, and she was then married to her agent and that she didn't want to take Kelly away from the only parents he knew. So we went ahead and adopted him."

"Why didn't you get in touch with me?'

"It wasn't our place. The baby was under her maiden name, and so that gave her full power to do whatever she decided."

"All these years I had a son and a daughter, but didn't know of them."

"I am so sorry, Alex. I don't know what to say."

"Now some things are making sense to me. Like why the word *marriage* was something Emma used to dance around. She couldn't be my wife if she couldn't be totally honest with me. Marrying me would have backed her into a corner, and it might have ended us, after all. We spent time together, and she always seemed to be on edge about something. She always told me that she worried about the old people she was working with, and I believed her. All the time this was eating away at her, and she just couldn't bring herself to tell me. Even in her last letter, she told me about Kate but never mentioned a son. The saying 'you don't really know anyone' is so true." He bows his head.

Chapter Twenty-Eight

---•---

The three men were in the lounge for one hour.

Dr. Collins and Kevin filled Alex in on what Kelly was really like, and they had pictures to show him. They were prepared to do this today in hopes of saving Angel's life and not wanting to destroy another.

Alex felt like he didn't know Emma at all. The one woman that he thought he knew and he loved more than life had secrets that went to her grave with her. It was going to take him time to understand what Emma had done, if he ever could. To say he would forgive her didn't matter; she wasn't here anymore. He still hopes that she was resting in peace although—knowing Emma—he doubted it. What does he mean, knowing Emma? He never really knew her.

The three men had decided to have Kevin be Angel's donor, and the surgery was set for the next morning. Alex was not all that comfortable about it as there were risks to this surgery, and he sure didn't want to see another wasted life. He had already lost his daughter to this, and now there's a good chance he could lose a granddaughter or grandson—or both. He knew there wouldn't be much sleep for him tonight.

Jake and Trevor were happy to hear of the donor. They, of course, did not know of all the details. Alex thought he would tell them when Angel was well enough to take part in the conversation.

In the morning, everyone was up and excited about today. Angel had woken up long enough to be told they had a donor. She gave them a weak smile and dozed off again. The surgery itself would take about three hours. So Jake, Trevor, and Alex waited it out together. Of course, for Jake and Alex, it would bring back bad memories of the day they lost Kate. This time, seeing how both the giver and the taker were young, they all prayed heavily for their recovery. The three had been asked to go outside for a walk twice as they walked the hallways steadily. None of them had much to say. They were heavy in thought, especially Alex. At this moment, he had enough on his mind to make him excuse himself from the others, and he went to the cemetery. He thought if he wanted to talk to Emma that would be the best place to be.

Sitting at the head of the grave, he didn't really know where to begin. He found this hard because he never had problems talking to Emma. Now he felt he was talking to a stranger.

"Hi, Emma. It's been a while, I know. Guess when you really think about it, it has been many years since we really talked. Some of today's feelings are my fault, but I found out today that I had two children—a daughter and a son. For the love of god, I don't understand why you didn't tell me. Thank you for thinking of my dream. But what about yours, and what about us and our dreams of a family and a home together? Was there ever an us? Was this not a worry to you all those years of knowing you had my children and perhaps I would find out?

"What about Kate? Didn't she have the right to know about her brother and her father? All those years that we were close and all the times of me helping Kate, you don't think it would have been better for her to know I was her father? Not her doctor, for crying out loud, Kate. She was my daughter. That just wasn't right. And you had no right playing god as you did. What about Kevin? Yes, I understand it's tough raising babies alone, but you didn't have to be

alone. Oh, Emma, our lives could have been so different. They could have been more fulfilled. I know mine would have been, and yours would have been as well. To go to your grave with such secrets had to have had your heart twisted with pain. Didn't you ever wish you would have told me? Even at the end, you told me only half the truth in your letter, Emma. WHY?

"Today, our granddaughter and grandson are under the knife. I pray that if you know this and can see us and have any power in making this all right, that you will do it. It is too late for you and me, but our grandchildren deserve a fighting chance. OUR great-grandchildren deserve their mother and cousin. They also deserved to know their great-grandfather.

"Will I ever forgive you? Probably, as I don't have many years left to carry a grudge, but I won't forget what you have done to US. Emma, it was us that you destroyed so many years ago. I do hope you are resting well with this, and please don't let me stop you from that. I only wished the best for you always. Oh, my darling, I don't know if I can go on anymore. All of this has drained me of everything I believed in."

Kissing his fingertips and placing it on her name plate, he gets up.

"I have to go now and see how our grandchildren are doing. Maybe we will chat another day."

Alex walks away from the cemetery with a heavy heart; he knew deep down that he would not be back anytime soon.

Alex found that surgery had gone well and that both were in their recovery rooms. He met up with Jake, and they decided they would go home. Trevor was going to stay and sit with Angel as soon as they would let him in.

Jake was dropping Alex off and decided he would ask.

"Alex, is everything okay with you?"

"Yea, why do you ask?" Alex had hoped no one said anything while he was gone.

"You look like you lost your best friend."

"You could say I did," he answered as he got out of Jake's truck and closed the door. Jake thought he would give him a couple of days then go back and talk to him. He was curious to find out what he meant by that.

Everything with Angel and Kevin went well. Their ages had a lot to do with it. Dr. Anderson was concerned that Angel was too run-down to make a quick recovery, but she surprised them all and was wide awake in three days and said she was very hungry.

Trevor brought the children in, and then he decided to put the ring back on her finger that had been taken off for surgery. He felt it was a great time, and to have the children there as well would please Angel. Tracy had stayed home so he could have his private time with Angel.

Once the children had hugged and kissed Mommy and talked her ear off, Trevor got them settled with crayons and books he had brought along.

"Now, Miss," Trevor says as he reaches into his pocket again and pulls out the ring. "I asked you once already, and I'm not in the habit of begging. But this time, I will let it go. Would you honor me and become my wife?"

"Trevor, that is so sweet of you to ask. What about the children?"

"What about them? We get along great."

"You really want to take on another man's children?"

"Only the ones that belong to you. We will all be great, and there is no time better than now to start a new life, Angel. You have been given another chance, and you should live it to the fullest, and I would like you to do it with me."

"I was so lucky that they found another live donor."

"You have no idea how lucky you really are."

"Do you think they will let me meet the donor?"

"We can ask and find out, but first, I would like an answer."

"YES, Trevor. I would love to be your wife."

"You would, just like that."

"With a ring like this, how could I go wrong?"

"It's not much of a ring. I don't make much on my internship yet. I promise you that when I do, you will get a nicer ring."

"This one is great, Trevor. I don't need a new one."

He leans over and kisses Angel and says to her, "Welcome back, sweetheart. I've missed you."

"I'm sorry I have put you through so much."

"Trust me, it wasn't your fault. I know all about Chris."

"You do?"

"Yea, you could say we met. I don't think you will ever see him again."

"I couldn't be that lucky."

"Oh yes, you can. And believe me, he has moved on."

Trevor wasn't going to tell her that Chris was still in the hospital thanks to him. He had been in and saw him, and Chris said he was moving on as soon as he was released. Chris wasn't laying charges; he knew he was going to be charged with causing bodily harm with the intent to kill. They had found his DNA on Angel, so he was going away for a very long time. He just never told Trevor where he was moving on too. Although he didn't want his children, he didn't want them knowing he had done that to their mother and was serving time for it. They had told him while he was away they would provide him with all the help he needed to turn his life around. He had thought maybe then he would make a trip and see Angel and the children, if Trevor would allow it. His prison time was cut if he agreed to take the courses and the counseling they offered.

The eight weeks went by fast for Angel, and she had done so well. The second day home, as they were sitting around the fire, the doorbell rang. She looks at Trevor, and he at her.

"Who can that be this late?" She asked.

"Not sure, but will go find out." Opening the door, Trevor found that it was Dr. Adams, Jake, and Kevin. He looked at them all strangely and said, "You want to come in?"

"Yes, we want to talk to Angel. And you if you don't mind us being here so late."

"No, not at all. Come on in."

When they were all seated with their coffees, Alex decided he would tell Angel the story. As hard as it was going to be, he felt it should come from him. Once it was all said and done, he said to Angel, "Do you have any questions?"

"So you are telling me that Kevin is my cousin and also my kidney donor, you are my doctor but my grandfather, and no one knew this until now."

"That is correct, Angel. I know this is a lot to take in and you will have to take your time in adjusting to it all. All I can say is I'm so very sorry."

"Sorry for what? Telling me I have family—that I'm not on this planet all alone? Yes, I'm disappointed in Grandma for not telling us sooner, but she must have had her reasons. Everyone does. Trevor was right. I was given another chance at life, and what a great one it is. I'm getting a great husband, grandfather, and a cousin. Why would I be any more than happy over all this?" Turning to Kevin, she says, "I'm trusting there's more family where you come from."

"Oh yes."

"Sweet. My children will get to know them all. And for you, Grandpa, you will have to spend more time with us now that you're not our doctor. My children have a grandfather, a great-grandfather, and cousin to get to know. I couldn't ask for anything more." She stops and turns to Trevor, saying, "Except for one more thing. A great father. Our lives are now as normal as everyone else."

Kevin speaks up. "Angel, my grandmother would love to meet you and the children."

"I think that can be arranged very soon."

"Thank you. I will let her know." Angel goes over and reaches her hands out to Kevin, and he stands up.

"Kevin, thank you for my life. I know that doesn't sound like much. All I can say is that perhaps someday I will be able to do a pay-forward that will mean just as much to them as you have done for me." She goes into his arms, and it felt strange yet super that she was hugging blood kin. At this time, she lets some tears fall; and for once in her life, they were tears of joy. Closing her eyes, she says, *"Thank you, Grandma. I know you had your reasons, and I still love you with all my heart."*

Angel and Tracy were busy making wedding plans. Alex had told her to go for all, he was paying and she had never been married. Jake was giving them a cruise to wherever they wanted to go. He told them it had to be for one full month so they were sure to get their new start in life off on the right track.

Rose was seeing to the meals; Angel had inherited two more mothers. She had only hoped that Tracy and Rose continue to get along as well as they do now. They work very well together.

Their wedding was going to take place at Jake's mansion. It was a little out of town and lots of room. Although Angel's family had grown some, it wasn't nearly as large as Trevor's. He said his mother was inviting everyone whether they be relatives or not, and she was enjoying this as much as a mother to the groom could do. He didn't have the heart to tell her no. It was the first wedding she had anything to do with, and she also wanted to make sure that money was there for whatever Angel needed. Trevor had expected words from his mother about him marring Angel. Surprisingly to him, she had kept a very closed lip on it all. This was not like his mother; she was one to speak her mind. He figured it was because of his dad.

Jake was surprised when Angel went to him and asked if she could wear her mother's gown.

"Are you sure you don't want your own gown to hand down to Elisabeth?"

"She too can wear Mom's gown if it fits her. I want to feel Mom with me on my special day. She has missed out on everything that should have been hers to celebrate."

"Don't do this, Angel. You are starting a new life. Please start it with no regrets, okay?"

Jake pulls her in for a hug then she whispers in his ear, "I love you, Dad. You are giving me away, right?"

"Not on your life. I will share you, but I will never give you to anyone. You will always be my little girl. Do you understand?"

"Thank you, Dad." She just folds into his arms for a longer hug.

She had to have her mother's gown shortened a little, and that was all. Kate loved to wear heels, and Angel liked her pumps or with a one-inch heels. Lord knows, she could have worn three-inch heels and Trevor would still have to look down to her. She never learned to walk well in high heels and didn't think her wedding day was a good day to practice in them.

Her bouquet was of the bright fall colors. They were getting married the weekend after the hard frost; everything was bright and beautiful. It made for great outdoor pictures.

Chapter Twenty-Nine

———•———

Jake's groundskeepers had done a superb job of the grounds and decorating.

Angel couldn't have asked for more, except for her mom and grandma to be there.

Elisabeth was her flower girl, and she was dressed in a burnt-yellow gown with her hair done up in curls and sunflowers. She looked adorable. Tracy had Gregory in his stroller, and he was our ring boy. The rings were attached to his soother. He played with them as he watched all the people.

Angel was getting dressed when a light tap came on the door. Thinking it would be Rose or Tracy, she just called, "Come in." To her surprise, it was neither. It was Trevor's mother. She had not spoken to this woman since the hospital. She pushed the door open just a bit and stuck her head in.

"Oh my, how beautiful you are. May I come in?"

"Yes, of course you may." Having words with Trevor's mother just before she was to marry him wasn't something Angel was looking forward to.

"I won't take up much of your time. I just wanted to say that I knew you were the right girl for Trevor when I met you in the hospital. You were a spitfire, and you weren't letting anyone walk all over you. I was proud of you that day. You showed me you had a spine of your own, and you weren't just out for a ride. I'm sorry to be so blunt, but I want you to understand. Trevor has had many girls wanting to be where you are today. They were all wanting a free ride. You know what you want, and you aren't afraid to go for it. I was a little worried about Trevor taking on another man's children, but it sounds like he has it all under control. The big thing is, he is very happy, and you and the children are all we hear about." Angel knew she was blushing now.

"Now look at this. We have a blushing bride and a beautiful one. There is one thing I want to ask you."

"What is that?"

"I would like to know if you would let the children call me *Grandma* right from the start. I have waited a very long time for this, and I would like to enjoy every minute I can. They are such darling little children. You have done a real bang-up job of raising them. I would be proud to be their grandmother."

This all floored Angel; she didn't know how to respond to any of it. So all she could say was, "It would be their pleasure to call you *Grandma*."

"Thank you. Now I will go so you don't have to keep our son waiting any longer." She pulls Angel in for a hug and then kisses her on the cheek.

"We will chat later, my dear daughter-in-law." She was gone. Angel had to sit on the edge of the bed for a few minutes. Had that really happened? Was Trevor's mother really going to accept them without a fuss? Guess time would tell.

The wedding went on without any problems, and they had a long day. Angel and Trevor stayed with the children that night, then left on their honeymoon.

When they got back, Trevor helped Angel set up the house the way she wanted. Alex had retired, and Jake had sold his little place in town and moved in. Angel wanted to take care of them till the end. Angel's cousin had moved into the mansion of Jake's, although he kept saying it was hers. Kevin had a big family, and it filled the house to the brim. This pleased Angel. She herself didn't want to live there; she felt it was best she and Trevor stayed on neutral grounds.

Tracy stayed on and helped her, and Rose stayed on with Kevin. Everyone seemed to be happy. It was nice to see Jake with the children. He acted like a child himself at times, and that made Angel laugh to herself. She could remember some of the things that Jake used to do with her. Now he does them with her children; they too laugh as she used to.

It took some time for Alex to come around. They all knew he had demons that he was fighting with, and it had seemed that perhaps he had finally put them to rest. He had also looked like he had aged ten years. Alex had no more life in him. So moving in with Angel and Trevor was the only smart answer as far as Angel was concerned. She had hoped that perhaps she and the children would brighten his days. She knew that they could not heal the deceit that he was feeling in his heart, nor could they give him back all those years he had missed with his children and grandchildren. Angel was so happy that she had a big family and that the ones that were dearest to her were all under her roof and in her care.

Kevin's family had also become her family. He also had a great mother, and his grandmother was so happy to have more under her wings.

Two years after they were married, Angel got pregnant. They had all but given up hope. The doctors didn't want her having a baby to soon after her surgery, but once they were into their second year of trying, Angel had accepted the fact that she and Trevor were not having a baby. Neither one thought any more about it because they all had a very full and busy life.

"Tonight, can we take our supper coffee out on to the deck and watch the sun go down?"

"We can do whatever you want, Angel."

"I want just the two of us, okay?"

"Are you all right, Angel?"

"Yes, just tired. And I just want to sit with you."

"Okay." They get their coffees and headed for the deck. Angel snuggles in close, and after a few sips of coffee, says to Trevor, "What would you like for Christmas?"

"Christmas? That a ways away yet."

"I know, but what would you like?"

"You know me. I like simple."

"How simple do you like to stay?"

"Why, what do you have in mind?"

Angel reaches into her pocket and pulls out booties.

"What are these for?"

"Pink for a girl, blue for a boy."

"Boy, girl—what are you talking about, Angel?"

"Trevor, we are having twins, and they will be here for Christmas. A boy and a girl."

"Are you for real?"

"Oh yes, my dear. They are for real," Angel says.

"Who knows about this?"

"Just us and my doctor."

Trevor starts to laugh and cry at the same time, squeezing Angel and kissing her till they were out of breath.

"All this time, you knew. Every time I asked if you were feeling okay, you would just say you had done too much and was tired."

"That isn't a lie. I am tired. I was just waiting for all the tests to come back to make sure there were no mistakes when they told me they thought there were two. I wanted to know for sure before I told you."

"Oh, sweetheart, you have made me even happier than I already am. This doesn't change anything with Elisabeth and Gregory. They are still mine, but now we have one more of each. The kids will be so happy. Let's go tell them."

"Okay. Are you sure you don't want to wait?"

"Are you kidding? We have waited long enough for this."

Trevor spreads his hands over her tummy and pulls her in for a hug. "You know the saying: all good comes to those who wait."

"Yes. My mom used to tell me that all the time."

Going in, they had asked for everyone to come into the sitting room. That was where Jake and Alex spent most of their time.

"Is something wrong?" Jake asked first.

"No, nothing is wrong. We just want to share something with you, that's all."

"What is it, Mommy?" Elisabeth asked.

"We are going to be having a baby."

You could have heard a pin drop. Trevor and Angel look at each other. This wasn't quite the reaction they thought they would get.

"In fact," Trevor spoke up and said, "we are having a boy and a girl for Christmas."

"Just like—" Alex was saying when Angel cut him off.

"Yes, Grandpa. Just like Grandma did."

Alex had a warm feeling go through him, and he thought: well there will be no more time for running. So, smiling at Angel and Trevor, he says, "Well, let the party begin."

EMMA'S LETTER TO ALEX

My Darling, Darling Alex:

Where to begin, I do not know. When you are about to tear the heart out of the one person you have loved and respected all your life. Alex, please keep an open mind while reading. Trust me when I say my heart is breaking for you at this very moment. I only hope that in the end you will forgive me and be able to move on.

I could never find the right time to tell you, and maybe now is not the time either. After so many years have gone by, it almost seems as though it was a dream.

My darling, the one dream that we had together was having children. Alex, we did have those children you and I dreamt about and talked about. Yes, Alex, we did. When I left for modeling school, I was pregnant. I would not destroy your dream, and our parents would have been so disappointed in us. Guess I was also ashamed that I didn't have better control of myself. Oh, Alex, I loved you so much. I didn't want to leave and not know what it was like having you make love to me. That last day stayed etched in my mind for months, and then when the babies were born, Kate was a constant reminder of your love to me.

Yes, Alex. Kate is your daughter. We also had a son. His name is Kelly. We were lucky to have one of each. I wanted so bad to call you, but I could not get the nerve. It had been some time since I had heard from you, and I thought perhaps you would be involved with someone else. Then as the time went by and I had to make some choices of what I was going to do, the only choice I could think of was to adopt Kelly out and raise Kate. I thought a boy needed a man in his life. I felt good about the couple that had adopted him. They were both doctors, and I knew he would have a great life.

I didn't know that getting married to my manager was in the cards; otherwise, I would have kept him as well. Too much time had gone by, by the time I had gotten married, and I was not going to take Kelly from the only parents he knew. I am sorry for the choices I have made, and it was hard to live with them. Once you and I were back in the same town, it made me rethink what I had done. I lived with a very heavy heart. I always wanted to tell you about them, but the time was never right. Good god. When is the time right when you are going to tear the heart out of another human? At this moment, I know you are thinking I don't have a heart. Please, Alex, I did what I thought was best for everyone. Now with my passing, I want you and Kate to be there for each other. I know she had always wanted you and me together. That was something I also wanted to tell her: that we had had our time, and time just slipped away on us. We cannot redo the past, I only pray that you and Kate will forgive me and take what you know now and live your lives to the fullest.

I have hurt you, my darling. Deeply. I know that more than anyone. For you to have one of your dreams, you lost another. In today's world, it would not have mattered. Back then, it was a whole different ball game.

I did not want to bring shame upon you and your family, and I'm sorry that you and the children have paid with such a price.

Perhaps together you and Kate can find Kelly and perhaps put some joy back into your lives that I have destroyed. Loving you now and from afar.

Always,

Emma xoxoxoxo

EMMA'S LETTER TO KATE

Hello, My Darling Girl:

First off, I want you to understand that you were always my first thought. There was nothing I wouldn't have done for you. I had to make choices, or at least I felt I had to when I was young and foolish. Sometimes our choices come back and bite us in the ass. Everyone learns to live with their choices, and others just have to accept the choices that were made. Please know there was nothing I didn't do that you weren't first in my heart. I have hoped that I provided a good life for you, and I only wish I could have given you the dream that you had always wanted while you were young. I hope that you will take that dream and make the best of what time there is left. I hope that when you have finished reading this letter, that I too will still stand in your heart as you have always stood in mine.

The gift that I am about to give you is long overdue. Please, Kate, forgive me. Once my choices were made, it was something I couldn't undo. There were too many lives at stake, and it would have brought a lot of pain on too many. Please take what I give you now and cherish it to the end. Make it the best time of your life and always remember that no one ever loved you more than I.

So the gift I give to you now, is that of the father you always wanted. Alex is your biological father. I hope you are smiling as I am right now as I write this. It actually feels very good, and a weight has been taken off my shoulders, to finally let it be known that Alex Adams is your father.

Kate, I could not spoil his dream of such a wonderful career that he had chosen over our carelessness in the heat of a moment, and he is great at what he does. You know that firsthand. He would have put that all on hold for you and me, and I didn't want any regrets for him or to have him hating me because I got pregnant.

I tried to keep in close touch with him so he would know you as good as you knew him. I was nervous at first. I thought he would figure it out. My mother always told me God protected single mothers and made sure the child always looked like their mother. That we did, hey, Kate.

So now that I'm gone, I hope that Alex can be there for you as well as Jake, and it will make my passing easier on you and Angel. I hope that you are able to find an easy way to let Angel know that she too has a biological grandfather.

Alex will be hurt for some time, perhaps even very angry, and I totally understand. There has been a lot of years gone by — wasted years, I know. I'm sorry, Kate; there was just never the right time to tell you, or Alex. I didn't want to be the cause of such turmoil. Even now, perhaps I should have taken it to my grave with me. I only hope this will help you all heal in one way or another.

I hope God himself will forgive me for my deceitful way. I pray that you and Alex will also forgive me for the selfish way I handled this. Please try to move forward, and together, the two of you will put the puzzle together.

Loving you now and from afar.

Your Loving Mother, xoxoxoxoxoxox

BE SURE TO WATCH FOR DARLEEN'S NEW NOVEL CALLED
BROTHERS and FRIENDS ALWAYS

CPSIA information can be obtained at www.ICGtesting.com
Printed in the USA
LVOW060055151111

254946LV00001B/16/P

9 781465 382603